THE TOWER OF TRAITORS

Emma Bradley

ISBN: 978-1-915909-34-3

For everyone who struggles to leave
places where they no longer belong.

And for Kainen, who really is trying.

CHAPTER ONE

The problem with living with a bird when you were afraid of birds was that the bird tended to hold dominion over you.

"No, outside!"

Molly stood in the far corner of her workshop, waving her arms ineffectively as Aurora, the bird who had chosen her as an unwilling host, pecked at a piece of wood. Molly usually let that kind of behaviour slide, but the piece of wood was one she'd been carving.

She could almost hear Sammy's voice in her head 'oh that's so cute! She thinks she's helping you!' But Sammy, usually fine with handling Aurora, wasn't there.

Molly didn't want help with her work either.

Aurora cocked her head, holding Molly's gaze with a defiant, inky eye as she lowered her head for one final, insolent peck.

Before Molly could gather her mental strength to approach, still convinced the bird would one day change moods and peck her eyes out, a shadow fell over the open doorway.

Molly tensed as Ru stepped inside, his thick coat pulled tight around his neck to ward off the chilly winter air. He ruffled a hand over his short dark hair, his blue eyes bright against cheeks pink from the wind outside. Even though the citadel had no access to the outside realm beyond the air vents, the powers that be insisted on keeping a regular routine of seasons through a complicated network of heating and air-conditioning.

"Trouble?" Ru asked.

Molly shook her head. "No."

Stuck between facing him and facing Aurora, she took a deep breath and shuffled a step toward the bird. As if she knew playtime was over, Aurora gave Ru a beady-eyed look, then clicked her beak and flapped away to perch on the edge of the mirror, her favourite spot.

Molly strode over to grab the piece of wood, surprised to see Aurora had at least stuck to the groove she'd been carving, although the effect was somewhat patchy.

Maybe she really does think she's helping.

Molly shook the thought away and grabbed a chisel, anything to avoid looking at Ru longer than she had to. While he managed to make good grooming look effortless, she'd not even bothered to brush her hair, and the blonde strands still in need of a wash kept catching on her shoulders.

"Nothing to report yet," she said.

He leaned against the doorframe, his hopeful expression falling. Every time he came to see her, he seemed to expect her to have softened, but she still couldn't get past the memory of him with a poisoned dart in hand and his victim falling dead seconds later.

"How's training going?" he asked.

She shrugged. "Not as quick as I'd like, but I'm rarely at full energy these days."

The accusation in her tone wasn't his doing, but since getting the opportunity to join the resistance, he was the only person she saw from the Menagerie, and she was still heartbroken he'd betrayed the promise he once made her.

No killing. She set the chisel and wood block down, folding her arms across her chest. *He promised me, and he broke it, and I'm just supposed to forgive him for that.*

"You know we could get you into training at the Menagerie," he suggested. "You don't need to keep going up to that crummy gym to get stronger."

Molly shrugged. She couldn't exactly explain to him that since the trouble at the Kayla Crane concert a few weeks before, her faith in the Menagerie had waned and now she was as much a part of their enemy's camp as she was theirs.

"Maybe, but I want this to be something I do on my own. The Menagerie can't police what gym I use. Besides, it's not that. I just feel spread too thin. I have the workshop during the day, training at night, I barely find time to sleep."

He smiled. "At least it's character building."

"No," she snapped. "It's not."

His smile fell, and she ignored the fleeting stab of guilt at being sharp with him. Not long ago, he'd been her closest friend. She missed that part of him, but he'd broken her trust with no way of fixing it again.

"Is that all?" she asked, forcing her voice to stay soft.

"I-" He grimaced. "Yeah. For now. There's a rumour

floating about that the enemy are planning to hit an import some levels lower down, so Celeste might well pull you back into rotation for surveillance."

She'd expected it to happen sometime soon. Celeste had her permission to take a short break from Menagerie duties to get herself together, but she was still indebted to them and they would want to make use of her again.

Then Ru's words registered.

"Import?" She frowned. "Since when are there imports? What's being imported?"

For as long as she could remember, the citadel was self-sustaining. It was more than a matter of pride, it was practically paranoia that the outside realms would creep in through any cracks and soon the royal dynasties would take control. Everything bought, sold, traded, consumed, grown, made, was done inside the citadel.

Ru sighed. "You know we don't ask those kinds of questions. I imagine it's some kind of safety precaution, but either way we need to ensure it's not disrupted. That's all I know."

Molly nodded, her mind whirring. So the Menagerie was worried enough to bring outside help in, not a good sign.

"Any news on the latest missing artificer?" she asked.

"I would have asked you the same, but nothing from my end."

"Nothing from mine either."

He hesitated. "I suppose that's it then."

"Yeah."

When she didn't venture anything more, he tapped a

hand on the doorframe and stepped back into the lane. She stood waiting as he opened his mouth to say something, she had no clue what, but he glanced sideways and pulled his hood up, disappearing without a word.

Molly didn't move for several seconds, half-expecting a neighbour to come striding in to chat, but nobody appeared. With a hefty sigh, she sank into her chair and checked the time.

"No time for a nap now," she muttered. "Hopefully training tonight will be short."

Aurora chirped in reply as Molly let her mind wander. She should be getting up to do the last few bits of some commissions she had, feeding herself, and seeing if Aurora needed to go out before she left for the night. She sat there instead, turning thoughts over and over in her mind.

The issue of artificers going missing still had no concrete answer. Celeste had hinted the Menagerie might have something to do with it for the 'greater good', and the resistance, what little dealings she'd had with them so far, intimated it wasn't their doing. Even Talie had insisted that nothing was what it seemed.

Molly groaned quietly at the thought of Talie. They hadn't seen each other much recently either, not that she was expecting to or anything. A few awkward glances in greeting as they passed each other, but the only other person in the resistance Molly had seen so far was Phoenix, and he'd been the one to recruit her.

She heaved herself to her feet and grabbed a leftover meat pocket from the small fridge. Her workshop and living space filled one high-ceilinged room, with most of the space covered by various projects and tools. At the back she had a screen for washing and changing behind, her bed and a small kitchen in the corner. Beyond that, she didn't need much.

She tore off the crusty edge of her meal and left it on the plate for Aurora to swoop on, then she ate the rest and pulled her coat on.

"Right, I am going out," she announced. "Either you go out and wait until I come back, or you stay in here until I come back. No pooping inside, got it?"

Aurora chirped and ruffled her wings. Molly cringed in on herself as Aurora took flight, but the bird sailed straight out of the open doorway.

Relieved she wouldn't have to be cleaning up essence of bird when she got back at least, Molly grabbed her keys and her orb along with a couple of pesanas in her pocket and left the workshop. She locked the door, glad the short alley she lived on was empty, and strode toward the main lane that lead up and down the levels.

Artificial wind whistled between the enormous metal pillars cladded with wood that held the citadel tower up, rattling loose tiles on roofs and sending shop awnings flapping. Molly glanced down various paved alleyways leading off the main lane on both sides as she passed them, able to see the endless sheets of glass that hemmed the citadel in on one side and the shadows of the core side alleys on the other.

Not long ago, she was wandering through the Oak Queen's gardens with real sunshine on her face, smelling flowers grown in real rain, not regurgitated water from high-up sprinklers.

Three levels up from her own, she walked into one of the inns and nodded to the man behind the bar. He recognised her now, giving her a nod in return as she slipped past the bar and through the door labelled 'toilets'.

Passing the toilets completely, she dodged into the storeroom and shut the door behind her. Even though there wasn't much chance of anyone finding her there, her heart still pounded every time as she readjusted the chair and hopped onto it to push aside the ceiling panel.

Hauling herself into the dark space between the ceiling and the girder of the level, she set the panel back over the gap and walked the narrow plank of wood that traversed a gap in the ceiling below.

The light was on at the far end, a bare bulb hanging over a door, which meant Phoenix was in his office. She knocked and waited, wondering what horrors he intended to put her through next.

It's because I'm exhausted. Normally I'd love any chance to practice fighting.

"It's open," Phoenix called out.

She turned the knob and pushed the door open, lifting her head and coming to a halt.

"Oh, sorry."

The sorry was automatic, but the girl standing beside Phoenix's desk had a weird effect on her normally sensible brain.

Talie raised one eyebrow, an artful flick that Molly could never get the hang of. Her shoulder-length black hair was tucked behind her ears, highlighting the less than impressed expression. Without a coat, her slender frame was visible beneath a muted red t-shirt, but Molly hadn't seen her arms bare before and had to force herself not to stare at the unexpected expanse of tawny skin.

For someone so waif-like, she's got more muscle than I expected.

She cleared her throat and turned her attention to the reason she was there instead. Phoenix barely looked up from the paper-strewn across the crate he used as a desk. His pale face was lined with tiredness, but he smiled readily enough from beneath his cascade of silver-blonde hair.

"Hiya, Molly. I've been… detained, so Talie's going to train you for a bit."

Molly blinked, not sure she was hearing him properly. Phoenix had insisted she needed to learn to fight with her fists as well as her gifts, and while he wasn't cocky about it, he insisted he was the best teacher she could find that high up the levels.

Molly had seen Talie fight once before, frantically against two grown men holding her, but even then she wasn't exactly sure this was a step up from Phoenix.

She gulped, determined to at least play nice, even though Talie didn't look overjoyed by the suggestion either.

"Er…what?"

CHAPTER TWO

"Don't look so horrified," Talie grumbled. "You've seen me fight before."

Molly nodded. "Yeah, sorry. Surprised that's all."

Talie gave Phoenix a withering look but he made no attempt to hide his grin.

"I'm sure you two will be fine." He looked up, silent for a moment. "Go straight to the gym, Talie. Molly needs to learn more of our shortcuts. Only a couple of hours though tonight. Take a rest while you can get it both of you."

Talie scoffed something under her breath then waved her hand at the door. Uneasy, Molly slipped through and waited until Talie joined her. Silence fell as they headed right through a gap in the wall that led to a small space behind a huge pile of boxes.

Learning about shortcuts would come in handy, but Molly had been training with Phoenix for a couple of weeks and he'd always taken them back out through the inn and along the lane to the gym's front entrance before.

"I take it you didn't ask for this," Molly suggested.

Talie shrugged. "Didn't offer, definitely didn't ask, but Phoenix is a busy man."

He was. Molly had seen a similar tiredness in his eyes

to the kind she felt, but maybe he thought Talie and Molly were friends considering it was Talie who'd led her to the resistance in the first place.

Clearly he's mistaken.

She wanted to ask if Talie had appreciated the small Yuletide gift she'd left for her with Sammy's the last time they'd spoken, but then Talie had made no attempt to go out of her way with a thank you. Sammy often ran down to the workshop now that she was close to finishing school, but she rarely mentioned Talie and Molly didn't want to give the wrong impression by asking.

Molly followed her around the edge of the boxes and into a narrow stairwell, their footsteps echoing as they started downward.

"Are we doing the whole interrogation while walking thing?" she asked.

Talie frowned. "The what?"

"Phoenix usually asks me things while we walk down to the training ground."

"Anything you tell him you can tell me then."

Molly bit her lip, tempted to be troublesome. Usually Phoenix asked her things about her workshop or general life, but this time it was more to fill the awkward silence than to actually get Talie talking.

"Well, I got a few new commissions this morning. Aurora hasn't used my workshop as a toilet in the last two, so that's a record."

Talie slowed until Molly matched her pace.

"I thought you meant he asks you for information," she muttered.

Molly grinned. "I know. The only thing I have heard is that there's still no information on who keeps targeting artificers, or why, but that there's apparently some kind of import coming in."

"Import? We never have imports, not even your Menagerie uses imports, not that we know of."

"I know, that's what I said."

Molly ignored the 'your', because she wasn't sure the Menagerie was where her allegiance lay anymore. She couldn't trust the resistance either after they took her on despite knowing who she was working for, but then the Menagerie were using her too.

Talie sucked in a breath and grumbled something inaudible.

"If anyone is bringing in imports, it's not going to be for the masses," she said.

Molly snorted. "It never is. Doubt the nobles far down would be needing anything much either. I figured some kind of protection."

Talie walked ahead to open a door and paused as she looked back.

"Protection against what? What could the enemy possibly be planning that would need higher levels of protection than they already have?"

"How should I know?" Molly shrugged. "If it's something to do with the missing artificers, maybe whoever is doing whatever is building something here."

"Weapon of mass destruction?" Talie suggested drily.

"One can only guess."

As Talie smirked and threw the door open to reveal the

back of the gym, Molly steeled herself for a gruelling few hours. The vast warehouse was teeming with people, some clashing and clanging on the weights while others ran the circular track around the edge of the room and a few practiced fencing in the far ring.

Molly had learned early on that the best place to hide was out in the open, but the sheer ingenuity of the resistance to meet each other in public places still amazed her. Mostly, everyone was going about their business, but using the abandoned tunnels and decaying forgotten passages for more clandestine events.

Talie grabbed a couple of sparring pads and carried them to a spare patch of space in a far corner. Molly shrugged her coat off and settled her feet into the ready stance Ru had taught her long ago.

Talie raised one eyebrow. "Block my punches. Ready?"

"Of course. Ru taught me everything he knows."

Talie lunged forward, her fist arcing toward Molly's face.

Molly flinched back, eyes wide as she lifted her arm to block.

Talie's fist landed on her elbow without any real punch and she shoved it off, adrenalin kicking in.

"Didn't he teach you how to move your feet properly?" she asked.

Molly ducked as Talie swung again. She managed to wisp a knuckle past Talie's ribs before they were apart again.

"Hands up higher, don't let them hang around."

Molly gritted her teeth and obeyed, wanting to ask how

Talie could be so quick with her movements. She blocked a punch and hissed through her teeth as Talie's calf kicked smartly against her hip.

"You also have this thing called a lower body," Talie barked. "Guard it."

Spectators gathered around the edge of the ring. Molly inhaled deeply and blocked a punch and a kick. No sooner was Talie's foot on the ground, it was bouncing up again for a second kick. Molly grunted as Talie's boot hit her thigh and she stumbled back, arms out to keep her balance.

Even as Talie rounded on her again, punch, kick, punch, Molly dodged and lashed out, barely managing to land a single tap.

"This is impossible," she muttered. "You're not teaching me anything. Is this what you do all day, attack people?"

She didn't intend for Talie to hear her, but immediately Talie's posture stiffened.

"What do you think I do for hours while Sammy's at school?" she spat. "I train. Hit them before they wield over you. Catch them before they ward. This isn't some fanciful human tale where you throw a few punches and magically become a champion."

The derision dripping from her tone rankled Molly enough to send her storming forward. Talie folded her arms, haughty glower firmly fixed.

"I have no intention of being any kind of champion." She jabbed her finger against the swell of Talie's shoulder, her own heaving with frustration. "I just want to survive."

Molly caught the stillness a second before the danger

registered. She looked down at the offending finger. Talie looked down at the offending finger. Lifted her hand.

Molly flinched as Talie pinched it between forefinger and thumb and removed it from her shoulder before letting the contact drop.

"Calm down," she added.

Molly clenched her fists, the roar of anger drowning the chant of *'don't punch her, don't punch her'* dancing in her head. Mainly because if she punched Talie, she might never see another day. She whirled away, sensing the emotional explosion a second before it burst. Her hand slammed onto a sparring pad and she swung around to throw it before the thoughts of why it was a bad idea had fully formed.

Talie grunted as the pad hit her chest. She stumbled back until she fell and a bunch of jeering rose up from the ropes. Molly stood, chest heaving from unbridled rage laced with trepidation as Talie got to her feet.

"Good." Talie kicked the pad back toward her. "Again."

Molly hesitated as her pocket warmed against her leg. Holding a hand up to stop Talie advancing before she was ready, she reached into her pocket and pulled out her orb. Although Celeste had insisted on taking hers as a trade for a new gift, Phoenix had given her a new one. He hadn't said she should keep it secret either so she gave the details to her neighbours for emergencies.

"Libby?"

She frowned at the familiar face of her neighbour loomed as a pearlescent grey image in front of them.

"Are you around?" Libby looked frustrated. "I need to

go to work, but Beryl's about to pop."

A bloodcurdling scream tore from the orb, startling several people around the gym.

"If you don't tell her to get here this instant, *I'm not naming the baby after her!*"

Her next door neighbour Beryl's voice shattered every eardrum in the vicinity and Molly winced.

"What does she think I can do?" she asked.

"I don't know but she's asking for you."

"Why me? Where's Harvey?"

The vision twisted away from Libby's face, swirling until it settled again.

"Oh." Molly stared at the image of Harvey out cold on the floor. "But... her sisters..."

"Still stuck somewhere else. I wouldn't leave her but-"

"I know, I know, you can't miss this shift. Argh, okay, I'm on my way. I'll pick up someone on the way down who actually knows what they're doing."

She swiped her thumb over the surface of the orb to stop the vision and shoved it into her pocket.

"Sorry, I have to go."

Talie nodded. "For once I don't envy you."

Molly scowled and grabbed her coat, not bothering with a goodbye as she jogged toward the main doors and out into the lane. She pulled her hood up against the rain, calculating who might be wise enough to handle a hormonal Beryl about to give birth. She couldn't think of anyone except Mary, and Mary would be working.

"Crud, crud, crud," she muttered, dashing past people.

She had absolutely no experience with babies, children

or pregnancy. Clearly Harvey didn't either, but at least he could stay conveniently unconscious until the coast was clear. She skidded into her lane, ignoring Aurora's indignant squawk from the doorstep as she hurried past.

Pushing the door to Beryl's home open, she grimaced at the sight that greeted her.

So much for an early night.

CHAPTER THREE

TALIE

"You so have a crush on her."

Sammy's smirking face wasn't something Talie relished first thing in the morning, especially when Sammy still had her nighttime hair wrap on.

She arrived home from the gym shortly after Molly's impromptu departure to find Sammy already asleep, so she'd bolted down a meagre meal and settled into bed. Now on waking, she'd considered not telling Sammy about Molly rushing off to deliver a baby, but it would only result in her getting louder later when she inevitably found out.

"That's not- I don'- you have no idea how I feel so leave it alone," Talie grumbled.

Sammy's grin almost reached her ears. "Fine, fine, I know what I know and that's more than enough."

Talie groaned as Sammy leapt off her pallet bed and moved to grab her shoes.

"I'm going to see if she needs any help."

Talie stood before sensible thought could take hold.

"No, don't."

"Why not?"

She hesitated. "Birth is gross, and you're loud. Neither of those things should go together right now."

Sammy unravelled her hair wrap, easing the black strands free as her grin upended into a frown.

"How would you know? Have you ever seen anyone being born?"

"No, but I know enough from hearing stories."

"Well, one of us should go." Sammy's dark eyes flashed with wicked intention. "She's my friend and she'll be exhausted. I can pick up some food on the way down for her. She works in the workshop all day, then you two are out doing whatever I'm supposed to not know or ask about at night. When does she get time to rest?"

Talie rubbed the back of her head, eying the door over Sammy's shoulder.

"Argh, fine, but I'll go. I'll drop off some groceries and things, stuff she would need, and tell her you insisted she have a rest, happy?"

Sammy nodded. "Yep. Are you sure you don't fancy her? You gave in so easily."

"Leave it."

"You should, you know. She makes the meat pockets better than Mary at the kiosk does, with all the extra melty cheese and everything."

"I can make meat pockets," Talie muttered.

"Can you though? Melty cheese, that's all I'm saying."

Talie rolled her eyes, determined to get Sammy off the subject.

"Even if I did, it's ridiculous," she conceded. "Molly's

got so much stuff going on and I'm hardly a perfect match for her."

"Why not? She tolerates you, and that's most of the battle."

"Ha ha, very funny."

Sammy grinned. "I thought so. Oh, I'm going into school to singing class this afternoon, by the way."

"Okay. Be careful." Talie headed toward the door, bending down to shove on her boots. "No wandering anywhere else."

"I know, I know, like I have anywhere to go anyway."

Talie sighed and patted her chest to make sure her key was safe around her neck. A trick she'd learned from Molly, infuriating though her existence was.

She closed the door to their one-room home and set off toward the lane, dodging the patch of broken glass now stomped mostly into shards. Everyone muttered so often about needing to clean it up that it had become a sort of landmark for their alleyway. Only three levels down, Molly's lane was at least kept clean in comparison.

Talie shook her head and stepped onto the main lane heading downward. The faux winter season sent blowy winds down from the vents along with the synthetic scent of dirt and mulch, at odds with the faintest hint of sunshine peeking through cracks in the tint covering the citadel glass.

She slipped a hand into her pocket as she reached the next level down. Molly no doubt got her groceries from Ford's, but Talie only had a handful of pesanas until Phoenix paid her, so whatever Butch had on the shelves would have to do.

"Hiya, young Talie." Butch stuck his head over the counter. "Back so soon?"

Talie smiled. Beyond ancient, Butch had been at the citadel arguably before it was anything more than a fledgling row of small buildings. He openly admitted he didn't bother to glamour his white hair or the wrinkles around his eyes, insisting instead that it gave him a legendary status. Beyond that, he refused to talk about his past but he held a fondness for all the 'young ones' that entered his store. Sammy had once asked him how young was young, and he only grinned and said, "younger than me".

"Picking up a few bits for a friend," she said, eying the shelves.

Butch followed her gaze with a grimace. "Yeah, less and less every season. Can't afford to buy stock from the lower levels with prices rising, and the upper levels aren't faring so well."

"You think it'll come to rations or something?"

"I doubt anyone in power cares enough to bother."

Phoenix cares. She grabbed some dried meat, plover onions and powdered nutrient stock. *It's the one redeeming quality he has.*

Too cocky by half for her as a person, but Phoenix had his reasons, one of which was his determination to bring about a fairer citadel.

"Still saving up for your escape fund?" Butch asked.

Talie shook her head. "Not for a long while. Every time I save a handful, I end up having to buy things."

Her escape fund had seemed possible years ago, a childish dream that she could buy herself and Sammy a ticket through the skip-way to another realm, somewhere with a future. But as everyone knew, there was no escape from the citadel, especially not for Fae as far up the levels as she was.

She looked up from a box of plum tomatoes as Butch shunted a large wooden crate across the floor.

"Bit early for reductions, isn't it?" She hurried across to help him.

He winked. "Never too early. Go on, get first fill."

She almost wanted to hug him. Sammy would have done. Eying the tubs and containers inside the crate, she knew he was doing her a kindness. The reductions usually went out later in the day, full of produce just past its prime or with the odd minor defect at a cheaper price, but it looked like a good haul.

Talie grabbed a bushel of mixed salad barely even beginning to wilt, then a loaf of frozen bread. As two men walked through the shop door, Butch leaned slightly closer.

"Might be some cheese right down at the bottom."

Talie dropped her armful to the floor, angling her leg around it protectively. With both hands, she dove further into the crate.

"Hey! Reductions are already out!"

"Grab what you can, quick."

Talie grimaced, feeling around until her fingertips grazed something solid and cool. She hauled out an entire block of cheese as the man jostled against her.

"No shoving, you know the rules," Butch snapped.

The man barely even noticed. With a sigh, Butch grabbed a hand-bell from the side of his counter, threw open a window looking out over the lane and shook as hard as he could.

Talie winced at the loud clanging and grabbed her stuff before the man could pinch it from her. He didn't even look up or move himself out of her way, so she let her foot accidentally swing into his ankle as payback.

Butch returned the bell and came to price up her items.

"I hate reduction time," he grumbled.

Talie chuckled. "Then don't do it."

"And let the good Fae of Faerie starve? Never. That's six pesanas."

Less than he could have asked for, she knew. Handing it over, she waited for him to finish placing her items into her basket as what looked like the entire level cascaded into the shop, elbows shoving and mean, piggy faces snarling at each other.

"Go while you can," Butch suggested as he settled the cover firmly over the top of her basket.

Talie nodded. "I will, thanks."

She battled through the squabbling crowd, sucking in a deep lungful of air the moment she was back on the lane.

Six pesanas less left her with more money than she expected. She wound down another level, slowing her pace as she passed the park. The delicious scent of sizzling food wrapped around her, and she turned across the grass toward Mary's kiosk.

"Hello there, what'll it be?" Mary smiled over the

counter.

"Two meat pockets, with extra cheese please."

She counted out the three pesanas needed, hesitating as Mary turned to sort the food.

"Has Molly been by lately?" she asked.

Mary stilled. "Molly? Not for a little while. Poor thing, she's always busy with something or other. I always told her she doesn't need to help me, but she'll do it in exchange for a bit of food. Hates having to cook. Oh, this isn't for her, is it?"

"Yeah."

"Oh, well I probably owe her a fair few. I'll throw in some fritters too. Tell her to come and collect the rest herself though. Always too peaky-cheeked that one."

Talie nodded even though Mary had her back to her.

"She's been busy," she agreed.

She could well imagine Molly spending a day hunched over her work-desk forgetting to eat, then not wanting to face making food when she did finally surface. Peaky-cheeked wasn't exactly how Talie would have put it though, more like a flower that needed care and watering to be fully vibrant.

Mary spun around with the meat pockets and a huge paper tray full of hot fritters. As she slid them into a bag, she frowned.

"It was horrible what happened to her guardians. She never let on that she was breaking inside but she must have been."

"Was she close to them?" Talie asked, a lump forming in her throat.

Mary shrugged. "They weren't the most devoted but they gave her what she needed, food and structure and all that. They were all she knew growing up, them and little Ru. Not so little now though. He had a huge growth spurt a while back, but you'd always see them together."

Talie took the bag in her free hand, her other still clutching the basket to her chest. Thoughts of Ru weren't her idea of a good time, but he was Molly's friend so she had to keep him in mind.

He's obviously deep in with the Menagerie, and the further he goes the further Molly might be tempted to follow.

"Remind her to come see me," Mary insisted.

Talie handed over the three pesanas with a nod.

"I will, thank you."

She set off toward the lane. If Molly wasn't in, she could wait a while. She didn't relish the idea of going into birthing central to drop off a care package.

The thought dredged a smile to her lips.

Maybe Sammy would have been the better choice for delivery girl after all.

CHAPTER FOUR

MOLLY

"You can't name her Molly!"

Beryl grinned, her smile bright despite her pink cheeks and exhausted eyes. Even her purple hair looked wilted.

"Why not?" she asked.

Molly wiped a hand over her face, horrified.

"Weren't you going to name it- *her* after your sisters?" she added hopefully.

I should be honoured, but I don't even know them that well.

Her mind sloshed like soup, soggy fragments of thought colliding, but it was late morning and both mother and baby were fine.

"Don't you have any kind of more Fae-like extension to your name?" Harvey asked. "Is Molly short for anything? Or even a nickname might do."

"Why don't you go and have another lie down?" Beryl gave him an acidic look.

He grinned. "I'm fine, oh light of my life. I have to admit, calling her Meryl Cheryl Molly Hutchinson is a bit… unfair."

Molly didn't even have the energy to laugh. She leaned against the doorframe, determined not to get any more sucked into their family chaos. She needed a few hours' sleep, although she had commissions piling up, then she probably needed to do extra training after to make up for rushing out on Talie the night before.

"It's just Molly," she said. "The closest I can get to anything that's remotely like my name is Molinia, but that's a grass I think, not a flower."

Beryl smiled down at the tiny, slumbering bundle in her arms.

"Molinia. It's not the worst name."

A brush of softness and a whisper of air passed Molly's cheek. Before she could cringe away, Aurora flew past her and landed with innate grace on the arm of Beryl's wooden rocking chair.

"Hello, bird," Beryl said. "If you peck my baby, I will wring your neck."

Molly grimaced. "Her name's Aurora. She's kind of adopted me, I think. I'm not too fond of birds but she won't leave."

"That's a Greater Spotted Hump Warbler," Harvey announced. "They're meant to be extremely loyal."

"What do you know about birds?" Beryl scoffed.

Harvey shrugged. "I know that much. My uncle used to raise birds."

"This is the uncle who used to drink half a bottle of *Beast* and try to fly?"

"Well… nobody said he was sane, but he knew a lot

about birds."

Beryl huffed, but her attention didn't stray from the baby as Aurora opened her beak and something small dropped onto the baby's blanket.

"She's brought her a silver button, look!" Beryl cooed, her brow furrowing. "Aurora Molinia. I like it. Any objections?"

Harvey grinned. "I wouldn't dare, but you're telling your sisters."

"Fine."

Beryl's eyes closed, her head tipping back as she fell asleep with the button still in hand. Molly ducked as Aurora took flight again and soared over her head out of the door.

Harvey pressed a finger to his lips and shuffled her out as well, closing the door behind him.

"I'm going to the shop before they wake," he whispered. "Want anything?"

Molly did, but she couldn't think what she needed. Her fridge was basically empty and she couldn't remember the last time she'd eaten. She reluctantly shook her head.

"No thanks. Congratulations."

She left him at the workshop door and shut it behind her, contemplating locking it. It would be just her luck for Ru to come and summon her, or take advantage of her addled state and talk her into forgiving him.

She eyed Aurora already snoozing on her mirror perch, then looked longingly at her bed.

Sleep or work, those were her options. The thought of journeying to the shop made her frustratingly tearful, and her commissions would only begin to pile up if she didn't start them. She needed to complete a few and get the payment for materials before she started another as well, so she sank into her chair and reached for what she needed.

I'll make a bit of progress, then go for food, she promised herself.

Her eyes were almost closing when the knocking started. Startled, she almost took her thumb off with the chisel.

If I ignore them, they'll go away.

She didn't want to talk to Ru, or celebrate with Beryl and Harvey. She wanted sleep that she didn't have time for, and food that she didn't have in her fridge. She couldn't even stomach the idea of Sammy's effervescent company, or she might have begged a favour and asked Sammy to bring her a meat pocket.

Door's closed. Everyone knows to leave me be when the door's closed. Even Beryl knows that.

The knocking continued until the sound hammered into her brain and she got to her feet, storming across the workshop to throw the door open.

"WHAT?!"

She froze with her mouth hanging open as Talie held up a bag.

"Food. Figured you wouldn't think to eat."

Molly refused to cry, even as her eyes watered traitorously. She couldn't fathom why Talie of all people would even think of her, let alone think to bring her something kind.

"You didn't have to."

Talie pulled the bag away. "I can take it back if you want?"

"No! Um, no, it's fine. Did you want to come in or... You don't have to."

Baffled and in no mind for company, Molly tucked loose straggles of hair behind her ears as Talie brushed past her and headed for the kitchenette.

"I wasn't sure what to get. There's fridge stuff, but figured you'd need one of these."

She held up a meat pocket in a paper bag, the cheese oozing over the edge.

Molly hurried over to take it and dug in without a single thought for manners. She didn't even fuss over Talie quietly putting away the shopping for her, or flicking on the kettle while opening a new pouch of *offke* with her teeth.

"Strong or weak?"

"Huh?" Molly stopped halfway through licking crumbs off her fingers. "Oh, strong as it goes. Thank you for the food. You didn't have to."

Talie shrugged. "Figured letting Sammy come would wreck your brain. Girl or boy?"

Molly scrambled for comprehension for several seconds as Talie found two mugs, washed them briskly and poured the *offke*.

"The baby," Talie prompted. "Girl or boy?"

"Oh, a girl. Aurora Molinia."

Talie froze. The *offke* almost spilled over and she hissed in annoyance a second later, her gaze drifting to the mirror where a pair of intelligent inky eyes were watching them.

"Yeah, I know." Molly huffed. "Not what I would have chosen either. There's still time for her to change it though. Naming your kid after someone's random fowl houseguest is probably leftover hormones."

"And Molinia?"

Molly shrugged. "They wanted to name her Molly. I don't have a Fae name based on anything natural so the closest we could think of to that was Molinia, which is-"

"-a type of grass."

"Exactly. Aurora like the sky and Molinia like the ground, with everything in between."

Talie snorted as she handed over a steaming mug. Molly blew on it and risked a sip, pulling a face.

"Too strong?" Talie asked.

She shook her head. "Hot. Faerie knows why Beryl wanted to name her after me in the first place, but I did end up doing… yeah, I don't even want to think about it."

"They haven't been here that long, have they?"

Molly frowned. "No, less than a year."

"And they're from a different level?"

"I never asked. Why all the questions?"

Talie sighed into her mug and eyed Molly over the top of it.

"Would you rather I stood here saying nothing?"

Molly scowled and drained her drink, burning the roof of her mouth.

"Just asking."

She washed the mug out and reached over to tip fresh water into the cracked plant pot base Aurora used as a water dish. And a bath.

"You can skip training tonight if you want," Talie offered.

"No thanks, I need it."

"You look like you need sleep more like."

Molly sniffed, stubborn determination rising.

"My looks are nothing to do with you. If I say I'm fine, I'm fine."

Talie threw up the hand not wrapped around her mug. "Fine."

"Fine." Molly echoed sarcastically.

She risked a glance at Talie, not sure if it was utter despair on her face or the tiniest hint of a smile.

"Can I make one suggestion without you biting my head off?" Talie asked, setting her mug down and heading for the door.

"One, yeah."

She paused in the doorway. "Shower and fresh clothes. I don't even want to imagine what you've got on yours."

Molly opened her mouth to retort something suitably witty, her mind wading through the sludge of exhaustion. Luckily, Sammy bulldozed through Talie before she had to, knocking her sister into the doorframe.

"Wow, Molly you look..." Sammy squinted. "Industrious."

Molly snorted. "Is that wordy for tired?"

"I would never." Sammy glanced over her shoulder at Talie. "That man who I'm not supposed to know exists was very specific about not telling me he was looking for you. Well, you and 'the other one', which I assume is Molly as he definitely didn't mean me."

Talie grimaced. "Phoenix summoning us is never a good thing."

Molly sagged, exhaustion needling over her skin.

So much for a shower and fresh clothes.

She didn't even care about freshening up, not entirely. She wanted sleep, days and days of it. The thought of escaping up onto the girders filled her head, just her, a blanket and a pillow.

"I can cover the workshop if you like?" Sammy offered. "I'm sure I can figure out what end of the hammer does what."

"Um, no." Molly had to laugh. "I love you, but no."

Talie closed her eyes, Molly assumed in torment, then opened them with a sigh.

"We'll give you ten minutes to wash and change. Then we'll have to go find Phoenix."

Ten minutes wouldn't give her much, but as Talie hustled Sammy bodily out of the workshop and closed the door behind her, Molly grudgingly decided it would have to do.

CHAPTER FIVE

TALIE

Molly said very little on the walk up the levels. Talie honoured that silence but she glanced Molly's way occasionally, noting the straggles of wavy blonde hair scraped back into a hair ribbon. The ribbon was one of the ones Talie had gifted her for Yuletide, very much at Sammy's insistence. She was glad of it in the end, because the flawless slim dagger Molly had gifted her in return was even now strapped to her wrist beneath her sleeve.

Even her eyes look like the colour's faded.

They were usually a soft mid-blue, like the hue of the morning skies over the endless green forest outside the citadel on summer mornings. She couldn't be sure that wasn't just the tint over the citadel glass, but even so, it was usually a fitting enough match.

Conscious that Molly was running on no sleep and barely had time to pull on fresh clothes, it took all her effort not to make a glib joke about Molly following her without comment for once.

She led the way to the gym, holding the door open for

Molly to go through first. A rhythmic thudding filled her ears and she rolled her eyes to find Phoenix mid-spar inside the ring, a weaving mass of bare skin slicked with sweat. He finished throwing his fists into a sparring pad and wiped his forearm across his forehead, tossing his silver-blonde hair back as he threw a grin in their direction.

"Took you long enough."

Talie shrugged. "Molly was delivering a baby."

"I- what?" Phoenix wrinkled his nose. "Never mind. I need someone to go and check the cargo coming in."

Talie frowned, instant confusion giving way to wariness as she folded her arms across her chest.

"And you're asking us?" She hesitated. "Both of us?"

Phoenix grinned and grabbed a bottle of water.

"Problem? I would send someone else, but there isn't anyone, so you two are it. Five down, and I'll orb you the rest of the details."

The desire to demand he explain why he'd chosen them, Molly especially as she knew nothing of the cargo, not that Talie could tell, was squashed by the realisation that Molly was in no state to be creeping around the levels.

But if I say that, it'll only make her more determined.

Talie sighed and lifted an awkward arm to indicate Molly go first.

"After you then," she said.

Molly blinked. "Where am I going exactly? Which way?"

Good point. Talie turned toward the back of the gym. Phoenix gave her a wry grin as she passed then returned to punching things, the thud echoing behind them. Talie glanced sideways, noting the tiny wince Molly made with each hit.

She led them through to the rear hallway, past the pile of boxes that hid the entrance to the tunnels and further along to a small hatch in the floor. It led into a shaft diving downward, and again she looked Molly's way doubtfully.

"It's a short drop down to the chute," she said. "Are you going to manage?"

Molly flexed her hands and dropped with an ungrateful thud to sit with her legs dangling in the hole.

"I'll be fine."

She shuffled forward and twisted into the gloom. Talie winced as Molly's hands slithered over the cool wood, clawing to find a grip. Although there was a flat surface a short way below the hatch, Talie hurried down beside her in case she stumbled.

"Shuffle along then." She pointed to the waiting rubbish chute.

Molly did as she was told, but Talie kept her attention on her as they walked toward the waiting rubbish cart.

Molly's shoulders sagged the moment they entered the cart, and Talie gave her a critical glance as she shut the gate behind them.

"Dare I ask what exactly we're meant to be doing?" Molly asked.

Talie pulled a pearlescent, pale blue orb from her pocket and slid her thumb across the surface with a frown.

"We're going down to where they're apparently taking in the imports, to try and figure out what they are."

Molly blinked. "Wow, okay."

"Problem?"

"No, but... I'm surprised they'd trust me with something like that."

Talie pulled a face. "Because of your super cool double agent status?"

"No, well yes, but more because none of you've known me long."

"I wouldn't worry, Princess. Phoenix prides himself on judging character."

"Are you sure?" Molly asked.

"As much as anyone can be. He certainly is, why?"

Before she could fathom the line of questioning, Molly's face broke into a smile, a tiny spark amid the exhaustion.

"Let you in, didn't they?"

Talie stood frozen, fighting the sudden desire to laugh. It bubbled up, strange and somewhat alarming, but she managed to tamp it down again.

"Funny, you should do comedy. Will you be alright to hold the gate?"

Molly nodded, irritation scrunching her face. "I'll be fine, stop fussing."

Talie released the gate and grabbed the rope tied to the wall, looping it around her hand and elbow a few times to take the strain of the cart. She watched Molly clamp a hand to gate to hold it shut and shoved the button.

The gust of wind and stench of decaying rubbish swept over them as the cart shot downwards, but Molly didn't twitch a rigid inch the whole way down.

I'll speak to Sammy and ask her to find a reason to draw

us out of training tonight. I'm sure she can make something up.

Molly needed an early night and an excuse for too much food. As the cart bumped to a stop, Talie unwound the rope and tied it to the edge of the cart, ready for it to be pulled upward again.

Molly undid the gate, her fingers fumbling with the latch, and Talie followed her out. She took the lead, mindful to keep her stride brisk but her steps shorter so Molly didn't guess she was slowing their pace on purpose.

"You take me to the most glamorous places," Molly muttered.

Talie had no idea if she was supposed to have overheard that or not, and she fought the urge to grin. Their forced proximity didn't exactly make them friends, and there was an unfortunate part of her that would prove Sammy right if she ever had the slightest chance of being anything more than that.

She deserves so much better. I'm not exactly a great match for anyone as it is, let alone her.

The thought curdled inside her gut, a long-simmering burn. She inhaled sharply and winced as the tunnel's stench assaulted her nose.

"Do you know anything about these imports?" she asked, more in hope of a distraction than anything else.

Molly frowned. "Only as much as you do. The citadel doesn't do imports, we all know that. It must be some kind of rare item or substance, but why? What does someone here need that the citadel can't provide?"

Talie snorted, the noise echoing off the bare brick.

"So trusting."

Molly stopped and wrapped her arms around herself.

"What's that meant to mean?"

"Never mind."

"No, go on." She glowered. "No sense having manners now."

Talie shrugged. "There are only two factions of any renown in this place, and the resistance aren't the ones importing anything."

Molly wiped a hand over her face. Those brief flashes of determination quickly gave way to the lidded eyes of utter exhaustion, and Talie promised herself they would get the task done fast so that she could drop Molly home for a proper rest.

"Let's just get this done," Molly muttered. "It's bad enough I'm being pulled in all directions night and day."

"As you say."

They walked on in silence, but Talie did her best to keep one eye on Molly without making it obvious until Molly threw a random question her way.

"When's your birthday?"

Talie frowned. "My what?"

"Your birthday, the day you were born."

Talie bit her lip as tension crept over her shoulders. "Why?"

"I'm just asking." Molly shrugged. "We can walk in silence if you want."

"No need to be touchy, Princess. I don't have a birthday. I mean, I obviously do, but I don't know what it is. I grew up in the home, remember?"

"Oh. Does Sammy have one?"

"Yeah, but she's never been pushy about it. I take it you know yours? Suitably fond memories of each?"

She couldn't keep the glaze of bitterness out of her voice as Molly sighed.

"Mine is Midsummer," she said.

Talie snorted. "Of course it is."

"Problem?"

"No." She shook her head. "No problem."

"We should pick one for you then," Molly suggested.

"You want to pick a birthday for me?"

"Not really, but you should pick one yourself. Why not?"

It had a weird sort of sense about it. Talie had no idea who she was in terms of blood family, no official birthday to call her own as proof of it either, but she had been choosing her own path her entire life.

Why not choose a birthday too?

"Dawning Day," she announced quietly. "The days are getting a bit lighter after Yuletide, and if you really squint hard, you can see bulbs pushing through the snow outside the citadel."

Molly nodded. "Okay. We'll celebrate your birthday on Dawning Day. It's as good as any and fits your sunny personality."

Talie's chest squeezed tight at the hint of humour in Molly's voice. Nobody, not even Sammy, had thought to suggest she name a day for herself. Most Fae were said to celebrate their birthday, but Talie never had that luxury. She'd tried for Sammy's but it only seemed to make them both sad, so the tradition faded over the recent years.

The vulnerability she fought so hard to slay lifted its head, so she shoved her hands in her pockets and set her gaze on the gloom ahead.

"Handing out birthdays, Princess? What's next, presents? Titles? Gifts?"

"Not likely." Molly snorted, the sound echoing in the narrow tunnel. "Reject it if you're not interested. Otherwise, you'll get a barely edible cake because that's probably all I'll be able to manage."

Talie's lips lifted. "If you say so. Any more noble declarations?"

"Not for the moment."

"Probably best. We're here now anyway."

She led the way to a door at the end of the corridor, squinting against the sudden flow of light as she pushed it open. The door led out onto a wide girder high above a courtyard between several warehouses and alleys. The citadel glass let in enough daylight to see below but was supported by several overhead lamps at the edges of the courtyard, so from their vantage point they could see clearly enough.

Talie eyed Molly warily. Given the gentle wobble as she inched closer to the edge of the girder, her lack of sleep was affecting her perception. Talie sidled closer, one arm tensed ready to grab if anything happened.

"Sammy thinks you work too hard." The words slipped out.

Talie tensed as Molly lifted her head, her narrowed gaze darting away from the knee-wobbling height and piercing

Talie's face instead.

"It needs to be done. The resistance aren't exactly employing me, the Menagerie give me a pittance, so the commissions keep me alive."

"You wouldn't rather be free of all of it? Just leave it all behind and focus on the shop?"

Molly laughed, a sad echo. "I can't do that. You know I owe them a debt."

She didn't need to say who she owed. After the fight months ago in the Menagerie offices, Marcus had announced that Talie knew something about the night Molly's guardians died. The knowledge hung between them, and for all her hoping and wishing, Talie couldn't find any way around it.

I can't get past the swear-block they put on me, or I'd tell her what happened back then, but I can put us on more of an even footing.

She nodded, the movement exaggeratedly slow.

"I know. That makes two of us."

Molly froze. Talie could almost see the sluggish calculations whirring in her mind, that the Menagerie were aware of who Talie was and that she was part of the resistance, yet they let her go.

A flicker of movement down below caught her eye as Molly's confusion turned into accusation.

"Wait, so are you-"

A swirl of purple-grey plumed through the courtyard.

Of all the times... Talie grimaced. "Shhh."

Molly's eyes widened. "Don't shush me! How can you not-*mmmph*!"

Talie panicked and pressed a finger to Molly's lips. Molly almost inhaled it mid-splutter, but the moment she stilled, Talie nodded to the skip-way below and removed the offending finger.

It took all her effort, despite the precarious situation and the secrets still stuck between them, not to smile as Molly gave her a furious 'this is not over' glare before directing her attention downward.

CHAPTER SIX

MOLLY

"They're... people."

Molly stared in confusion, scanning the single file procession of Fae being jostled into being from the swirling grey and purple of a skip-way.

"Are they carrying anything?" she asked. "Perhaps they're importing something small?"

She sought for items in their hands even as realisation dawned, the positioning of their arms tied behind their backs telling her what she really didn't want to know.

"They're importing Fae," Talie muttered. "Utter orb-munchers, why am I even surprised?"

Molly's horror kindled to fury, even as she eyed the surrounding girders and pillars down to where the Fae in boots uniforms had rounded up their captives. She didn't need a sight gift either to see the frightened faces, but if the Menagerie were kidnapping people then she needed to find out why.

"Molly! Come back here," Talie hissed.

Molly ignored her, already creeping across the girder

toward the nearest pillar. She hadn't had much time to practice the stealth gift Celeste had given her, but it would have to do.

I can't believe Celeste is aware of how bad things are. This has to be down to Marcus, unless Celeste is a better actress and word-tangler than anyone ever suspected.

Molly bit her lip. She'd deal with that later.

She pressed her hands to the pillar while mentally scoping out her way down. As she lifted a foot toward the nearest foothold, something snared around her shoulder. Talie hauled her around, her hazel eyes flashing bright enough to look almost amber.

"What are you doing?"

Molly scowled back. "We need information and we won't get it up here."

"It's too dangerous."

"I won't get caught, trust me." Molly shook Talie's hand off. "If I'm not back in a few, take this information to Phoenix."

Before Talie could stop her again, Molly swung onto the ridges of the pillar and scrambled downward. She reached deep into her Fae connection and cloaked the subtle hum of stealth around her, manoeuvring across the girder and down. Her muscles screamed with each movement, her fingers burning from the tight grip she had to hold, but she reached the ground unseen and hid behind the closest courtyard pillar she could risk getting to.

No chance of me making it back up to Talie, but hiding and waiting out the enemy is sometimes safer than running anyway.

The nearest Fae in a boots uniform lifted his hand to shove the shoulder of the captured woman passing him, his laughter bouncing off the courtyard stone as she stumbled into the person in front.

"By the crates, stand together," another barked.

He stood beside the first as the group of shackled Fae clustered close together, frightened faces alongside furious ones.

Molly froze, her heart pounding and her adrenalin stuck inside her jittering limbs as the boots stalked closer to where she stood. She swathed her stealth gift around her, ready to use charm, or even compulsion if she really had to.

"Bloody fairies. What do we want to bother with them for?" the first man muttered.

The second shrugged. "Useful for their gifts, I guess. Tainted by the human half so they barely even count as Fae, but the boss knows people who can use them as resources."

Molly grimaced, shrinking even smaller behind the pillar. The first scratched his chin as the second pulled out his orb.

"They're late picking up. Why are they always late picking up?"

The first laughed. "Got somewhere to be? We're not meant to ask questions. Grab them and pull them in, that's the end of it. Whatever the boss wants to use their gifts for, we're better off knowing as little as possible."

"Rumour I heard was that they aren't using the gifts."

"What do you mean?"

"Ah come on." The second one stifled a yawn. "What does anyone want in this day and age? Transferable skills. Transferable and therefore sellable."

"So, they're going to be selling them? The gifts or the fairies?"

"Not a clue, who cares? Not even sure how they'd be able to get the gifts out of them in the first place." He blew on his hands. "What I wouldn't give though to get something like permanent warmth."

"Or permanent wealth. That'll piss of the nobility if gifts are being traded for pesanas and percats now, rather than solely as their honour to bestow."

"Not if they think they're the only ones buying."

A loud clatter of cartwheels echoed from a lane on the opposite side of the square. Molly let out a soft breath as both men stomped off toward it, one of them aiming a not-so-subtle kick at one of the fairy's legs as he passed.

Molly bit her lip, searching for any way she could possibly set all seven fairies free before the boots saw her. The alternative was taking to the levels and following the cart, but even pushing away from the pillar had her muscles struggling.

She took a step back, determined to try, but something firm clamped over her wrist.

With a grunt she dropped into a crouch, tearing herself free and spinning sluggishly with one leg out, but her assailant hopped clean over them. Molly lifted her head, ready to pull on her charm, or fight, but the glowering face pointed down at her had her huffing an irate breath.

"Don't sneak up on me like that!" she whispered.

Talie rolled her eyes. "Whatever you're thinking of doing, don't. Ah orbs, they're headed this way."

Molly didn't even have a chance to look over her shoulder as Talie grabbed her hand, hauled her to her feet and pulled her stumbling further into the alley. She almost went face-first into the wall as Talie swept her into a doorway hidden behind another pillar. As Talie claimed the space right in front of her, Molly swallowed down a squeak of alarm.

"Shh," Talie murmured.

Unable to keep her breath from heaving, Molly lifted a hand and pressed it over her mouth as Talie's arms settled either side of her shoulders. She stared at the smoky amber eyes mere inches from hers, so close she could feel the subtle puff of Talie's breath sweeping over her knuckles.

Close enough that in any other situation, with anyone else...

She needed a distraction, fast. The sound of the cartwheels clattering again caught her ears and she grimaced.

"We need to follow them," she insisted.

"No. Too many guards. We wait until they're gone. You're in no fit state to climb either."

Molly scowled, fighting the urge to argue even though it was true. She stared down the lane instead, anything to avoid Talie's unwavering gaze.

"Don't you ever blink?" she muttered.

Talie didn't reply, stoically silent until Molly had to look back at her, half rueful over being snappy and half reluctant. A clump of hair flopped in front of her face and she lifted a hand to swipe it away, her fingers brushing Talie's as they moved to do the same. Butterflies exploded inside her gut and her gift tingled over her skin as exhaustion and awkwardness spilled over.

Talie sucked her bottom lip between her teeth, her hand still frozen between them.

"I think they're gone," Molly said.

Talie stepped back as if burned.

"Yeah. Will you be able to walk up?"

Molly nodded. "Walk, yes. Climb, not so much."

Talie set off toward the end of the alley, her coat fluttering around her thighs and her boots making no sound on the stones. Molly heaved herself forward with a groan, not wanting to think about how many levels they would need to go up before she could finally tuck herself into bed.

Except I can't yet, because I need to report this to Ru. She slowed as Talie checked the square was clear. *Or do I?*

She fell into step with Talie as they crossed the square.

"Go on, let me have it," Talie said.

Molly frowned. "Have what?"

"Whatever's circling that incessant head of yours. Your face goes all scrunchy when you overthink. Let it out. It might help."

She'll take it straight to Phoenix. Molly hesitated. *Or what was it she said before the fairies appeared, she has a link with the Menagerie too, like I do?*

The confusion swirled around her and she focused on each step as they joined the main thoroughfare, gaining several uneasy looks from folk dressed far finer than either of them. But it was a few levels upward yet and she had to hope Talie would give her answers if she ventured some thoughts of her own.

"Are you working for the Menagerie?" she asked.

Talie tilted her head, a strangely jerky movement.

"I can't tell you things."

Molly let that sink in.

Not, 'I can't tell you that' or anything specific.

She couldn't press the issue either, or Talie would probably clam up completely.

"Okay. I'm not sure if I should tell…" She hesitated before mentioning Ru. "I'm not sure who I should tell what to, if anything. I have no idea who's targeting those fairies, whether it's the resistance, the Menagerie or someone else entirely. Whoever it is, those fairies don't deserve whatever's going on."

"You should tell whoever you need to," Talie said. "Don't take risks for anyone but yourself, ever. I'm guessing your boyfriend has a hand in all of this too."

Molly sighed. She'd sell the workshop before admitting Ru's attempt to have a relationship with her to Talie, even though it was probably easy enough to work out. But she couldn't exactly out him as her Menagerie liaison either.

"He's not my boyfriend. He's my friend… or was. I don't know anymore. He did something I can't forgive, and he's upset that I can't forgive him for it."

Talie stopped dead. "Did he try something?"

"What?" Molly slowed, blinking in confusion. "Oh, no, nothing like that. Just… I can't say what it is."

The thunder on Talie's face took a few seconds to fade,

her eyes flashing gold in the lamplight as her lips pressed thinner than Molly had ever seen.

"But you're safe enough around him? He's not forcing himself on you or anything, is he?"

"No, of course not." Molly sighed. "He'd be missing his bits if he tried."

She flinched as Talie snorted loudly.

"Ouch, Princess. You're not as sweet as you look, are you?"

Molly sucked in a startled breath as her cheeks heated.

"I do what I need to for survival, Sunshine, don't you worry. Look, that cart's going up."

She hurried toward the nearest cart rattling past and reached out to catch the lip of the cart. She almost let go again in her feeble state, her fingers shaking around the wood and her arms straining to lift her. She swallowed a groan of torment as Talie vaulted up onto the wheel-guard beside her with a ready arm at her back to push her all the way on. Molly clung to the cart and closed her eyes as the air ruffled her hair back. She would get herself something to eat and keep the workshop door open a while. It was late so if Ru wasn't waiting for her, she likely wouldn't see him until morning and could risk doing a bit more work before turning in.

Even if he does turn up, he can wait for me to eat something.

She braced herself as familiar sights whizzed by, until it was time to let go of the cart. The impact jarred through her knees as she dropped to the ground and she winced, forcing herself upright before Talie could do something awful like offer to help her. At the entrance to her lane, she hovered as Talie scrunched up her shoulders and shoved her hands in the pockets of her coat. An awkward moment passed and Molly cleared her throat.

"I take it you'll tell… you know," she said.

Talie nodded. "I will. Rest tonight. Training tomorrow as normal."

Molly fought the urge to smile. Something about the gruff tone, the way Talie wouldn't quite meet her eyes, it was oddly endearing.

"Okay. Tomorrow."

She turned on her heel and ambled down the lane. The dimmed lamps would gutter soon but she had no fear of the darkness. Even without light she wouldn't have missed the figure skulking in front of the workshop door.

"Out late?" Ru asked. "Or did you need an escort back from training? Did something happen?"

His dark hair was rumpled around his temples, his skin ghostly in the shadows. Molly reached under her t-shirt and pulled out her door key.

"Training." *Among other things.*

She unlocked the door and squeaked, crunching in on herself as the flutter of wings soared overhead from the girder above the lane. Or would have soared overhead, if Aurora hadn't decided to land on her shoulder instead.

"She's not going to eat me, she's not going to eat me," Molly muttered, inching into the room.

"You need to be firmer with her," Ru suggested.

Molly scowled. "Why are you here so late?"

"Waiting for you."

"Why?"

Ru sighed. "I don't like it when you're so hostile like this. Whatever's happened-"

"You know exactly why I'm hostile. Anyway, I'm tired. I'm not discussing it. I've had a late night as it is with Talie, then Beryl's baby last night, workshop stuff, I don't need you hounding me."

She sagged with relief as Aurora fluttered from her shoulder to perch on the back of her chair instead, clicking her beak in Ru's direction. He remained in the doorway, one broad shoulder pressed against the frame.

"Fine." He sighed. "I know you've been out of commission, but I can always tell when you're hiding something."

Molly turned to the kitchenette, eying the groceries Talie had brought her instead of answering.

"Molly." Ru's tone was like granite.

She curled her fingers around the tin of *offke* as Talie's words flowed back to her.

Don't take risks for anyone but yourself.

If both sides wanted to play each other and she was merely a tool to do it with, then she didn't owe any of them anything. If she told Ru what she'd seen and made it seem like a chance occurrence, she could give him something without betraying who she'd been aligning herself with more recently.

"We were walking a few levels down," she said, her tone curt. "I didn't get much information about why. We saw a couple of Fae in boots uniforms pull a bunch of fairies out of a skip-way, shackled and being pushed around. Said something about only needing them for their gifts, to take them or use them."

She turned to face him, eying his expression. It was locked down tight, no sign of movement, but that was all the more worrying for the absence of horror.

"Who's we?" he asked.

She hesitated. "Talie and I."

"You're spending a lot of time with her considering what you know about her."

"Sammy's my friend. Talie kind of comes as a package deal with her. She's not the friendliest but she's not all bad."

All said without a single lie, and it surprised her enough that she didn't prepare for his next question.

"Are you seeing her?"

She blinked. "Like visually in front of me? She's not invisible."

"You know what I mean." His eyes narrowed and his mouth twisted thin. "Are you dating her?"

Her responding snort was likely loud enough to wake up baby Aurora. She covered her mouth with her hand, a stray giggle burbling out.

"Orbs alive, no I'm not. She'd never consider it in a million years. Don't be dim." She sobered instantly. "Wait, don't try and distract me. Explain to me why people in boots uniforms, who we both know the Menagerie controls, are kidnapping fairies through skip-ways?"

Ru tilted his head, his body falling still. She recognised the subtle signs of his mind working, figuring out how to 'handle' her.

"It's a valid question. I'll take all this information back and have it handled."

Molly folded her arms across her chest, her instinct surfacing as her gut sank.

"Handled? How on earth can this be handled? I didn't manage to get any names, or where the cart was going. If the Menagerie are somehow involved in kidnapping, what's to say they aren't taking the artificers as well?"

She narrowly avoided dropping a casual mention of killing in as well, because reminding him of the reason they were barely on speaking terms wouldn't get her any answers.

Ru stepped back into the lane, she knew he wouldn't be giving her any information in exchange for what she'd given him. Whatever he knew, it was something he wouldn't ever trust her with.

He's no more my friend than Celeste or Phoenix or Marcus are.

"Like I said, I'll speak to Marcus and we'll handle it. Leave it with me."

She held her silence and his gaze, refusing to back down until he frowned and reached in to grab the door handle.

"Maybe things aren't as clear cut as they seem, or you didn't get a clear idea of what was actually happening there. You look tired enough to drop as it is. Get some rest, Molly."

Desperate to scream and rage, or at least throw something, she stuck her tongue out as he pulled the door shut. No doubt he would go straight to Marcus, who according to most rarely slept.

Just because he doesn't, doesn't mean I can't.

She hurried across the room to lock the door, then pulled off her clothes and found her softest pyjamas. Washing would be for the morning. For now, short of the citadel falling down around her ears, she was going to take Talie's advice and put herself first.

As she cobbled together a plate of random ingredients, her mind drifted back to Talie's instant fury when she thought Ru had hurt her. Then her memories spiralled to unflinching eyes and a raised hand frozen between them. If it had been anyone else, she'd have assumed some kind of affection was in the air.

Molly slid into bed and allowed herself a quiet giggle. Talie actually fancying her instead of seeing her as an unfortunate liability was the biggest laugh she'd had in a long time.

CHAPTER SEVEN

TALIE

I can never tell Sammy she was right.

Talie skulked up the levels with her hands in her pockets, her head ducked down against the gust of synthetic wind barrelling against her.

It was bad enough she had a hand in Molly's past, then got herself entangled in Molly's situation with the Menagerie.

It was absolutely orbing inconvenient to walk into Molly's workshop after she'd returned from wherever she'd disappeared to for weeks with literal royalty, and know without a shred of a doubt that the tightness and fluttering in her own chest was attraction.

Any kind of relationship is out of the question. Other than Sammy forcing hugs and unwarranted advice on me, I don't deserve affection. Or consideration. Not after all I've done.

Molly's kindness and innate morality would wither around someone like her, she knew that much. Molly was sunshine while she wasn't even the glamorous kind of darkness.

I'm the gloom that leeches away anything good.

She had to consider the problem of whatever Ru had done as well. She couldn't wipe the memory of Molly's haunted face from her mind, the suggestion he might have done something physical driving her mad. She clenched her fist in her pocket and turned along the wider stretch of lane that led toward the gym.

Phoenix asking her to spend more time with Molly was dangerous as well.

I don't need another person to worry about and protect. Sammy gives me enough grief as it is.

Molly didn't need protecting exactly, but with so many secrets flying through the citadel she definitely wasn't safe either.

None of us are.

Talie hadn't missed the not-so-veiled threats the Menagerie had made against her either, which affected Sammy too.

It's all such a mess.

She couldn't distance herself from Molly physically, but she could do her best to chill the unexpected feelings that had cropped up. Standing all pressed up close behind the pillar had set her heart thundering, a complication she really didn't need.

Working her way through the main floorspace of the gym, past the boxes and up between the levels to Phoenix's office, she sorted through what she wanted to say in her head. He needed to know about the fairies, but she also wanted to see if there was any way of extricating Molly from the firing line.

She knocked on Phoenix's door and leaned wearily against the frame when he didn't answer immediately.

"Talie? That was quick?"

She turned to find him coming up behind her.

"We saw more than enough."

He unlocked his door and stood aside to let her go ahead of him. Only once the door was shut and he'd seated himself behind the box he used as a desk did he give her the nod to continue.

"The boots realm-skipped a bunch of fairies through, scared ones," she announced. "Only two of them, but about seven fairies. They said about being used for their gifts, and transferable skills."

Phoenix sighed. "So the Menagerie aren't only stealing artificers now, they're also stealing fairies from other realms. Did you see where they went?"

"No, they put them in a cart and rushed off. Molly wasn't... well she needs a break."

She grimaced as the words came flying out, not wanting to make Molly sound weak because she wasn't.

She's probably one of the single-mindedly strongest Fae I know.

"We all do," Phoenix agreed. "I'd love to give you both a break but we do what needs to be done. The Menagerie won't be slacking for breaks."

"Nobody's slacking-"

"Molly made her choice with the Menagerie. You made your choice too, remember?" His expression softened.

Talie sagged. "Molly didn't have a choice."

"We don't know that. She's a good girl but we only have what she tells us. Never make the mistake of believing words."

For someone who has that as his mantra, he's using an awful lot of words.

She couldn't say it to his face, but then he didn't know as much as he thought he did, not about Molly's past or about Talie's hand in it.

"Remember what you asked of us," he added.

Talie nodded. "Safety for me and Sammy from the boots, and whoever runs them."

"Have we let you down since then? Sammy goes to a good school, you have a roof over your head and money in your pocket. Nothing runs without trade or sacrifice."

"I know that. I am aware of it every day, believe me."

She held firm as he reached out and patted the side of her arm, the urge to flinch away from the contact clawing at her insides.

"When the Menagerie burst into being, the citadel wasn't as prosperous as it is now, but what's the point in massing wealth if it only benefits the elite?"

She nodded. "I know. Even Butch says he's beginning to struggle."

"Butch is getting on a bit." Phoenix grimaced. "He's old even for an ancient Fae, but in that respect he's right. If the Menagerie are stealing gifts then they're plotting something big. Possibly something that will be hitting soon, and we all need to be ready when it does."

Talie thought about the gym downstairs. She should get

the chance to train while Sammy was at school. Then she thought about Molly, probably back at the workshop finding 'just one more thing' that needed doing instead of having a proper sleep.

I need rest too. If something's coming, I have to be fit enough to protect them.

Phoenix tilted his head, his gaze narrowing as he stared at her. She hated when he went utterly still like that, as if he was zooming right into the very depths of her soul.

"Maybe we should be watching the artificer's guild again as well," she suggested.

He frowned. "We've done all the watching there we need to. Why would we bother going back? We don't have the manpower to track every artificer in case they're next on the disappearance list, and we know where to find them when they need their minds wiped after. We can't risk the Menagerie fiddling with their minds and letting them loose."

Talie clung onto her mental thread. They'd had the argument before, that the artificers guild couldn't be trusted. She didn't even know exactly how much Phoenix knew about the absences either, only that when one went missing, he would find them on their way out and fetch her to the warehouse to wipe their mind. She'd assumed he had someone watching their house for their return, someone with the power to guide them away before they were seen.

But the Menagerie were using them for something, and he'd never once let her be in the room while he questioned them, or be alone with them while she was wiping their memories. Then the Menagerie had to know she was the one doing the wiping, unless they had another person with the same gift hidden away.

Then again that's possible, considering...

"Don't worry about the artificers for now," Phoenix added, his tone utterly decisive. "Focus on keeping Molly on side. Train her to fight. When the time comes for her to choose a side, we want her on ours."

The question burned on Talie's lips, *why,* why Molly, why not Ru or any of the other Menagerie minions. But she wouldn't get any answers by asking about it. As far as Phoenix knew, Molly only had stealth and charm gifts too, nothing overwhelmingly unusual. Whether he knew the whole truth or not, she would need to be patient to find out.

But Phoenix knew her more than well enough, and he would expect some kind of glib grumble in reply, so she had to give him one.

"She's not exactly graceful for fighting," she muttered.

He grinned. "Just do your best. When the time comes, we want her on our side, grace or no grace."

Talie opened the door and let herself out, closing it behind her before letting the sigh tumble out. She would need to go home and spend the remainder of the night with Sammy being extra fizzy, assuming she was still awake. Even though she'd spent the first half of the evening with Molly, she couldn't shake the disappointment that they wouldn't be training together for the rest of it.

"Talie! Come spar with me."

She looked up to where Nia was standing in one of the training rings.

Spar a while and work out some aggression, or go home

and try to stay calm so she didn't snap at Sammy for being her usual bouncy self.

No contest.

She shrugged off her coat and dropped it by the edge of the ring.

"Just for a bit," she said.

Nia chuckled. "Sure. No Molly tonight?"

Talie tensed. She didn't want to talk to anyone about Molly, Nia least of all. Crushing on the woman who was given the task of training you had its ups and downs, but Nia was flirty with everyone.

Even as Talie looked at her now, she felt the familiar flicker of emotion. It was faint, weirdly so, but still there. Nia lifted her arms to scrape her long brown hair back into a bun, tanned skin and toned muscles on show. Talie swung under the rope and hauled herself into the ring, pulse quickening.

Nia wasn't anywhere near as shapely as Molly, taller too. Her nose was straighter as well, and large eyes with lids that fluttered all too often.

Why am I comparing them?

Her cheeks burned as the image of Molly came into her mind. She steadied herself and rolled her shoulders as Nia squared up.

"No Molly tonight?" Nia repeated.

Talie shrugged. "She's got stuff on."

Like sleep. She ducked a punch, more than used to Nia's fighting tells. *I'll get Sammy to go and check on her tomorrow, make sure she's okay.*

She landed a jab of her own, thoughts of Molly

spending time with Ru, boyfriend or not, sending a rush of jealous adrenaline through her limbs.

"You're not usually so chummy with people Phoenix asks you to deal with, that's all." Nia grinned. "Wondered if you and her were stepping out."

Talie twisted sideways and aimed a kick. "Phoenix asked me to deal with her, so I am."

"And that's all?"

Talie stepped back. "Yes."

Because that's all it can be.

She re-firmed her stance and threw a string of punches as Nia ducked and weaved even faster.

"Hmm. Not sure I believe you." Nia held her hands up for truce. "But she does seem like a nice kid. I know someone who'd probably be interested in her if you're not."

Talie held her fists at her sides, chest heaving as she battled the savage urge to launch forward and punch the smug grin off Nia's face.

"She can see who she likes," she spat.

Nia grabbed a towel hanging over the ropes and wiped her face.

"Try unclenching your teeth when you say that, sweets. I'm done but if you want a piece of advice, tell her how you feel before someone else does."

Talie stood welded to the spot as Nia ducked under the rope and sauntered off in the direction of the back rooms. She didn't usually get so triggered by Nia's teasing.

Orbs, normally I'm just trying not to make a fool of myself.

With the realisation that at least one ill-chosen crush seemed to have died an eternal death, Talie left the ring and threw on her coat.

As she walked out of the gym and into the cold, she pushed the embarrassment aside and settled on the uncomfortable truth.

Nia asking her about Molly meant Phoenix was asking her about Molly, and considering it had happened straight after she'd reported in to him, that meant Phoenix had asked Nia to check in with her before that.

He knows Molly's sworn to the Menagerie, and he has an interest in getting her on side. He's sending me on tasks with her, then sending Nia to ask me about her.

She sighed as she turned into her alley.

"Hey Mister Boots," she muttered as she passed.

The orange cat hissed back at her but she ignored that and paused outside her door. She would need to keep everything from Sammy, but there was no harm in absentmindedly mentioning Molly so Sammy would insist on going down to see her in the morning.

She unlocked the door and pushed it open.

"Only me."

Sammy lifted her head, her entire body wrapped in her blankets.

"Hi, Only Me. There's leftovers on the side."

Talie locked the door behind her again and trudged over to the kitchenette, swiping up the bowl of Grain-O-Bake.

"Thanks." She bit into the crumbly bar and waited.

"So…" Sammy wiggled her eyebrows. "You and Molly get on okay? You didn't kill her or anything?"

"Nope. Returned her to the workshop in much the same condition I found her. Exhausted and belligerent."

Sammy huffed. "Well she was up for a whole day and night delivering a baby, then you're dragging her Faerie knows where straight after. I'm surprised she didn't kick you in the shin. I'm going to go down in the morning and make sure she's okay."

Easy as anything.

Talie grunted and chewed an extra large mouthful to hide her smile. She thought back to what Nia had said about Molly being a nice kid. She wouldn't have used those exact words, but Molly did deserve someone who would look after her, fight for her.

She imagined Molly hunched over her desk tinkering with random gadgetry, probably working far too late into the night. She'd stagger to bed in the early hours, likely not bothering to remove clothes.

Or if she does, she might end up- Nope. Not going there.

She shook the thoughts away and finished the rest of her food. After washing her hands and face in the tiny square of bathroom they shared, she clambered into bed and decided she would wake early for a proper clean.

Then Sammy might appreciate company on the walk to the workshop, just to be safe.

CHAPTER EIGHT

MOLLY

Molly walked into the gym the next evening with a clear head. She managed to sleep after Ru left, waking later than usual when Sammy turned up to hammer on the door. Talie didn't say much of anything about the previous night, but Molly managed to exchange a weary shared glance with her when Sammy accidentally upended a whole box of screws that needed picking up.

She even finished a couple of commissions after Talie dragged Sammy away, then ate three full meals and whiled away a quick chat with Harvey, who was looking for somewhere to hide until Beryl found the clean nappy cloths. After a relatively normal day, she was ready to train.

"Hiya, Molly." Phoenix stood in one of the nearby training rings. "Talie's up the back."

Molly nodded to him but ignored the directive and stopped to watch in astonishment as he faced an enormous silver bear. When he saw her gawking, he grinned.

"I'm training her to block," he explained.

The bear rose onto her hind legs, reaching out a paw to bat gently at the arm Phoenix threw her way.

"Is she…" Molly hesitated.

The word 'pet' was a word used by the lower-downs and the nobility from what she'd heard, but she also hadn't come across a bear before, and as far as she knew a bear was a bear and therefore not exactly able to sit down around the card tables or for a mug of *Beast*.

"She was rescued from one of the lowest levels. They wanted to use her as a peculiarity because of her colour, but she was rescued and now she hangs around with Finola."

Molly hadn't met Finola yet and opened her mouth to say as much, but a persistent sniffing around her calves caught her attention instead.

"Oh, hi."

She smiled to find an otter nosing around the fabric of her trousers and over the lines of her shoes, the broad black whiskers twitching.

"That's Mina," Phoenix said. "Finola has a habit of collecting those that need a home, but she draws the line at keeping Fae."

Molly's smile froze as a loud caw filled the air. She tensed, recognising it seconds before the flutter of wings brushed the side of her head.

Aurora landed at her feet, her beak weaving a series of warning pecks at Mina's inquisitive nose.

"She's protective of you." Phoenix lifted an eyebrow. "Not the animal I would have imagined for someone like you, but still."

"What kind of animal would you have imagined?" Molly asked.

Poor Mina gave Aurora a dismissive huff and a flash of her rear end before sauntering off, scampering up the bear's outstretched paw to sit on her shoulder. Aurora chirped and craned her neck, but even as she eyed Molly's shoulder, she seemed to think better of it.

Phoenix shrugged and crossed the training ring to lean on the ropes with a roguish grin.

"You strike me as a cat girl. Me? I'd be paired with a lion or a wolf. Now Talie, she'd be a-"

"I'd be a nothing. I don't want any animals, or to be compared to one."

Talie appeared at the corner of the ring, her expression decidedly grumpy. Molly failed to smother her smile in time as Talie turned the withering look on her, but the sight of Sammy popping up over Talie's shoulder made the evening even better.

"Hiii Molly." Sammy grinned, hurrying up to her. "I'd be a cat."

"Yeah, you are half-feral," Phoenix joined in. "What does Talie need an animal for when she has you?"

Sammy pulled a face at him and followed it up with a hand gesture. Molly choked over a surprised snort as Phoenix roared with laughter.

"That's what they teach you at school now?" she asked.

"That, and how to survive this twisted tower we call home. Oh, and a load of stuff we don't need. Like, today I discovered the exact shade of Talie's eyes."

Molly blinked. "Er... okay?"

"Don't you think they're a pretty colour?"

Trap, definitely some kind of trap.

Molly scrambled for a suitable answer, because the truth was unlikely to get Sammy to stand down on whatever mad assumption she'd somehow arrived at.

Talie scowled. "Sammy, enough."

"Don't you?" Sammy ignored her.

Molly nodded slowly. "Sure?"

"Pretty like amber, that's a golden type of brown, warm tones." Sammy gazed around at the confused stares. "There are so many better descriptions for brown than 'your eyes look like a lump of wood'."

"Your brain's a lump of wood," Talie muttered. "Go home."

Sammy's eyes grew wide, her lip extending for the ultimate pout.

"But Molly's here. Can't I watch? I won't bother anyone."

"You'll bother me."

"Won't."

"You absolutely will."

"Won't."

"Will."

"Won't."

"Urgh, fine. Not a word, got it?"

Sammy beamed. "I promise. Oh! Before I forget, Molly I wanted to introduce you to Daisy. She's an assistant teacher at school but you won't know her. She only started this year. I was speaking to Nia who works here and she mentioned you and Daisy would get on."

Talie's jaw dropped so violently that Molly was torn between following Sammy to see how low it could go, or asking if she needed some kind of crank to help wind it back up again. Sammy eyed her sister.

"Orbs alive, it's literally two minutes, calm down. It's not like I'm marrying her off."

Molly squeaked as Sammy grabbed her hand and hauled her past an incensed Talie.

"You're surprisingly strong," Molly muttered.

Sammy ignored her for all of two seconds before stopping in front of a surprised young woman with immaculate hair braided into a crown of chestnut gold. She looked as uneasy as Molly felt at being thrown into a random conversation.

"Daisy, this is Molly. I told you about Molly. She's my friend."

Molly managed a weak grimace. "What exactly have you been saying about me, Sammy?"

"Nothing bad! But Daisy said she likes birds, and you have Aurora, and well, birds!"

Daisy extended her hand, giving Molly a 'what else can you do?' smile. Molly shook the hand, because what else could she do, and clung to the one thing Sammy had given her.

"So, birds?"

Daisy nodded. "Yours is impressive. Don't think I've ever seen a Greater Spotted Hump Warbler in person before. Is she friendly?"

"I have no idea. I'm… not a big bird person. Actually, I'm kind of absolutely petrified of them."

Daisy's eyes widened, the tension of awkwardness leaking from her shoulders.

"Why do you have her then?" she asked.

"She chose me, Faerie knows why. Literally can't get her to leave, and I did try in the beginning. As long as she does her thing outside though, and doesn't peck my eyes out in my sleep, she can stay I guess."

Daisy chuckled. "They're not a breed that's known for being partial to eyeballs, don't worry. Crows on the other hand…"

"Seriously?!"

"No, not really. I'd love to meet her one day, if she's amenable to it."

Molly glanced over her shoulder but Aurora had vanished, apparently done issuing warnings to the other animals for the day.

"I have a workshop a couple of levels down," she said. "Just past the grocers through the lane on the right, *Molly's*. She tends to spend the days with me and fly out at night, unless I have to leave and lock the d- *OW*."

She winced as something hit the side of her face and looked down at a fabric sparring pad now lying by her feet. It wasn't sturdy enough to hurt, more like a glove, but the *thwack* of it still smarted on her skin.

With one hand still clamped to her ear, she ducked to grab the pad.

"Sorry, I didn't realise you had a girlfriend," Daisy said, amusement in every word.

Molly glared. "I don't. Excuse me."

She whirled around to find Talie still beside the ring,

arms folded and hip cocked to one side, irritability scrawled across her face.

"I don't have all night," she snapped. "We're here to train, not lounge around flirting."

Molly pulled the sparring pad onto her hand as she stalked toward her.

"How is that flirting? We were just being friendly," she hissed.

Talie rolled her eyes. "I don't care what it is. Do it on your own time, not mine."

"She was asking about Aurora. That is not flirting. Why do you care anyway?"

"I don-" She huffed. "I don't want to hear the excuses. Three rounds, three chances to land a hit. Go."

Molly raised her fists, settling her stance ready. She was fed, rested and now, thanks to Talie's charming personality, spoiling for a fight.

She swung out a fist the moment Talie was ready, but of course Talie dodged, one arm lashing out to bat the attack away.

Molly feinted the next strike with her left hand and punched with her right, but of course Talie was ready for both. Without waiting, Molly shifted her balance onto one leg and kicked up with the other. Even as Talie's arm came down to defend against her knee, Molly swung sideways and used the arc of her leg to knock Talie off her feet.

Talie twisted and fell forward instead of sideways, her entire weight bearing Molly down to the mat. Molly closed her eyes ready for the thump as pressure settled on the back of her head.

"Not bad."

Talie's voice brought her eyes open again and she blinked at Talie staring down at her. There was the tiniest hint of a smirk on her face, the rings of gold around her hazel eyes blazing.

Amber. Molly smiled.

Talie clambered to her feet and held a hand out. Molly took it and let Talie haul her up, preparing herself for another round.

"Everyone out."

Phoenix's voice echoed louder than any of the background noise. Halfway through swinging her next attempt to punch, Molly heard the directive after Talie did and almost landed a savage blow to her chest, twisting and stumbling to avoid it at the last moment. Talie grabbed her shoulders and hauled her upright. Her gaze lifted to Phoenix as he climbed one of the posts at the corner of the ring.

"Gym's closing," he added. "Sorry folks. Open again tomorrow."

Molly frowned as he jumped down amid the grumbles of folk already grabbing their stuff to head out.

"Something bad?" Molly asked.

Talie frowned, her gaze following Phoenix as he strode off toward the back of the gym and disappeared out of sight.

"Could be something, could be nothing. Unless we're called, we may never know. Come on. We'll have to pick up training tomorrow."

Molly wiped a hand over her face, then realised it still

had the pad on it. Grimacing, she hauled the pad off and dropped it in the nearby box full of them.

"I guess I'll see you tomorrow then," she said, pulling her coat on.

"Yeah."

Molly took that as the dismissal it was, heading for the door without bothering with goodbye. The fans were happily simulating soft drizzle and a chill as she stepped outside, and she pulled up her collar against the elements. Another night in was a luxury she didn't get anymore, so she would make the most of it.

CHAPTER NINE

TALIE

Talie watched Molly leave the gym as a sense of foreboding settled around her. She hadn't missed the meaningful look Phoenix had given her. He would expect her to hang around while he interrogated whichever poor soul needed to have their mind wiped after.

"Take it this means me as well?" Sammy asked.

Talie grimaced. "Yeah. I don't have time to walk you back I don't think."

She looked to the door, half wishing she could run after Molly and ask her to see Sammy home.

"I'll run, don't worry."

"And lock the door behind you when you get in."

Sammy rolled her eyes. "Yeah, I know. Happy doing whatever it is you do."

Talie grabbed her coat and pulled it on as Sammy walked away. She slid her hands into the pockets and clenched them into fists, watching Sammy walk out of the gym.

"Talie, follow me," Phoenix called.

He beckoned her over to the door that led to one of the class studios and she hurried to join him.

"Things are becoming increasingly unorganised," she muttered. "I don't like Sammy walking home on her own."

He nodded. "I know, but it can't be helped. I want you with me while I question this one."

"What? Why?"

"Because you're the one who's been interested in the artificer's guild. Come on."

He pushed the studio door open and strode through. Talie had to follow or have it swing shut in her face, her mind racing as they approached the storage room.

"Not a word," Phoenix warned. "Let me do the talking. When I give you the go ahead, you can remove the memory."

Talie nodded as he reached for the storage room door.

"Wait, we're not doing this in the warehouse?" she asked.

"Not this time. With Molly in our midst, the less we show her about where our bases are, the better."

Talie bit her lip as he opened the door.

No need to tell him how Molly and I met, or where. Knowing her, she could be waiting outside to follow me when I leave.

That thought alone made her smile, although she smothered it immediately. Among the mats, weights and bits of old gym equipment, a woman sat on a wooden chair. She looked up at them with a mixture of nerves and defiance in her bright blue eyes. A shaking hand tucked russet hair behind her ear, and she cleared her throat but didn't say a word.

"I'm told you had something you wanted to share?" Phoenix asked.

Talie risked a glance at him, the wide stance and folded arms giving off no hint of friendliness.

The woman's shoulders squared instantly.

"I think there's been some mistake," she said. "I don't have anything to say to Fae I don't even know who stand there glowering at me."

Phoenix lowered his arms.

"Apologies. It's been a long day." His tone softened. "If you do have anything to share, it could really help us."

The woman didn't relax, but she did settle back against the chair a small amount, her narrow-eyed gaze fixed on him.

"I'm all for progress," she said, her tone still defensive. "As part of the guild I need to be. We managed to not only isolate the components of gift use some time ago, but came up with a theory for replicating them."

Phoenix nodded. "I have heard some rumours of this."

"Rumours are everywhere. What we have are facts. That's where things get tricky. I've always been interested in fairies. Breeding humans with no known ability or skill and Fae that have an abundance of it, well, you're bound to get curious results. We figured out the necessary markers for replicating gifts almost a year ago now, but of course the ethics of trialling it were somewhat murky."

"What markers would these be?" he asked.

Her gaze sharpened. "Confidential ones. I have no intention of sharing guild secrets."

"Then why are you here?" Phoenix voiced exactly what Talie had been thinking.

"I'm not sharing guild secrets. Menagerie ones however, those I have no love for. I was sent toward the core yesterday to give some updated information, but what I saw…"

She looked away, disgust scrunching her face.

"Anything you can give us will help, no matter how gruesome," Phoenix prompted. When the woman's gaze flickered to Talie, he sighed. "She's more than acquainted with the darker side of the citadel's dealings, don't worry."

Talie nodded, fighting to keep her face expressionless. She had some idea what the woman might be about to say, and she'd craved for so long that Phoenix would trust her with the questioning.

Now, it sickened her to be involved at all.

"I'll spare the gore." The woman sniffed. "They're using them like mindless test subjects. The injuries, the noises… I'll have nightmares forever. There are ways of Fae that even the old traditions didn't cross. Torments that weren't even levelled on mere humans in the old days, or so the stories say."

"I remember," Phoenix said.

"I thought you might." The woman nodded. "I know who your family were, who you are."

He cocked his head. "You do?"

"Of course. You make very little effort to hide it. Why else do you think I brought this information to you?"

Talie fought the urge to launch questions at him. He'd never mentioned having any kind of notable family, not that he needed to tell her, but she hadn't even heard any rumour or whisper of it.

"The Menagerie might have their uses," the woman continued. "But at least when your family ruled, the citadel fared by the old ways. What is the point of keeping the balance between rich and poor, Fae and fairy, if those meant to serve are being hacked like bits of wood?"

Talie kept her fists firmly in her sweatshirt pocket, her jaw aching from keeping her mouth shut as astonishment urged her to splutter out questions.

"I couldn't agree more," Phoenix said smoothly. "What use is gift replication if the group using it are planning to throw it out to gain the wider world of Faerie? The citadel is self-sustaining and we have no need of the realms outside. Long will it continue. The Menagerie have been using this place as a resource for far too long."

Talie kept her gaze welded to the woman's shoulder. Any moment now, Phoenix would give her the nod to remove the woman's memories of the whole thing. She would need to word-tangle what the woman did remember so there weren't any gaps noticeable by others if they asked, but it proved one thing: Phoenix's words about the citadel and the Menagerie were for her benefit. She just didn't know why.

It's to do with Molly. She bit her lip. *Ever since he took her on, he wants me to train her, watch her, guide her to his side. He wants me to see things like this so I'm convinced we're on the right side.*

She almost missed Phoenix turning his head and nodding at her. Hating herself for having to do it, she dredged her mind-wipe gift forward, letting it settle like a catch in her throat.

"So let's just make sure we all understand each other," she said. "You went to the core to deliver something?"

The woman nodded. "Yes, I went to deliver some updated markers."

"But you witnessed something worse."

"I'll never forget it, never." She shuddered, a hand pressing to her chest. "The screams, the sights through those glass doors."

"And then you left, on your own?"

"Yes- well, apart from the guards. The entrance through the Menagerie hall is extremely well guarded, but once you get through the double doors, you only get one guide."

A bit of bonus information there. Talie pulled her gift back with her heart already in her shoes. *Do I tell Molly this?*

"Tell me one more time," she commanded.

The woman frowned. "Tell you what? I came to tell you…"

"You came to tell us you had nothing to report, didn't you?"

Talie offered the excuse quicker than she might have done normally because she wanted out. She had to make sure Sammy made it home okay, and she wanted nothing more than to wash the awful day off her skin.

"I- must have done," the woman agreed slowly. "This is an odd place to meet."

"You must understand we have to ask these questions," Phoenix added.

Talie nodded. "We do, but if there's nothing you need to share with us, I'll show you out."

The woman stood and Talie led her through the studio, slipping her gift around her again.

"Have you seen that storeroom before?" she asked.

The woman shook her head. "No, first time. Why?"

Talie opened the studio door and led the woman back out into the main centre of the gym, letting the silence swill as her gift unwound the woman's recollections of the studio and the storage room beyond.

"I think you have the wrong place," she said the moment they were at the door to the lane. "It's a nice enough place here but no offense, you look like you could afford to go to the gym five levels down."

The woman looked around, her frown fading.

"I can see that. I don't know what I was thinking. Excuse me."

She strode downward, her pace increasing until she was almost running.

Talie let the gym door close behind her. She should go back inside and double check Phoenix didn't need to mull the whole thing over with her, but she felt heartsick and wanted to go home.

I didn't even know that woman's name, and I took her mind like it was nothing.

She wiped a hand over her face and glanced over her shoulder. No sign of Phoenix, so she made the decision for herself.

Striding through the drizzle being dropped from the vents, she let the pace calm her jittery limbs.

Telling Molly was the right thing to do, but if Molly took it back to the Menagerie, whether by choice or by necessity, Phoenix would know she told. She walked a very dangerous line every time she disobeyed him, because he was the one currently paying for Sammy's schooling.

Not much longer and we won't need him for that anymore.

She turned into her lane and dodged the broken bottle, nodding automatically to Mister Boots lounging on a nearby bin.

She pushed her key into the lock and opened the door to find Sammy surrounded by sweet wrappers on her bed, the scent of food lingering in the air.

"I made soup," Sammy announced. "It's not great, but it'll do. It was either that or go out for something and I know you hate me doing that on my own."

Talie locked the door behind her, tugged her boots off and went straight to the counter. She grabbed the soup leftover in a big mug and downed it without bothering to taste it. Nutrients were all the same hot or cold.

"Did you have fun doing whatever it is I'm not supposed to know you're doing?" Sammy asked innocently, not looking up from whatever she was reading.

"Fun doesn't come in to it."

"Not even if Molly was involved?"

Talie huffed. "Please don't. Molly's…"

She couldn't say friend exactly, but admitting she liked Molly's company to Sammy, even in the slightest, would be the absolute end of any peace she might have ever again.

"Don't worry, I won't say a word tonight." Sammy

cackled unconvincingly. "You look wrecked. Perhaps you need a holiday."

Talie sank onto her bed with a sigh. She had no hope of any kind of holiday, not from Phoenix or the citadel or any of it.

I wonder if there's any way for Sammy though. The thought curled enticingly in her mind.

She turned on her side to face the wall, exhausted enough to drift straight to sleep.

Molly might be able to help, considering she had all her fancy friends like the lords and ladies.

If I can find a way to get Sammy out of the citadel, at least she'll be safe from whatever's coming here.

CHAPTER TEN

MOLLY

"Sanctuary!"

Harvey burst through the workshop doorway, his purple hair stuck on end and his eyes rolling wild. Molly pushed out of her chair, wild thoughts of the baby or Beryl in trouble filling her head until the word registered. Harvey shut the workshop door and pressed his back against it.

"What did you lose?" Molly asked, easing herself back down.

"Me? Absolutely nothing." He grinned. "I'm just seeking the quiet company of my neighbour who isn't likely to throw soiled nappies at my head."

"She does have a good aim to be fair," Molly agreed.

Harvey pushed away from the door and strode over to take the chair opposite hers. With the desk between them, and him looking exceedingly comfortable slouched there, Molly wondered how long he was planning on hiding out.

She had no idea what to say to him and continued sanding down the little trinket box she was working on. Harvey glanced around at the workshop, from the shavings at her feet to the dust on the ceiling.

"Is it a good living, the workshop?" he asked.

Molly shrugged. "It does what it needs to. If I'm short I work harder, sometimes I can work less. Depends on what commissions come through really, but it does okay."

No sense telling him there weren't any rental rates, and that her ownership of it depended on the Menagerie's good will not to take it away from her, especially as he had no idea who the Menagerie were.

"I've never been very handy," he said. "Beryl's got a good elemental gift on her, good for shattering things, but I'm mostly charm and defensive skills. I can catch something before it breaks, but often doesn't help when I'm the one breaking stuff."

Molly smiled. "You do seem kind of clumsy, no offense."

"None taken. It's all I can do not to drop the baby, not that I ever would. She at least seems to like me."

It was all said with a grin and a swagger, but none of that hid the dark circles under his eyes.

"It must be tough," she said.

He shrugged. "There are so many people out there far worse off than any of us."

Thoughts of the fairies taken by the Menagerie filled Molly's head, and of Talie constantly worried for Sammy's safety.

"Can't disagree with that."

Harvey tilted his head to the side. "Sounds like you're speaking from experience."

"Could be better, could be worse. That's the case for

most I reckon. Rumour has it there are fairies in some realms who get targeted simply for their human blood."

She left the subject hanging, wondering if he would fill it. She knew so little about them, and it hadn't occurred to her until then to ask, but the chances of them somehow being spies were slim.

And it doesn't matter if they're Menagerie or resistance spies, as I'm on both sides anyway.

"I've known humans."

He announced it so casually.

Molly stopped sanding the wood in her hands, eying him in amazement.

"Actual humans? How? Where?"

He smiled. "I've travelled here and there. Less said, the better. Humans are no different to Fae. They don't have gifts, granted, but they have skills of their own, of a different kind."

"Like what?"

It occurred to her she should have offered him something to drink, but now she was so amazed she couldn't bring herself to interrupt the subject. Nobody in the citadel had ever seen a human, not that she knew of. The nobles might have on their travels, but most Fae were born in the citadel and humans were from somewhere other entirely.

"They have flying carts called planes, like your bird except made of metal. They have carts that go amazingly fast too, called cars. Their food isn't half bad either, what they can do with basic ingredients is magical."

"That sounds... fictional." She frowned. "Whoever

heard of metal that flies? How does it even stay up? Is it like huge wings they have to flap really fast?"

"Nope but it's complicated stuff. Fae think humans are mindless animals because they don't have gifts, but Fae get lazy with them. The worst thing I can imagine is being in a world where people who can feel pain, whether human, fairy or Fae, are used like objects and resources."

Molly thought of the fairies, her blood boiling.

"Fae don't exactly see humans as more than objects, or even fairies," she admitted.

"Some Fae don't. The more progressive ones are getting the hang of it though. The orb-casts are all about the new Holly Queen outside the citadel breaking down the old ways and trying to make Faerie fairer."

Molly bit her lip, trying not to smile. Harvey had no idea she'd actually met the queen, and she couldn't tell him. He probably wouldn't believe her even if she did, or would think her delusional and not safe around the baby.

"It's an admirable thing to do," she agreed. "There are those who want fairness here too, but things have been weighted toward the nobles and the powers pulling the strings for so long."

Harvey sighed. "True enough. All we can do is keep being kind to those around us where it matters. Like sheltering a wanted man from his beloved."

Molly snorted. "She probably knows you're here."

"Probably. Which means it might be safe to go back, because she's probably asleep." He groaned to his feet. "Thanks for hiding me briefly. If you ever need a place to hide, from Fae, fairy, human, or other, you can count on us."

His eyes twinkled as he said it, and Molly grinned as he ambled to throw the workshop door open. She wouldn't bring any of her chaos down on him or his family, and she knew how to take care of herself enough to stay out of total peril.

But those poor fairies.

Her mind wandered as Harvey left. She didn't want to even think about what the Menagerie might be doing to them, or why they were even inside the citadel at all.

The only way I'm going to find out is either by asking, which is madness, or by doing what I've been trained to do.

Spying on the Menagerie seemed like madness in itself, with so many people going about the place she'd be spotted anywhere she wasn't meant to be. The guild however…

She rubbed a hand over her face. The guild was guarded but there were ways inside, and ways through that didn't exactly scream 'someone might be hiding in here'.

"What do you think?" she murmured to Aurora. "Guild? Maybe I should invite Talie."

Aurora crooned softly before tucking her head under her wing. It wasn't a yes but it wasn't a 'click-of-her-beak' no either.

Inviting Talie was dangerous, but then Molly couldn't exactly ask Ru to keep lookout.

He'd be through the first open window to Marcus after forbidding me to leave the workshop.

A shadow loomed in the doorway. Half expecting Harvey to be back, she lifted her head. The smile died on her face.

"Why was the door shut?" Ru demanded.

She tensed. "Harvey was hiding from Beryl next door. Why is that a problem?"

Ru stalked into the shop, his gaze flicking around the room. Aurora's head reappeared from under her wing, her beady eyes clamping on him with dedicated intensity.

"I came by to talk and you never shut your door during the day, unless you're out."

"So? I could have been out. Wait, have you been watching me?"

Thoughts of what he might have seen or heard if he had followed her cascaded through her mind.

"I don't like you being so prickly with me," he said.

No answer is as good as a confession.

She shrugged. "I don't like you killing people. It was the one thing we said we'd never do. Kill one for whatever reason, then all are fair game if the reason is right."

He glanced over his shoulder but didn't shut the door like she expected him to.

"I wish you could understand, but this goes deeper than even I comprehend. I trust Marcus will keep us safe, and that's what matters. And Celeste, she's always been kind to you, hasn't she?"

Molly nodded. "She has, but that still doesn't excuse killing random people on their orders. What if they asked you to kill me, if I strayed beyond the bounds of their control. Would you do it then? Or what if it was one of my friends, would that be okay?"

"Have you strayed?"

She stared at him, pulse pounding. For the first time, possibly ever that she could remember, she pulled a protection warding over herself in his presence.

"It was a hypothetical question. You're nothing more than a mindless assassin now to them, willing to kill if they ask, which makes you nothing more than that to me."

A flash of pain passed over his face, his fists clenched at his sides.

"You don't understand. That man threatened- He would have hurt so many in the long run. Would have hurt you."

"I don't even know him."

"You would have in time. This is all for you, Molly."

She shook her head. "It has nothing to do with me. I might work for the Menagerie, but even that's because they all but own my service. No more Menagerie means no more workshop, no more place to live or earn my living. They ask me to track the artificers going missing, I do it. They ask me to go to the queen's court and spy, I do it. What has killing whoever that man was got to do with me?"

Ru wiped a hand over his face. Another glance over his shoulder and his pained expression faded.

"You'll understand eventually."

She pushed her hands on the desk and got to her feet, barely flinching as Aurora left her perch atop the mirror to settle on the back of her chair instead with a warning caw.

"What is there to understand? The boots are controlled by the Menagerie. The boots were pulling frightened looking fairies through skip-ways and throwing them into carts to be taken Faerie knows where. You're running around killing people."

Ru's mouth thinned. "So you're on the enemy side now? A few days hanging around with that, that… *girl* and you're one of them?"

"I'm not one of anybody!" She seethed in a sharp breath to keep the tattered threads of her self-control. "Until I know the reasons, I can't support killers. You've always known that about me, always. Do I think the Menagerie's enemies are going to magically turn out to be the good guys? No, but the Menagerie aren't exactly painting themselves in the best light either right now."

It would be just her luck to have Talie walk in at that moment. She almost expected her at the door but Ru blocked it, his face cast in a semi-shadow of sadness.

"I wish I could explain, but I can't," he said. "Remember you still need to report anything important though, whatever your delusions. The Menagerie is still your employer and I'm still your liaison."

She nodded. "Well aware. The Menagerie comes before all else, or else, I know."

He opened his mouth to respond, to retort something suitably patronising, but after a moment he simply shook his head and left the shop.

Molly sagged back in her chair, wailing quietly when Aurora ruffled her feathers right above.

"Please don't peck my eyes out," she murmured, shutting them tight. "I think I've had just about enough of everything for today."

Aurora chirped something withering and fluttered back to the mirror, but Molly kept her eyes closed.

She couldn't trust Ru to keep her safe anymore, perhaps she never could. She couldn't exactly trust Talie either, or Phoenix, but someone needed to find out what was going on, if only to raise the alarm outside the citadel for those poor fairies.

It started with the artificers' guild, so I need to be looking there.

She remained in her chair, eyes closed as she ran over the potential plan and pitfalls. It couldn't hurt to see if Talie wanted to go along with her, just for safety's sake.

CHAPTER ELEVEN

TALIE

Talie ducked a punch flying at her face, her arms up a fraction too late to defend. Seething through her teeth in frustration, she squared up to Nia and managed to land a jab of her own.

"Good," Nia said. "Take five."

Talie shook her head. "Don't need five. Go again."

Nia nodded to something over Talie's shoulder with a smirk. Talie twisted, her thudding pulse squeezing tight. Not only was Molly fresh-faced with her blonde waves swept back in a high ponytail, but she was all bright-eyed too, standing hesitantly at the edge of the sparring ring.

Talie wiped her wrist over her sweaty forehead, then down her cheeks for good measure. Her ragged t-shirt clung to her skin and she glanced down at the holes in her trousers.

Ridiculous, none of that matters.

She approached the edge of the ring, mindful of Molly's fingers curled around the top. Edging to one side, Talie braced her forearms on the rope.

"Early for you, isn't it?" she asked.

Molly nodded. "I need to speak to you."

The slight calm in Talie's adrenalin shot back up again. No sign of obvious distress or injury, if anything Molly looked ready to raise hell. Her lips twitched and she assessed the sparsely populated gym before nodding and heading toward the water station. She grabbed a cup and filled it, then picked up her threadbare towel to wipe her face.

"What's going on?"

Molly hesitated. "I've thought about it and all the links seem to go back to the artificer's guild as well as the Menagerie."

"What are you suggesting then, that they're working together somehow? Sacrificing some of their own for the wider cause?"

"Well, I wasn't thinking that, but I am now. No, I'm going to go and spy on the guild."

Talie blinked. "You're what?"

Molly glanced around before shuffling closer. Still breathing hard from the exertion, the subtle scent of verbena gusted up Talie's nose and it took all her willpower not to close her eyes and sniff deeply.

Weirdo. She let that self-assessment slide as Molly lowered her voice to a murmur.

"I'm going to have a look, maybe a listen if I can get close enough. There are certain entry points which are often unmanned in most buildings, and I need to practice my stealth gift anyway."

"If you need to practice stealth, sneak up on Sammy,"

she suggested. "She's mostly harmless."

Molly rolled her eyes. "If I had all the time in Faerie I would, but I don't. I'm not asking permission, I'm letting you know."

"Why?"

Even as the question burbled out, Talie wasn't sure she was prepared for the answer. It definitely wouldn't be the one she wanted deep in the pit of her wilted heart. Either way, if Molly was going then so was she.

"What do you mean why?"

"It's a question, used to ascertain the reasoning behind an action or intention, Princess."

"Orbs alive." Molly turned away. "Forget I said anything."

Talie smiled. "No. You've told me now. I'm coming with you."

"Don't bother."

"Too late, I'm going. Lead the way."

Molly scowled at her for several seconds, but Talie couldn't contain the sudden excitement at the one thought thundering through her head.

She came to find me.

There was absolutely no reason for Molly not to go alone. She wasn't incapable, if anything her time with the Menagerie had given her ample skills for sneaking around, yet she chose to seek her out.

"You need to change then," Molly said, her tone flat. "Or at least start breathing normally. They'd smell and hear you a mile off."

Talie cocked her head. "Ouch. Alright, give me five

minutes."

She left Molly hanging around the gym and dipped into the changing rooms. Her cheeks were fast losing the flushed look, but her hair was a state and she didn't have a change of shirt.

The door burst open while she was still despairing at the state of herself.

"Here, don't say I don't do anything for you." Nia breezed past to drop a clean dark blue t-shirt on the counter beside the sink. "I'd at least finger-brush your hair as well."

Talie swiped up the t-shirt with a disgruntled glower. "Thanks."

She raked her hands through her hair several times before the bizarre situation registered.

"Wait-"

Nia cackled. "Wherever you're going with Molly, you don't want to do it stinking like a pit fight and looking like a haystack. Trust me, girls notice."

"Why would I care if she notices or not?" she asked, teeth gritted as she pulled out a puff-case of deodorant powder.

Nia hopped onto the sink with a smug grin.

"Do you?"

Yes. "Why would I?"

"You know constant questions are as good as an admission, right?"

Talie shoved the deodorant case onto Nia's lap and hauled off her grimy t-shirt, replacing it quickly with the blue one while mumbling through a conveniently placed mouthful of fabric.

Nia chuckled. "Yeah, you continue pretending you don't fancy her. Sure she's already figured it out."

Talie scraped her hands through her hair again and gave Nia an arctic look.

"You're infuriating."

"Thanks. Remember that next time you try to punch my bad shoulder."

Talie let that reminder fall with a tiny smile of thanks in reply and left the changing rooms with her old t-shirt in hand.

She managed two paces before she saw Molly, then who Molly was talking to. Irrational jealousy rose hot inside her chest and tightened her gut into writhing knots.

Daisy's objectively good-looking in an overly confident way. She scowled as Daisy laughed at something Molly said and pushed her shiny chestnut hair from one shoulder to the other. *It's not like I'm the kind of pretty anyone would be interested in.*

Somehow, it had never mattered much to her before. She valued effort and smarts over beauty, but now the sensation of being naturally lacking burrowed deep into her mind.

Clenching her hand around her dirty t-shirt, she walked up behind Molly. Daisy saw her first, her smile becoming amused instead of animated.

"Hello. We didn't get a chance to meet last time."

Talie nodded. "Hi. Molly, are we going or what?"

"First you make me wait around while you change, now you can't get out fast enough, what's with you?" Molly grumbled. "See you around, Daisy."

Each step away from Daisy eased the hideous tightness in Talie's chest that little bit more, until she felt sane enough to answer properly.

"You told me to change, it wasn't me making you wait around."

Molly shrugged. "Maybe, but I don't understand what you've got against Daisy. She's not… one of the other side, if you know who I mean."

"The other side? Not your side? Interesting." Talie pulled the gym door open.

"I don't have a side anymore. Maybe I never did. The whole point of choosing a side is exactly that, you get to choose. I haven't been allowed to choose any of this."

"I think it's hard with all the skulduggery going around on all sides," Talie agreed. "Can't be sure who to trust these days."

She didn't miss the sneaky sideways glance Molly gave her, or the tiniest upward tilt of her mouth as they reached the lane and started downward.

"That makes two of us."

Echoing what I said yesterday. Talie smiled.

"Nice try, Princess."

"What? It does."

"You have a terrible innocent face. You know there are things I can't tell you."

Molly frowned. "Can't or won't?"

"Can't." It was as close as the swear-block placed on her head would let her get to spilling secrets.

"Oh what, someone put a swear-block on you or

something?" Molly joked. When Talie didn't answer, she grimaced. "Seriously? Orbs, that sucks. I wondered whether it was that or if you were just being difficult."

Even nodding was a huge effort, and she wasn't sure if Molly saw it, but it would have to do.

"Unless you're simply saying nothing because you can tell me, but won't, and you don't want to have to word-tangle about it," Molly added.

Talie sighed. "You'll have to make your own mind up about that."

"Well, what can you tell me then?"

Talie thought back to her conversation with Phoenix.

"Phoenix is worried about the fairies being brought in. The way he was talking, it sounds like he's expecting something big to happen soon. I've spoken to him before about watching the artificer's guild but he's always said we've got it covered or we've already done what we can there."

A vague answer, now that I think about it.

Talie bit her lip as they passed Molly's level and continued on downward. It would have been quicker to take the rubbish chute route, but Molly didn't suggest it so Talie didn't either, content to spend the afternoon walking at Molly's side.

She smoothed down her clean t-shirt, relieved now that both Molly and Nia had hounded her into making the small effort. The artificer's guild was several levels below, and passing through lanes that far down would probably draw all sorts of disgusted looks their way.

"Did you know the artificers live in the guild itself?"

Molly asked.

"No, but there's like a thousand of them in various skillsets. That must take up a lot of room."

"Exactly. You can climb, right? Like up the pillars?"

Talie nodded, even though her climbing skills weren't exactly well-practiced. Molly hooked left down a wide alleyway, stumbling to a halt when two women started toward them. Talie brushed her shoulder alongside Molly's with her heart sinking. One of the women looked familiar and was smiling right at her.

"Hello again," the woman said. "Fancy seeing you twice in as many days. What brings you here?"

Talie caught the subtle note of suspicion in the woman's voice, even as Molly turned to give her a badly veiled look of accusation.

How do I tell her what happened last night?

"We wanted a chance to talk to each other." She word-tangled quickly. "It's chaotic at home and we're both so busy. Walking's good for getting time alone."

The woman nodded. "Fair enough. These alleys are part of the artificer's guild though, so I wouldn't hang around on this level, or any of the below, not without a reason."

"Of course, thanks for warning us," Talie said.

"After you giving me the heads up about your gym yesterday? No problem at all."

She dodged around them with her friend in tow as Molly faced Talie, the edge of their focus fixed on the mouth of the alley. The moment the women were out of sight, Molly folded her arms.

"Let me guess, another thing you can't tell me about?"

Her nostrils flared when she was angry and Talie had the ill-timed urge to laugh. She shouldn't be telling Molly anything, definitely not about the reason Phoenix had closed the gym early the night before, or her part in the whole thing.

"So, Phoenix closed the gym last night, but I didn't leave straight away. He had a job for me to do."

Molly frowned. "Keep talking."

"Remember when we first met, when you fell out of the rafters? Well, there are some tasks Phoenix needs me to do, and what I was doing that night, I was doing last night too."

"Wiping memories?"

Talie hesitated. She didn't want to have that conversation with Molly of all people, even though Molly had more rights than most to demand it. When she didn't answer immediately, the dip in Molly's brow deepened.

"You wiped my mind, right?" she prompted. "You told me that much already, about what happened to my guardians. Guessing that wasn't a one-time skill. Seymour was an artificer, the one that died in the park. Lady Carrington was affiliated with the artificers too, but you and the resistance aren't."

Talie wiped a hand over her face. Her first thought was to run to Phoenix and tell him Molly knew way too much, but the scrunchy look on Molly's face, part pout and part withering determination, held her in place.

"So, you're either part of the reason they're going missing," Molly concluded. "Or you're part of the reason the truth isn't going public. Which one is it?"

"It- I can't say."

"Of course you can't." Molly stamped a foot and rotated away, moving a few paces away before stalking back again. "Maybe it's best we don't do this then, not together at least."

Talie's heart sank.

"I don't get to be in the room when the discussions are going on," she said bitterly. "I just ruin their lives for them afterward."

Molly sighed, the scrunchy expression unfolding a little.

"Do you by any chance have a super easy way into the guild without us being seen?" she asked.

Talie shook her head. "Never been. That woman only recognises me because it was last night. In a few days, I'll be a fuzzy part of her mind that she associates with a distant dream or something."

"Can I trust you?"

Talie stilled. The question threw her off guard. She wanted so badly to say yes, but it wouldn't be the whole truth.

"As much as I have choice over my own actions, you can."

Molly nodded. "Thought as much. I've learned not to trust anyone, but I wanted to see how vague your answer was."

"Suitably vague enough for you, Princess?"

"Eh, I've heard worse. Come on then, but if we get caught I'm blaming you for leading me astray."

Talie smiled, unable to help it. "I'm sure everyone

would believe you."

Molly only rolled her eyes, then vaulted onto a long wooden box beside the nearest pillar. With steady hands and secure feet, she dug into the grooves and surged upward.

Talie gritted her teeth, eying the foot and handholds Molly had used, one determined thought revolving in her mind.

If I don't manage this, she'll never let me live it down.

She hauled herself up a few spaces, the muscles already sore from training protesting. One quick glance upward and Molly was already on the girder below the next level. Talie renewed her determination, a burning wave of panic passing over her when she almost missed a handhold.

Molly didn't comment when she finally hauled herself up, but for someone more used to moving through old service tunnels and interconnecting resistance backrooms, balancing on a girder barely wide enough for them to stand side by side wasn't her idea of fun.

"See that window over there?" Molly pointed. "If we creep in through there, it should take us through the eaves and into the chimney network."

"And these chimneys are…"

"Redundant now." She set off toward the window. "Most of them, at least. They're part of the older structure the Menagerie wanted cleared out."

Talie scowled as she stepped cautiously after Molly, the artificial wind strong enough to make her feel unsteady even though her balance was firmly centred.

"Oh, there's not much space," Molly added. "And

they've removed the chimney flue, so it's just a sprawling mass of air. Oh well."

She swung in through the window and Talie hurried after her, desperate to get away from the yawning drop into the alley below. She crawled through, went to take a step and grabbed Molly's arms.

"What the-"

She stared down at an even deeper drop than outside, her stomach lurching.

A tiny smile etched itself across Molly's face.

"I told you they removed the flue," she said. "Don't worry, we can shuffle to the corner there. See that hatch? It'll lead us into the wall-space. Don't make any loud noises and they'll have no idea we're even here."

Reluctant to let her go, Talie released her grip on Molly's arms.

"How do you know all this?"

Molly shrugged. "The benefit of who I work for, and I don't mean myself. I guess where you and the resistance have your inside tunnels, the Menagerie have the outside roofs and chimney stacks."

Talie watched the steps Molly took to reach the corner of the rafters, the wooden beam they were standing on barely deep enough to fit the length of a foot.

Inching sideways, Talie focused on Molly, already peering into the hatch, her golden ponytail tumbling over her shoulder.

"Do you think-" she began.

Molly pressed a finger to her lips, then pointed to the hatch. As Talie crept closer, she heard the subtle hum of voices.

"Can you pressure climb?" Molly whispered.

"Can I what?"

"Pressure climb. You know, push hands against one side, feet against the other and use that leverage to work your way upwards?"

Talie stared at her, almost forgetting the perilous drop right beneath her until she accidentally looked down. Tipping her head back with a rough gulp, Talie closed her eyes.

"No, I can't pressure climb."

She would learn though, if only to wipe the insufferable smirk that was no doubt lighting on Molly's face.

"Okay. Back in a minute."

Talie opened her eyes in time to see a swish of blonde getting swallowed by the gloom of the hatch. Her heart lurched, breathless nausea bubbling up. She shuffled as quickly as she dared to the edge, peering in.

Already a fair way down, Molly had her back to one side of the brick wall and her feet braced against the other as she wiggled downward like a determined caterpillar.

Talie pressed a hand to her forehead while clamping the other tight to the lip of the hatch. In that one aspect of skill, Molly had her beat hands down. Her orb burned in her pocket and she pulled it out, dreading the thought of having to explain to Phoenix where she was if he was summoning her.

Molly's name curled around the shimmering blue surface. Astonished, she swiped her thumb over the orb and held it up as Molly's face shadowed by darkness filled the air in front of her.

She's letting me hear what she's hearing. Talie bit her lip. *She might not trust me, but she's willing to level the field between us, even though I can't tell her things.*

"-nothing." A man's voice filled the air, distant and tinny. "Two more infusions."

"One more should do it."

"I said two."

Molly's exasperated face flashed into view again, moments before the orb-cast changed to a view of what Talie realised was her neck. Given the tiny clinking noises, she had the orb keyring between her teeth.

"I told her, she's out of her orbing mind if she thinks he's in any way interested in her."

Talie waited as flashes of conversation drifted past as Molly made her way further down.

"-and then I said, how many legs does one need for that?"

"Sometimes, I think she's just testing me."

"-legend of the citadel's core is one many have taken interest in over the ages."

Talie tensed but Molly was already stopping, the orb-cast slowing it's rocky pace.

She had to be one-handed at some point to get the orb out. How much strength is she hiding?

Talie shook the thought aside and leaned the tiniest bit closer to the gaping hole Molly had disappeared into.

"We must let the powers that be fight amongst themselves," a woman replied, her tone dripping with amusement. "Much like the nobility, we will ensure our longevity while they're all squabbling for a brief taste of ruling. The guilds are needed by all."

"If it is the core they're seeking, what's to say it won't swallow the whole citadel in time? I've heard horrific stories about wells of power."

"What's to say they haven't found it already? Everyone knows who holds dominion over the citadel's core, but whether they've discovered its secrets or not, who knows? No, best we keep both sides singing sweetly. Outward impartiality and inward favour both ways. Whoever wins, we will be there to celebrate among the spoils."

"As it should be. We can discover more at the meeting tonight."

"Same boring old voices harping on. What time?"

"Seven, in the Rose Room."

"Hopefully it won't last long. Oh, did I tell you Primrose came top of her class again this week? She'll pass the guild entry exam with no problem at this rate."

"Assuming you remain in favour, she won't have to bother with it."

Their laughter filled the air, and thoughts of Sammy striving at school without influential connections filled Talie with untameable rage. The image from the orb-cast started bouncing again, a slower, more defined bob that suggested Molly was on her way back up. Peering down again, Talie could see the faintest outline of her pressure climbing slowly.

Almost at the hatch, Molly leaned her head back against the wall, the sheen of sweet covering her flushed face.

Talie shoved her orb back in her pocket and held out a

hand ready, her skin fizzling when Molly grasped it with her burning one.

The moment Molly was out of the hatch, Talie turned both her hands over with a frown. Molly flinched at the contact, but glanced down at the raw pink skin on her palms with a shrug.

"Necessary evil of climbing. Let's get back onto the girders. We can take a shortcut back."

Talie started her slow shuffle back toward the window, not sure if the queasy buzzing in her knees was in any way healthy or normal.

If she can shunt herself halfway down what must have been at least two levels, then back up again, I can get to the window.

She climbed out onto the wider girder and sagged against the wall. Molly clambered out behind her and sighed.

"I take it you heard what they were saying?" Molly asked. "I wanted to go down further and see if I got anything else, but I know when I've hit my limit."

Talie frowned. "That was insane. You're like some kind of weird stick insect."

"A *what?*" Molly choked over a surprised laugh. "I can't believe you called me a weird stick insect. I almost think that's worse than Princess."

"Princess was never meant to be an insult," Talie muttered. "It fit with old stories I've read, that's all."

"Get hold of old stories much?" Molly asked.

Talie shrugged. "I got a library card from Phoenix to do his dirty work. I couldn't help hanging around a bit to read whatever I could find."

She waited for the inevitable scoff of derision, or the soft laugh like Nia had once given her when she mentioned dipping into the story section of the library.

Molly smiled. "You're lucky then. I wish I could have one. Maybe you can tell me some stories one day."

Astonished, Talie bit her lip, her mind venturing through the levels to the cruddy hand-bound bits of paper she'd collected.

"I can, if you want. I'm not allowed to take books out of the library without permission, but I wrote some of them down on scraps of paper."

She'd chosen the best ones for telling Sammy on the nights where the shadows loomed dark or they couldn't afford lights or candles in the very early days. Sometimes, when nightmares crept in, the stories had also kept them both sane. She'd turned a blind eye to Sammy 'borrowing' glue from school to bind the paper into book form for that reason alone.

"That's so clever." Molly said it without a shred of mockery in her voice. "So, are you taking all this information back to Phoenix?"

Talie hesitated, still swimming in the unnerving inner warmth of having been praised for something.

"I have to. Are you taking it back to the Menagerie?"

Molly looked away, staring out over the rooftops of the level and beyond to the setting sun beyond the citadel glass.

"I should, but then I'd be in trouble for snooping without permission. I could do with getting into the library next actually, to find out if there's anything about this well of power or the citadel core."

"You don't know who built their entire fortress around the core then?" Talie asked carefully.

"No, I'm guessing you do." Molly sighed. "And I'm betting one guess, it's not Phoenix."

"The Menagerie is built around the core. Not many know that, but Phoenix has mentioned it before. He said the core was meant to be full of old storage from ancient times, blocked off to everyone to keep it safe. The Menagerie formed around it slowly, creeping into businesses and homes bit by bit."

Molly turned toward the nearest pillar and stretched her arms against it with a groan.

"I'll have to go there next then."

Talie pushed away from the wall, conscious that Molly looked like she was lagging from the exertion, her eyes lidded and her shoulders hunched.

"Give me some time and I'll go with you."

Molly snorted. "In case you've forgotten, I'm part of the Menagerie. You're not. You'll stick out, or I'll get in trouble for bringing you in."

"Nice try." Talie folded her arms. "I can be sneaky when I need to be. You can't go in alone, even if you are one of them. It's too dangerous."

"Well it's definitely too dangerous for you. Besides, I'll need to find a way into the guild first for that meeting."

Talie's jaw dropped. "You what?"

"You heard me. If you're worried about me not sharing information with you-"

"Worried you'll get caught more like." The words tumbled out before she could stop them.

Molly's brow lifted, surprise scrawled across her face.

"I have ways of going undetected, I'll be fine."

"Well, so do I. I'm coming with you."

"Oh really? How are you planning on getting in then?"

Glowering at each other, Talie both respected and despaired at Molly's stubbornness.

"Okay, how about this." She forced her tone to calm. "Go back to the workshop for now, lay low. I'll come find you once I've sorted a couple of things that might help us."

She held out her hand. Molly stared at it, then back at her face.

"Why?"

Talie had absolutely no logical reason, but she'd be cursed if she let Molly know that.

"Because we both want to know the truth, but you need a rest first. That was some serious climbing."

Her face burned and she was convinced Molly could see right through her. After a long, excruciating moment, Molly ducked her head and chuckled.

"If you were anyone else, I'd have assumed that was a compliment. Fine, I could do with the rest. I'll go home, but if you're not there by six tonight, I'm going in without you."

"Absolutely."

Talie moved to lower her hand at the same time Molly reached forward to shake it. Her pulse jumped as they made awkward contact, fizzles shooting from her chest to her elbow and right down into her fingers, the sensation buzzing. Molly dropped her hand but Talie couldn't see any sign of surprise or emotion on her face.

"Come on then." Molly sighed. "Several levels to climb up yet."

Talie smiled even though her insides were still rioting.

"Far be it for me to tell you what to do, Princess, but you could just walk up the normal way with me."

CHAPTER TWELVE

MOLLY

Molly ambled down the lane with plans brewing in her mind. Talie had left her at the entrance to her lane with the insistence that she didn't leave for the guild alone. She lifted her head, hoping for a couple of hours rest, which she wouldn't tell Talie about. Her amusement died the moment she turned into her lane.

Ru stood leaning against the workshop door and turned to face her as she slowed her pace, stopping a few steps out of reach.

"No training?" he asked.

"Cancelled."

"Just as well then. You've been summoned."

Molly's insides flared hot before the inevitable chill of foreboding set in. If Marcus was summoning her, it could be for any number of reasons, but given her doubts she wouldn't be able to word-tangle her way out of the truth if he asked her about her allegiances.

I can't refuse though.

She cast a look around and vaulted up onto the

neighbour's rain barrel to get up onto the girders. Ru kept a pace or two behind her as she traversed the familiar route toward the Menagerie window entrance, honouring her mood by not saying a word.

Perhaps there's not much he can say anymore. The thought didn't comfort her any.

She hopped through the Menagerie window without waiting for him and headed toward the double doors of Marcus's office. She inhaled a sharp breath, but Ru brushed past her and opened one door without knocking, standing aside to wave her in.

"Ah, Molly, come in."

She inched through the door, a sudden onslaught of nerves hitting her square in the chest. Marcus looked up from his seat behind the desk, his dark hair raked back from his face and his shoulders in their usual stiff set.

Celeste stood in the far corner by the window overlooking the lane, her long caramel hair pinned back without a strand astray. She threw Molly a fond smile but said nothing by way of greeting.

"What have you found then?" Marcus asked.

Molly hesitated, reluctant to glance at Ru.

Is he asking because they don't trust me to have told them truth, or don't trust Ru to get it from me?

"Pretty much everything I told Ru."

Marcus arched an eyebrow. "Enlighten me."

Molly did, recounting as best she could the situation with the Fae without mentioning Talie or the resistance. Marcus didn't as much as twitch his expression once, leaving her talking into an impassive abyss until she trailed off.

"I'd wager the resistance could be hoping to target the citadel's precious gem collection." He looked Celeste's way. "If they have any way out of here, those would fetch any price needed."

Molly frowned as Celeste sighed loudly and turned away from the window.

"It's difficult to know what's going on without sufficient intel," she said. "Molly, your friend hasn't given you any indication of plans, or potential targets maybe? We know she's one of them, so she may have let something slip, no matter how minor."

Molly wiped a hand over her face, forcing the bubbling froth of angry words back down until she could summon up a suitably contrite response.

"No. I joined the same gym as her and she says I need more training. Always more training."

Celeste smiled. "Training is important."

"What about the stolen fairies though?" she asked. "How does any of this relate to the missing artificers, or the dead ones?"

Her mind whirled as the others stared at her. Everyone 'in the know' knew the boots worked for the Menagerie, the visible arm of an unknown entity that pulled all the necessary strings to keep the citadel running, in control.

Marcus and Celeste exchanged a look. As Celeste crossed the room to reach them, Molly wrapped her protection warding around her but tried to keep her stance relaxed. Marcus would be watching her, and she didn't want to risk giving them any indication that she suspected them of being at the heart of nefarious things.

"Whoever is stealing fairies probably hasn't managed to achieve whatever they're trying to yet," Celeste said softly. "They would have attacked by now otherwise, made a stand."

Molly shivered. "The citadel is in enough unrest right now as it is."

"Exactly. Open war isn't the simplest way to deal with insurrections, so we watch and we wait."

Marcus leaned back in his chair, the creak bringing Celeste around to face him.

"Then yes, there's the missing artificers," he said. "The ones that have returned with their minds wiped clean are still completely oblivious to whatever happened to them."

Ru nodded. "The need to wipe their minds does imply there is something worth hiding."

"They've all returned to their normal lives," Marcus added. "Except for the dead ones. Then again, the Artificer's guild has always been somewhat intransigent. Who knows how deep these things run?"

Always a question in place of a lie.

She couldn't escape the fact that the boots worked for the Menagerie, so either the ones manhandling the kidnapped fairies had gone rogue, or they were doing it on the Menagerie's say-so.

Which means Marcus and possibly Celeste have known all about it.

Molly inched her hands into the pockets of her coat, desperate to leave but too weary to find a suitable excuse. She needed time to sort out her thoughts, something she couldn't do with Marcus eying her the same way Aurora eyed a morsel of food.

She flinched as Celeste's hand landed on her shoulder.

"If there's nothing else, you can go," Celeste said, still all smiles. "We want to keep the lines of communication open, so we may ask you to check in directly more often. We won't bring you back into active duty yet, but do try to improve your friendship. She could guide us to the information we need, even without realising it. Oh, that's no slight to the trust we have in you, Ru."

Ru laughed. "I have no doubt."

He might not, but I do, a whole mind full of doubt.

Molly nodded awkwardly and managed a weak smile as she took a step back. They expected her to say something reassuring to round off the conversation somehow, but she had nothing to offer.

"I'll keep you updated then."

The phrase worked like magic as Ru opened the door and stood aside to let her pass. She hurried out and headed straight for the window.

"Molly."

She didn't stop to hear him out, clambering out of the window and onto the girder instead. If Ru wanted to speak to her, he could make the effort to keep up. His footsteps echoed steady behind her until they hit a slip of the girder where they could walk side by side.

"Tell me what you're thinking," he said.

She guessed he meant it as more of a request than the demand it came out as. The urge to use her compulsion gift on him to get him to leave her alone tugged at her, but she took a sharp breath and went for natural determination instead.

"Whoever is stealing fairies and artificers wants more than mere riches or gemstones," she said carefully.

Ru sighed. "I'd imagine so. It's not really our place to ask though, you know that."

"How convenient. They ask enough questions of us when it suits them."

She grabbed the nearest pillar and shimmied down, her shoes ridging with less coordination than usual on the grooves in the wood until she thudded to the worn paving stones of her lane.

"They're doing what's best for all of us, for the citadel. Don't you trust them?"

Ru followed her right to the workshop door. Molly unlocked it and ducked automatically before she even felt Aurora sail over her head.

"Do you trust them blindly?" she asked. "Anyone can be corrupted by power, and whoever is stealing these people will be near unstoppable at taking over the whole of Faerie if they keep going."

"That's a big leap. This is the citadel, not the rest of Faerie, and the Menagerie have kept us safe so far."

She shrugged, wishing he would leave. She had a few quiet hours before she had to call it quits for the night, and usually she'd settle down with some commission work, but tonight she wanted to climb up to the glass and watch the Fae sky outside the citadel.

"I know they have, but this is something big. The resistance don't seem to have much of the power either, not like the Menagerie do, or they'd have made a proper stand by now."

She bit her lip and busied herself at her desk, moving things that didn't need moving for something to do. Telling Ru the resistance weren't as strong was like a green light for the Menagerie to move against them, but then she didn't know how deep the resistance ran either.

"I don't want us to be enemies, Mol," Ru said, his tone softening.

She nodded. "I know that. It's just going to take time, I think."

"Time for your new friend to turn you against us?"

"She's not- It's not- it's complicated. She's not a horrible person."

She hasn't killed anyone. That I know of. Oh, orbs, what if she has? How do I even ask her? I can't go up and say 'hey, ever killed anyone?'

Ru frowned. "Appearances can be deceptive."

"On all sides," she countered.

"You can't seriously mean that. The Menagerie are protecting us! When your guardians died, they could have left you to fend for yourself, taken this place, done anything. Instead, they let you keep it and work for them. How is it that you can villainise them so easily?"

"So, you're absolutely adamant that the stolen fairies, the missing artificers, all of that, has absolutely nothing to do with the Menagerie?"

He sucked in a breath, the motion stalling. She folded her arms across her chest, warning blaring in her mind that she should stop now, keep her suspicions a secret, but anger drove her onward.

"See? You can't say it, because deep down some part of you doesn't believe it."

He shoved his hands in his pockets, his eyes narrowing.

"What's your great plan then? Seeing as you already know everything, I'm sure you have one."

Molly grabbed the back of her chair with both hands.

"I'm not sure who's trying to achieve what, but if we can corner both sides into admitting one way or the other, we'll know who the real enemy is."

"Oh, sure." Ru scoffed. "What are you going to do, arrange a dinner party? Both sides are well-practiced at verbal warfare I'm sure, and nobody's going to admit anything to you."

"Surely it's worth at least trying?"

He stepped into the lane, framed in the doorway.

"I'll believe it when I see it. You'd never pull it off. Stop being so ridiculous and start seeing sense. The Menagerie has to keep control somehow, and the enemy are fighting that for their own ends. Sometimes harsh methods have to be taken."

"Like killing people?"

Ru's expression twisted, his grimace pained as he took a step back.

"I didn't deserve that."

He turned on his heel and disappeared, but Molly stood by her desk a moment longer before moving to the door. She still wasn't sure she agreed with him on that.

Keeping her coat on, she walked to the open door and glanced out. Ru was gone, but she didn't exactly want him around right now anyway. She cast a wary eye toward Beryl and Harvey's, but there was both silence and darkness, which she chose to take as a good sign.

"In or out?" she asked Aurora.

Aurora chirped and stretched out her wings, a sign she wasn't hanging around. Molly stepped outside and tensed as Aurora wisped past her. She locked the door and moved toward her usual barrels, clambering up with a weary groan and vaulting back up onto the levels. She turned left along the beam under the level above and ambled toward the enormous sheet of glass separating the citadel from the rest of the realm.

So far, there were no signs of anyone finding her quiet place. Not many people would think to climb between levels, and those that did likely had their own haunts in other parts of the tower. Her wide, threadbare cushion covered with a sheet of plastic to ward off the seasonal damp from the vents was as she'd left it, and she nudged it aside before thudding down to sit.

She eyed Aurora warily, but the bird seemed content to perch beside her, staring out at the inky sky dotted with bright stars, and the ghostly grey trees waving between the glass and the horizon.

"You got yourself in," she muttered. "Yet you don't seem bothered about getting yourself out."

Aurora tilted her head, dark eyes burning as they fixed on Molly's face. One blink. Two. Then Aurora chirped and hopped closer to the glass, rootling across the beam for scraps.

Molly heard the quietest of taps behind her moments

before Aurora's head shot up. Leaning forward as close to Aurora as she dared, she tensed ready to sweep her leg out at whoever was trying to sneak up on her. Until a throat cleared, a soft noise almost like a chuckle.

"Nice spot you've got here."

CHAPTER THIRTEEN

TALIE

Talie waited for Molly to disappear down her lane after spying on the artificer's guild, determination firing as she turned around and started back down the levels. There was one benefit to being part of the resistance, other than the security Phoenix had offered for her and Sammy, but the library was a few levels down and she didn't have long before she'd have to go back to the workshop. She had no doubt Molly would go without her if she didn't make it back in time.

A tiny smirk flickered across her face at the thought as she approached the library doors. Molly hadn't even blinked twice at her mentioning stories. No snide comments about someone on her level knowing how to read either, which she'd endured here and there.

The cavernous entrance hall of the library was as much a place of comfort as the gym, its towering stone pillars and quiet rows of endless books untouched by the simulated weather outside. The library was always warm too, something she loved.

She pulled her library card out of her pocket and held it up to the brisk young woman at the reception desk. The woman glanced at it, at her, then back at the card before nodding.

Talie passed the desk and turned left through the endless stacks until she reached the cartography section. She yearned to get Sammy a library card too but Phoenix had never managed to secure a second one, and hers wasn't set up to take books out of the library, only to read them inside.

Molly wanted me to bring her stories too. Maybe I should write a couple of them up on neater bits of paper sometime. Then she can keep them.

She passed through the endless shelves of rolled tubes, scanning the titles until she found the one she needed. Pulling the rolled wooden tube toward her, she found a deserted desk and eased the delicate scroll of paper out.

The map unrolled across the desk and Talie frowned down at the lines and squiggles. Glancing over her shoulder, she bit her lip. The cartography section was technically authorised access only but as long as nobody found her, it wouldn't matter.

She trailed a finger across the paper, marking out the blueprint of the citadel all the way to the rooftop flue entrance Molly had taken her through, then scanning down from the main entrance. With a smart tap on the room she needed, the route to it marked out, she rolled the map back up and slid it into the tube. Her plan was absolute madness, but one determined scowl from Molly and apparently that was enough to make her risk it.

Creeping back through the stacks, she peered around the

end of the row, scoping out the route to the exit. The reception desk was empty as she started toward it, thoughts of proving herself not entirely useless in Molly's eyes filling her head.

"Wait right there."

A dominant voice echoed behind her. Her chest squeezed tight, her heartrate picking up as she eyed night still falling outside. Turning slowly, she lifted a hand to swipe a non-existent strand of hair behind her ear.

"Excuse me?"

The receptionist stalked toward her, her tumble of brown ponytail swishing like an angry tail.

"What were you doing in the authorised section? You don't have clearance for that."

"You remember everyone's clearance?" Talie asked, unable to keep the scepticism at bay.

"I saw your card five minutes ago. You don't have clearance. What were you doing?"

With a sigh, Talie let her gift unspool, the blade of guilt flipping in her gut.

"What did you say, sorry?"

The woman folded her arms. "I saw you going into the authorised section, you don't have clearance."

"I don't have what?"

"You don't…" A frown of utter confusion settled over her face. "Do you have clearance to be in here? Let me see your card."

Talie hesitated, surprised the woman wasn't succumbing completely. The side-effect of her gift was often a lingering sense of obedience, many Fae minds deep down needing to align themselves to a strength which she provided by default through each exchange. This woman had an edge of steel to her mind however, and she wasn't one of the regular librarians Talie knew by name.

Reaching into her pocket, she pulled out her card.

"Here."

The woman scanned it, frowning deeper as she handed it back.

"What were you here for?" she asked.

Talie frowned. "That's my business surely?"

"If you're in the library, it's library business. There are so many rumours, we've been told to be on high alert to any signs of deviancy."

"Coming into the library is deviant now?"

"Obfuscating while being asked questions by library authorities is, yes. What were you here for?"

With another tug of her gift, Talie forced her muscles to relax, to take the calm stillness of dominance.

"What was the question?"

The woman huffed. "I insist you tell me… tell… what are you doing here?"

"Sorry, I'm here doing research." Talie held up her card. "I found what I needed, thanks. Do I need to sign out?"

"I… no, I sign you out when you leave. Haven't you been here before?"

Talie reined her gift back in. "I have but you look really busy. Thanks."

She strode toward the exit, half expecting to be called back and finally letting the unease settle when she wasn't.

The woman wouldn't remember the altercation in a few minutes, just a needling sensation of forgetting something that would be lost to time, explained away as a passing blip.

Small uses of her gift didn't bother her, not if it got her what she wanted. She'd promised herself never to use it on Sammy, or for frivolous things, but to keep Sammy safe, or Molly?

When did Molly wiggle her way into that category?

She lifted a hand and rubbed her chest, powering through the lamplit lanes.

"Offer on *Beast*, young Talie?"

She lifted her head, slowing as Fern ambled toward her with a small cart on wheels, the gnarled hands around the wood belying a fiendish strength. Fern insisted on changing her hair-colour the same frequency others changed their trousers, and today it was a chaotic nest of deep magenta.

Talie risked a smile. Faerie save anyone who tried to pull one over on Fern, but much like Butch at the shop she was fond of those who were kind to her.

"I…" Talie hesitated, an idea forming in her head as she eyed the contents of the cart. "Are those *Akiai* charms?"

Fern nodded. "A token to present to the one your heart desires. I'll do you two bottles of *Beast* and a charm for three pesanas."

Talie couldn't stop her lips lifting. Madness, but considering two bottles would usually cost her three anyway, Fern was offering her the small charm for free. No doubt there would be some small trade, a tease about who she might want to give it to perhaps, but it was a generous offer.

"That's kind. I'll take it. *Beast Lite* please."

She found three pesanas, her pocket getting ever lighter, and handed them over. Fern passed her the bottles but cast a hand over the cart straight after.

"Pick your charm, lovely. I hope whoever receives it appreciates it."

Talie smirked as she eyed the small red charms. Fibres woven from the *Akiai* plant were tough but once pulped and dried, they could be stripped into strands or moulded into shapes. Fern had several shaped charms, stars, orbs, but it was the single heart right in the corner Talie picked up.

Molly would probably prefer the raw Akiai to work with. She tucked the charm in her pocket. *Not that I'm actually going to give it to her, but it's worth it for the drinks anyway.*

"Thanks."

She took a step back, the necks of both bottles clutched between her fingers.

Fern grinned. "I won't ask who the charm is for. Off you go."

Talie lifted the hand with the bottles in farewell and set off up the lane again. She reached the corner of Molly's alleyway and turned the corner with a tinge of hope. No beam of light spilled out from the workshop and the door was shut, but a flash of movement caught her eye from the lamps above.

She watched as Molly hauled herself up onto a crate,

then scaled a pillar onto the girder above. They had some time before seven o'clock yet and Talie's heart sank. Before she could call out and let Molly know she'd caught her leaving without waiting, Molly turned away from the rest of the citadel and headed toward the glass.

Talie shoved a bottle in each pocket, eying the crate and the pillar.

Maybe she doesn't want to be found. She bit her lip. *Or maybe there's another way through the citadel I don't know about.*

She scanned the lane and clambered up onto the crate, hauling herself up the pillar. Her fingers ached from so much climbing but she pushed on, determined not to let Molly get away.

She tiptoed across the girder until she saw the shadow of Molly seated on a cushion. Keeping her distance, she watched Molly murmuring to the bright white bird she kept, unsure if to approach or go back down and wait. Disturbing her quiet space seemed intrusive.

Unless it's a place she shares with him.

The mere thought of Molly's Menagerie friend made her insides burn and her feet start moving. She pulled the bottles out of her pocket and her fingers skated briefly across the *Akiai* charm as she approached.

Molly tensed up ahead, ready to spring away or attack, but Talie couldn't squash the slight chuckle that broke free.

"Nice spot you've got here," she said.

Molly hid her astonishment well, her face illuminated by the sinking golden glow of the sunset beyond the glass. Talie stopped several paces away and held up the bottles of *Beast Lite* hanging from her hand.

"One of those for me?" Molly asked.

Talie nodded. "Be a bit mean to bring two and drink both myself. Here."

She held out the bottle for Molly to take and waited while Molly made a show of shuffling sideways, although there wasn't much room on the edge of the cushion. Talie crouched down and sat beside her, half on the cushion and half on the ledge. As Molly cracked the lid on her bottle, Talie turned her gaze to the realm beyond the glass.

"How did you know where to find me?" Molly asked.

Talie shrugged. "I didn't. Workshop was shut and you didn't pass me in the lane, so I figured you'd be up here somewhere. Either that or you tried to escape for espionage before I could get here, which would have been dim."

"How so?"

"I know where the room the meeting is in will be, and how to get there without being seen."

Molly straightened, her eyes sparking. "How? Where did you even get the info from."

"I have my ways." She smiled. "Library has old maps. It's the third guild level down. Once you get inside, there's a circular corridor with rooms leading off and a large hall in the centre, that's the Rose room. You go in with stealth while I glamour. I only need to get a short way in."

"What for?"

"You'll see. You hear what you can while you're in there, and I'll do the rest. I'll even get you a way out too."

Molly's brow lifted. "If you say so."

She heaved to her feet and Talie lifted a hand to steady

her, retracting it hastily the moment Molly was up. In the small space, the scent of verbena wafted between them.

With a deep breath, Talie pulled her Fae connection around her, ignoring the subtle leap of her mind-wipe gift sneaking up. She pushed it down firmly. The last thing she wanted was to take anything more from Molly than she already had.

Recalling the woman from the gym, she wound a glamour over herself, from the long blonde hair to the brown eyes and wider, shorter build. It was uncomfortable to stand in the shape of someone else's body, but for the look of awe on Molly's face, she would have contorted herself into a thousand awkward shapes.

"Wow." It took Molly a long moment to stop staring. "I never manage to hold a glamour for more than a minute or two, my mind always wanders off and it slips."

Talie shrugged, uneasy at the sheer burst of pleasure that lit up her insides at the praise. She took a healthy step backwards before twisting to keep the drop below in sight.

"Do you have a way in for yourself?" Molly asked.

Talie didn't answer until she was contemplating the drop down onto the boxes in the lane below.

"I have. You need me to get you in?"

"Nope. I'll be fine."

Talie sat down on the edge of the girder and swung around to hang below. She dropped onto the boxes with a thud and a grimace, lifting her head to see Molly smirking down at her, the lamplight from the main lane haloing one side of her face.

"Aren't you coming?" Talie asked.

Molly's smile widened. "You go your way, I'll go mine. Assuming we make it out, we can swap info."

Before Talie could ask questions, her heart squishing tight, Molly was off across the girders and vanishing into the shadows.

CHAPTER FOURTEEN

MOLLY

Molly jogged across the girders, the tiny smile not budging as she focused forward. Grabbing one of the pillars just beyond the main lane, she shinned down and dodged along the alleyway until she reached the small set of stairs leading to the underside of the level.

She'd expected Talie to show up, if only to get more information for Phoenix, but there was a subtle ease to her movements that suggested they were on some kind of secret-sharing basis now.

Heading downward, she mapped out the route into the guild.

Maps and books. She shook her head. *Talie's full of surprises.*

The guild levels were already buzzing with activity, and she crouched on the girder above the highest one. Reaching into her Fae connection, she let the stealth dribble over her skin like a cloak of cool silk. Well-dressed guild members were arriving in suits and skirts, but not one lifted a head or flicked a look in her direction as she dropped silently among them.

She moved with the people, twisting and dodging to avoid being touched. If they touched her, they'd notice. If she breathed on them or made a noise, they'd hear it, but the stealth was like a visual cloak from the rest of the world.

Slipping past the guard on the door who stood to greet members, Molly bit her lip and inched into a spare space beside a large urn full of fragrant flowers.

The corridor ran ahead on both sides, a circular curve exactly as Talie had said. Doorframes and paintings were gilded in gold, and the rich dark red wallpaper was soft to the touch, but there was a hint of peeling on the skirting board and a badly-hammered nail pinning a block onto a wobbly table leg.

A loud bonging noise filled the air and people milling in the hall turned like a wave toward the nearest door. Molly tiptoed after them, mindful to keep her breathing quiet.

The large hall dropped down to a stage in the centre, a circle of tiered seating surrounding it. Amid the abundance of red wallpaper, the arches over the all the doors were gold and expertly carved. Molly bit her lip, about to start interrogating the craftsmanship but she forced herself to remain focused.

She had no idea where Talie was or what the 'extraction plan' might be, but she had made it far enough without an accomplice.

No matter how trustworthy she is or isn't, I can't risk it.

The door slammed shut behind her, each one thudding

closed after the other until the entire circle of the Rose Room was shut.

Eying the ornate statues and vases full of bright flowers between each doorway arch, she inched around the edge of the room until she reached a large wooden clock, slipping herself behind it. She couldn't see any sign of Talie, glamoured or otherwise, but as a woman walked into the centre of the room, everyone fell obediently silent.

Molly squinted around the edge of the clock, but she didn't recognise the woman, middle-aged with blonde hair perfectly pinned and a stern but social smile that radiated around the room.

"Welcome, members." The woman rotated on the spot, catching eyes and commanding all attention. "This meeting has been called to confirm some rumours and lay to rest any nonsense that has been circulating of late."

Molly tensed as someone in the back row of seats leaned sideways to their companion.

"Third meeting this month," the man muttered. "With the guild in league with the Menagerie now, who's really controlling who?"

His companion shushed him, but Molly tensed her gut muscles to keep herself centred. If she could hear them muttering, they would hear any loud breathing from her.

The woman swiped a hand over her hair as her voice projected into the expectant silence.

"The Menagerie are closing in on the gift replication, I have it on trusted authority. Once this process is finalised, then the bottling and even selling gifts will begin."

"Who owns the rights?" someone called out.

Good question. Molly's heart sank.

She looked down at the tiny silver scar of a spiralling cage on her wrist, a sign of her allegiance to the Menagerie, and resisted the needling urge to somehow scratch it off her skin.

"There will be discussions of course, but the guild will retain exclusivity for production and the Menagerie will most likely see to distribution. It will be a collaboration unlike any the citadel, or even the wider realms of Faerie, have ever seen."

A clamouring of chatter broke out.

"Likely story," the man in front muttered. "The guild will eventually be strong-armed into servitude, you watch."

Again his companion shushed him, but there was no mistaking the look of doubt on his face.

"We're replicating, but how exactly are the Menagerie planning to contain and store gifts?" someone else hollered, distaste clear in their tone. "It would take a source of great power to contain them without a host."

The woman held her hands up, her expression utterly calm.

"You have questions of course, and they will be answered as soon as we can. We all know that the citadel is centred over a source of great power, a well in the very fabric of the nether. Storage won't be an issue."

"Where are these gifts going to come from exactly?" someone else asked.

"Replication is all well and good, but what about consent and clarity?"

"Never mind that, what about security? If the realms outside the citadel find out, you'll have half of them clamouring to take over and the more progressive half hauling us all off on trial!"

Chaos broke out as people started to clamour louder, all ignoring the woman calling for calm.

Thoughts of the fairies filled Molly's head, along with a clawing realisation that the Menagerie were neck deep in whatever horrors were going on.

The woman's gaze lifted over the crowd. Molly flinched behind the clock as their eyes made contact, her skin tingling as she forced every effort of her stealth gift around her. Seconds later, a shrill whistle pierced the sound.

She eyed the nearest door, shut and no doubt locked until the meeting was over. Tilting her head back, she assessed the ceiling, but there were no vents, no smaller or more secret routes of escape.

A loud wailing filled the air before she could figure out a plan.

Intruder alarm, it must be, orbs alive.

She tensed, ready to fight, to run, she wasn't sure which.

"An orbing fire alarm? Now?" The man in front of her shouted over the din. "This place is getting worse by the day."

Molly sagged, her hand resting against the clock as she dragged in a relieved breath. She peeked out again in time to see streams of disgruntled guild members flocking toward the now open doors. Tiptoeing out of her hiding place, she slid into the crush behind the man she'd been eavesdropping on.

"It's ridiculous," the man insisted. "One thing for the Menagerie to guide and advise, and to keep the rabble in check. But we are above their control. The moment they start tightening reins around us, it's time to leave."

"Where would we go?" A woman joined him as they swept through the corridor. "Other realms are governed by royalty now. The citadel has its issues but the Menagerie have never overstepped their boundaries before now."

"Never overstepped?! They were nothing fifteen or so years ago. They took the boots in hand, it's true, but the guilds should be independent, outside of mundane control. How else are we to have the freedom to do what we need to do?"

"I suppose they are doing what they feel is right," someone else muttered.

Molly crept behind them, still amazed nobody had spotted her or brushed against her yet. Whatever stealth strength Celeste had given her was immeasurably strong.

Even though she's part of the group stealing fairies and probably gifts too.

Her insides guttered so sharply that she almost gasped. She pinned her lips together tight, the realisation that her new gift she was using to spy on them might have belonged to one of those fairies.

How long have they been importing them without anyone knowing?

Her mind span as they walked into a courtyard full of fountains and sweetly fragrant flowers, candles hanging in jars alongside the ornate black lamps. The group she was following moved into a far corner and she melded into the shadows alongside them.

"This well of power, is it accessible?" the man asked.

Another shook his head, almost unseating the enormous top hat he wore.

"Of course not. It's deep beneath the citadel's core. Ancient stuff, not something anyone wants to mess with or go for a wander through."

"Are we still sure this isn't the work of something other than the Menagerie pulling strings?" the woman suggested.

"Oh don't start that again." The man with the top hat pinched the bridge of his nose. "The Omens are a myth, a fable. There's no proof of them ever having been unleashed or discovered, not here or any other part of Faerie."

"What even are the Omens?" the first man asked.

The woman grimaced. "The Omens sprang from the fabled well of power, a cavernous pit of gathered nether. They're meant to be essences of a sort, power, freedom, things like that. As the tale goes, they bewitched several realms into madness until the situation was contained."

"Contained how? Where is this well of power?"

"Nobody knows," she said. "It's a fable, a myth. If there were vast entities of power rolling about, I imagine Fae would have tapped into it and drained it dry long before now."

"Even so, the Menagerie's power must be coming from somewhere." The top hat wobbled as the man glanced around. "Marcus and Celeste came out of nowhere from scant and dubious backgrounds, and Marcus is rumoured to be accomplished with many gifts."

"No more conversation for now," the woman insisted. "Fires are easily quenched here, and we have many talented artificers who can wield fire. If someone's pulled the alarm, it's for another reason."

Dark looks passed between them.

"You think the Menagerie is spying on us?" someone else muttered.

The woman shrugged, gazing over the assembled crowd. "Wouldn't put it past them, would you?"

Molly eyed the archways leading back inside to other areas of the guild. She might hear something more of consequence if she lingered, but the sensation of her stealth gift was beginning to scratch at her skin, a sure sign she was reaching the edge of her limit with it.

The mention of the Omens sounded vaguely familiar but she couldn't place it, and getting out had to be her main focus. Sneaking through the nearest archway, she tried to picture her way back out in her mind, but the courtyard could have been on any side of the citadel tower for all she knew.

Unless it's one of the communal levels and I've ended up on a whole different tower altogether.

The thought didn't bear thinking about. Of the five towers that made up the citadel, Fae rarely made it from one to the other, not without going down a whole load of levels first. She had no idea if the Menagerie even had control of the other towers, although she guessed they would. Allegiances at least.

She shuddered and slipped past a few milling guards in uniform. Taking a chance, she turned left and slowed to a halt. Up ahead was a familiar face, but she had no guarantee that the woman peering down the hall away from her wasn't the original rather than Talie still in her glamour.

Sneaking up behind her, she listened.

"Two more minutes," the woman muttered, her tone tellingly frustrated.

Molly let her stealth gift slip, ignoring the wave of relief and exhaustion. She would have to rely on charm if she was up against the original, but she took the risk.

"Two minutes until what?" she asked.

The woman whirled around, her eyes wide and turning golden as her glamour slipped momentarily.

"Don't do that!" Talie snapped. "Orbs, I got here and realised you didn't see the layout of the place like I did."

Molly shrugged. "I can handle myself. What's the magic way out then?"

"The fire alarm."

"That was you?"

Talie nodded, a tiny hint of a smirk lighting on her glamoured face. Beneath the façade, there were hints of her amber eyes shining through, the misshapen shimmer of taller shoulders forming like an orb-cast either side of her ears.

"Told you I'd get you a way out. The Rose Room locks for meetings."

Molly folded her arms. "You seem to know a lot about the particulars of this place."

"I get around, Princess. That, and I saw it happen when you all went in. Now, if we go this wa-"

The sound of voices coming toward them from Molly's direction silenced whatever Talie was about to say.

"Do the stealth thing, quick," Talie muttered. "I can't hold the glamour much longer but I'll brazen it out."

Molly didn't want to admit she'd hit her limit, but charm might not be enough to get them both out safely and she didn't want to show her compulsion gift if she didn't have to.

She eyed the dead-end over Talie's rapidly growing shoulder, then the curtain beside them.

Talie huffed as Molly grabbed her wrist and hauled her behind the curtain. There was only room enough for one person to stand behind it without an obvious lump, but they didn't need long.

Ignoring the ache climbing through her limbs, she dredged her stealth gift back over her body and stood at the gap, hoping with everything she had that her gift would keep her hidden and therefore Talie as well.

Standing so close, face to face with nowhere to go as the voices drew closer, Molly's heart thudded loudly. She pinned her lips between her teeth, closing her eyes against the battle of her gift against her depleted well of energy. Soft fingers wrapped firm around her hand but she kept her eyes closed, her mind focused on quiet breathing and on keeping the burning stretch of her gift around them.

I should have practiced with it more. I should have found time to rest as well. I'm no use to anyone like this.

Something soft dropped against her forehead but she

didn't have the strength to open her eyes as the voices passed, or to nudge the curtain or piece of hair away from her face. Seconds later, a warm fingers brushed whatever it was away. Gratitude swelled and gave her the extra ounce of strength she needed to cling on.

A door closed behind her and the hallway fell silent.

"Time to go," Talie murmured.

Molly didn't comment about Talie keeping hold of her hand, just opened her eyes and let herself be led on aching legs back down the hall.

"Left here," she muttered. "There'll be a service hatch. Short drop and we can get out onto the level below."

Talie followed the direction until they reached the service hatch. She threw open the door and Molly inched through the gap. Her arms and legs shook but she clambered through and found the floor with her feet, wincing as something cracked. Given the faint whiff, it was some kind of dump chute for plates and cups, but Talie was already closing the hatch and towing her along the narrow passage.

The chance that they might meet staff coming to clear the chute flickered in her mind, but the staff entrance to the chute was at the end of a long corridor. She tugged on Talie's fingers and pointed right to another hatch in the ceiling, and Talie didn't hesitate.

"I'll leg you up."

Molly nodded. She put her foot into Talie's cupped hands and made a sluggish leap, Talie's strength powering her upward to snag the metal catch of the hatch with her finger on the downward motion.

"Are you okay?" she asked.

Talie rolled her eyes, even though her cheeks were pink. "I'm doing better than you, Princess. Nice big jump now."

Molly huffed and jumped again, catching the lip of the chute. The artificial wind from a nearby fan ruffled her hair, but Talie gave her no time to take a breath, shoving up against her feet to propel her onto the gap between levels.

Molly hauled herself up with a groan, her arms almost failing her. She shuffled around and stuck her top half back through the hole, anchoring both legs around a nearby pipe.

Talie glanced over her shoulder at the sound of people approaching and Molly stuck her hand down through the gap.

"Come on, quick," she insisted.

Talie bit her lip. "No, go, I'll be fine."

"Don't be dim, just jump!"

Talie grimaced as she jumped. Her fingers slid over Molly's and slipped away.

"Hey!" A deep voice boomed from the far end of the corridor. "Stop right there!"

Talie leapt again and Molly strained to follow the arc of Talie's hands, grasping on with a determined grunt. She pulled but her strength was almost on empty.

"Drop me and go!" Talie huffed, opening her fingers.

"No you don't." Molly clung on. "Climb up."

More shouting echoed, accompanied by the stamping of feet growing closer.

"Talie, in the name of Faerie, do it!"

Talie swung sideways, letting go with one hand and reaching upward. Molly bent her arm, giving Talie a hook to climb with.

"Other side, aim to get your arm around my neck," Molly gritted out.

Talie scrambled through the swing, managing to get a hand on the hatch. Around her side, Molly saw the blur of dark figures racing toward them.

"Orbs, you're heavy," she muttered.

Talie snorted a laugh then bellowed a curse as she heaved herself against the hatch, scrabbling over Molly's back and tumbling onto the floor beside her. Molly flailed to get a hand back up into the hatch, wild thoughts of Talie abandoning her there filling her head.

Up on her knees already, Talie grabbed Molly's shoulder and slid an arm around her waist, hauling her up.

"Leave the hatch, come on," she insisted.

Molly held onto Talie's arms, barely able to get to her feet. With Talie's support, they stumbled along the girder until they hit the lane below and the citadel righted itself in Molly's head.

"I know where we are, but I can't climb," she said.

Talie wiped a hand over her face before securing it around Molly's shaking one. She scanned the lane below, then pointed down.

"Leave that to me."

CHAPTER FIFTEEN

TALIE

Talie struggled to breathe easy the whole way through getting Molly down into the lanes and up the levels to the workshop. She almost dropped her while helping her down from the beam, and she guessed the only reason Molly wasn't complaining about it was because the poor girl looked half unconscious. By the time they reached the workshop, Molly's body had at least stopped quaking so violently, but it took her two tries to get her key into the door.

She barely flinched as a disapproving caw echoed over their heads, the flutter of wings sailing past.

"Shut the door," Molly mumbled.

Talie glanced along the lane before she dropped the latch into place by hand to be safe, making sure there was no sign of Ru or anyone else lingering.

"*Offke*?" Molly asked. "Or I have some ancient bottles of *Beast* around somewhere, but it's usually too strong for me."

Talie pressed her back against the door, her pulse still

not entirely calm as she watched Molly trudge past the bird perched on the mirror to rifle through a collection of dusty cupboards.

"Are you sure you'll be able to find them?" she asked.

Keep it casual.

Molly stilled for a moment before muttering something unsavoury. Talie smiled. She'd take whatever Molly offered, but teasing her was the only way she could find to get them back on a normal footing. Her mind strayed back down the levels as Molly clunked about, memories of standing nose to nose and the softest brush of breath on her lips.

She slid her hand into her pocket and passed her thumb over the *Akiai* charm.

"Aha, knew they were here somewhere." Molly held up a bottle with a sluggish arm. "I know where my work stuff is, and that's what matters. You want?"

Talie nodded. She didn't drink and *Beast* packed a punch, but one bottle wouldn't kill her.

Molly opened the bottles and carried them to her desk, so Talie met her halfway.

"Are we sharing fully?" Molly asked.

She tipped her head back against her chair and took a long swig from her drink with lidded eyes. Behind the lids though, the gaze was piercing. Talie sank into the chair opposite and cupped her bottle in hand.

"The drinks?" she asked glibly.

Molly grunted. "No, the information."

"As much as I physically can, I will." She took a sip and grimaced. "Strong. I'll be honest, I didn't hear much.

When they were going into the hall though, they were talking about the Menagerie. Something about extending reach, and the merchant's guild folding like a pack of cards."

Molly blinked. "The merchants guild are flouting rules for their own gain then. I did hear rumour of that a while back."

"Or so we were told." Talie frowned. "We weren't able to work out why though. What rules did they break exactly?"

"I'm not sure. It wasn't publicised. I can see what they mean about extending reach though. One of the men in the meeting I was standing behind kept going on about the Menagerie taking over the guild eventually, muscling in."

She shifted in her seat, wincing enough that Talie put her bottle down.

"We can leave this until tomorrow if you want," she offered.

Molly shook her head. "It'll jumble if I do. The woman holding the meeting said the Menagerie are closing in on the gift replication, and once they're ready they'll be able to begin bottling and selling gifts."

Talie gasped. "How can that be possible? The only way to gift someone is by a kiss, and only if the giver is of the nobility."

"They can already do it." Molly scrunched up her face. "What?!"

"Well, yeah. That's how Celeste gave me my stealth gift. In a vial. Had me shove it against my head and in it went."

Talie grabbed her bottle and drained half of it, huffing a choked breath at the end.

"There's no known way to gift without a noble kiss. How do you not know that?"

Molly scowled. "Well, it happened. I know the rhetoric, but I assumed that was the usual fable Fae are fed as children to stop them hoping for one."

Talie saw the moment realisation crashed into Molly's mind. Her haughty expression cracked and sorrow trickled through. Talie fought the urge to crash around the desk and give Molly a hug, the unfamiliar sensation needling her insides as she struggled for something sensitive to say instead.

"It means the Menagerie, possibly others too, are already able to gift without nobility or kissing," Molly added. "Someone was asking who would own the rights, and apparently the guild owns production, whatever that means, and the Menagerie would be responsible for distribution."

Talie sighed. "That makes sense. The Menagerie are in with the nobles and probably used to placating them. The guild will get a lot of perks and allowances for making it possible."

Molly lifted her head, anguish shining so brightly in her eyes that Talie checked her cheeks for tears.

"Those poor fairies. They were talking about a source of power containing gifts and a well of nether underneath the citadel itself."

"Which we already worked out the Menagerie has built itself around," Talie reminded her.

"I know, I know." Molly groaned and dropped her head onto her arms over the desk. "I'm tied to them, I'm tied to your side, and I have no idea what side to trust. Ru... I can't trust him either. It's not like I can leave the citadel and go... somewhere else."

Talie heard the unspoken truths in each hesitation. Ru had done something Molly couldn't get past, and the somewhere else was a specific place Molly had visited. Thoughts of seeing the workshop shut a while flickered in Talie's mind, a few days before Molly turned up and dragged Sammy, or more likely got dragged by Sammy, to a Kayla Crane concert. Considering the concert was so far down the levels that they would have needed sixteen lifetimes to save the pesanas for a mere seat, Molly had to have made influential friends on her travels.

None of this will make her feel any better though.

"We know one thing," she said, helplessness driving her mad. "The Menagerie are importing fairies for gift extraction, and they're already able to gift without the usual constraints. The minds I wipe..."

Molly shook her head against her forearms, her sigh muffled by the desk.

"Don't tell me if you can't. There's no sense you getting into trouble for nothing. What can we do? Even if I go check out the Menagerie, what can I do about it?"

Talie bit her lip hard. She inched her hand across the desk and leaned forward to place bold fingers on Molly's elbow. Molly flinched at the contact, her entire body tense, but still she didn't lift her head.

"The minds I wipe don't give me much," Talie

admitted. "Phoenix sees to that side somehow, the questioning. But I heard enough to work out that the Menagerie have been testing on some and using the skills of others. The experiences I wipe are sometimes... tormented. Nobody should be on the receiving end of that."

Molly finally lifted her head. "And Phoenix, your lot, are trying to save them?"

"I really orbing hope so." Talie sat back. "Phoenix talks a good game about fairness and equality, but all Fae can talk nice when they need to. If it weren't for Sammy, I wouldn't be so obedient to any side."

"I get it. You probably can't tell me, but does Phoenix know about what happened to me? Or are you beholden to the Menagerie like I am?"

Talie opened her mouth, her tongue burning as she tried to say it. Her head wouldn't nod.

Molly sighed. "Swear-block? Don't worry about it. I don't need to know the truth to be wary of all sides."

"I'd tell you if I could."

"I know."

Talie pushed to her feet. Any longer and she would find herself inching toward other truths she really didn't want to end up admitting. Like how Molly's eyes, all round and shiny, were the strangest golden green in the workshop lights instead of their usual stormy blue.

"Get some sleep," she said instead. "Training tomorrow night but we'll take it easy."

Molly nodded and Talie strode to the door. Flicking the latch, she checked the lane was empty, although she and Molly spent more than enough time together in public to be considered friends.

"Talie?" The soft, almost broken tone had her freezing in place. "Thank you for at least trying to be honest with me."

Talie's insides churned, nausea creeping up her throat. She sucked in a breath and pushed aside the gruesome reality of just how dishonest she was.

"Get your beauty sleep, Princess," she said softly. "Otherwise I'll send Sammy down next."

She left the workshop and shut the door behind her before Molly could reply. Shaking the sombre thoughts away as best she could, she set off toward the main lane and upward.

Phoenix wasn't in the gym, but she dodged familiar faces and clambered up through the walls to his office. Exhaustion swamped her as she knocked softly on the door, but better she told him immediately.

When he didn't answer, she stepped back, but a muffled thud drifted under the door. She dredged up a warding and shoved the door open.

The light was on, the bare bulb bright enough to fully illuminate Phoenix wrapped so intimately around Nia that Talie had trouble working out which hand belonged to who. She waited for the inevitable stab of agony, for her unrequited crush to come burning in, but none came.

"I... sorry. I thought... you didn't answer."

She took a step back as Nia smirked and extricated herself.

"I'll be on my way, leave you to it," she said.

Phoenix sighed heavily. "Yeah. What is it, Talie?"

She almost sympathised with the snap in his tone as Nia chuckled and swept out. Almost. But while he was wrapping himself around people, Molly was half dead with exhaustion.

"I'll keep it short. Molly asked me to go with her to the artificer's guild and I couldn't talk her out of it." He inhaled sharply but she rushed on before he could waste time with the lecture. "You asked me to get her on side and I figured that meant keeping her safe. The Menagerie aren't just importing fairies, they're replicating gifts and talking about accessing some well of power to store them with."

Phoenix folded his arms and started pacing the short few feet from wall to wall.

"You heard this yourself?"

"Not exactly. Some of it, but Molly heard the rest. She snuck into their meeting to listen."

Phoenix puffed out a surprised breath. "How in the name of Faerie did she get in and out?"

Talie hesitated. She didn't know if Phoenix knew about Molly's stealth gift.

"She got herself in somehow, and I pulled the fire alarm to get her out."

"Orbs, Talie, that's risky."

"I know, but she's been trying to do so much. She didn't lose her guardians all that long ago, and she's had a hard time of it recently."

"We've all lost people because of the Menagerie, and it's up to us to stop them before they harm everyone in the citadel."

He really does think he's our avenging angel. Talie kept her expression as neutral as she could manage.

"I'm not so much thinking about those lost but those who are still here," she muttered.

Phoenix nodded. "There's sense in that, but the past is a hard thing to shake off sometimes. We do need Molly on side though."

"She's doubting the Menagerie, as she should, but she's exhausted."

"Never mind that. We're all running on empty in our different ways. You said the Menagerie are already replicating gifts, how can you be sure?"

She resisted the urge to say his way of recharging wasn't exactly helping the wider cause.

"Because Celeste, that absolute witch that runs around with the Menagerie, gifted Molly through a bottle not a kiss. Molly's as Fae as I am, so she can't lie."

He halted, arms dropping to his sides.

"She told you that?"

Talie nodded. "Molly did, yeah."

"If they're able to bottle gifts already, then it won't be long before they're able to steal them as well."

"That's no doubt what the fairies are for, and given what little I've heard from mind-wiping, it's not a nice process."

Phoenix flicked a distracted glare her way. "Sure, but if they're bottling, it means they've already gained access to the core."

"What core?"

His head snapped up, his gaze focusing as he looked her way.

"You need to stick with Molly, more now than ever. Scrap the training if you have to, but make sure she doesn't go anywhere near the Menagerie."

"How am I going to manage that?" She ignored the fleeting glee that bubbled up at the excuse to spend all her time with Molly. "If they call her to report in, or that absolute bog-brush of a boy comes calling for her, I can't stop it."

"I don't care. Take her somewhere they can't find her, or seduce her for all I care, just keep her clear of the place."

Talie flexed her hands at her sides to avoid her fists clenching.

He's planning something. She took a step back until her elbow grazed the doorframe. *He knows more than he's telling me too, about the core, the Menagerie, all of it.*

He had no responsibility to tell her, but the one-sided lack of trust rankled.

"Anything else?" he asked.

Talie shook her head. "No. I'll do what I can, but she's ridiculously stubborn."

"I wouldn't expect anything less. Just keep her away from the Menagerie for now. We're going to need her."

Talie left the room without another word, her mind thundering. She didn't notice the few nods or greetings people gave her as she walked through the gym, or the drizzle slicking her face as she started up toward home.

Why Molly? What can he possibly know that makes her so important?

"Hello there."

Talie slowed to a halt, her shoulders hunching

instinctively.

"What do you want?"

She gave Daisy a dismissive once-over, from the chestnut braid curled around her head to the bright green eyes and pert nose covered in freckles. When Daisy laughed, Talie felt it like needles on her patience.

"Just being friendly. I apologise if I stepped on any toes last time. Sammy dragged Molly over and I have no reason to be rude."

Talie shrugged. "No toes. No stepping. Sammy's heart is in the right place but she doesn't understand propriety."

"I wouldn't do her the disservice. I think she knows exactly what she's doing. I didn't realise you and Molly were dating though."

"We're not. She's…"

She still couldn't bring herself to say friend. It sounded so final.

"She's not my type, if it helps," Daisy offered. "I'm not here to get in the middle of anything personal."

Talie folded her arms across her chest.

"Why are you here?"

Daisy smiled. "I'm nanny to Molly's neighbour, actually."

"Didn't Sammy say you were hanging around the school?"

Daisy wiped a stray flick of hair behind her ear, a colourful bracelet catching the light from the lamps. Talie hunched further into her coat. She was wasting time talking when she should be planning. Or, better yet, sleeping.

"A girl can have two jobs. I work part-time at the school

helping out, and I look after baby Aurora when they need me to."

Talie hesitated. "Does Molly see you around much then?"

"You know, I haven't actually bumped into her yet. I'm sure there'll be plenty of time for that. See you around, Talie, right?"

Talie nodded without thinking, scowling as Daisy gave her an amused look and continued on down the lane. Talie set off again, her mind rioting.

She gets everywhere.

She reached her alleyway and trudged toward her door with a sinking feeling in her gut. Keeping Molly away from the Menagerie would be all but impossible, but keeping the truth from her was proving to be even more excruciating.

She let herself in and locked the door behind her before facing Sammy.

"I won't ask where you've been," Sammy said, as she always did. "There's food on the side. Anything you can tell me?"

Talie kicked off her boots and headed for the food.

"Thanks. Nothing much I can tell you- oh, turns out I don't have a crush on Nia anymore."

Sammy sat up with the bonnet around her hair unravelling.

"Really? Why? How?"

Talie grabbed a cold wrap and bit into it.

"Saw her and Phoenix getting into it and felt absolutely nothing."

Sammy clapped. "Yay! Finally. Now you can ask Molly out."

Talie choked over her mouthful.

"What?"

Sammy rolled her eyes. "Oh come on. You spend every day with her now, and sure there's dodgy stuff going on, I'm not dim, but you like her. You don't have to admit it. I know you do."

"That's…" she sighed. "That's irrelevant."

"So you do like her! *I KNEW IT.*"

Talie groaned. "Leave it, Sam, please. It's never going to happen."

"Urgh, fine. Are you seeing her tomorrow?"

"For training, yes, and that's it."

As she settled into bed with Phoenix's demands ringing in her mind, she really, really hoped that would be it.

CHAPTER SIXTEEN

MOLLY

Molly fought the urge to storm the Menagerie and demand answers throughout the day after her escape from the guild. She hunched over her commissions, working like a demon, until a knock at the workshop doorframe startled her out of her carousel of worries.

I should not be as happy to see her as I am right now.

The thought didn't calm the sudden fluttering of nerves any as Talie stepped inside.

"Am I not meeting you at the gym?" she asked.

Talie shook her head. "Mental training first. I thought we could find somewhere quiet."

She pointed upward, and Molly fought the stab of panic when she realised Talie meant her private space up on the beams.

"Okay." She forced her body to relax. "I'm about done here anyway."

She laid her chisel down and eased out of her seat, sparing a glance for Aurora.

"In or out?" she asked.

Aurora chirped and took flight, sailing over Talie's head and out of the door.

"You have her well trained," Talie remarked.

Molly shrugged. "It's an ongoing process. I'm mostly trying not to get my eyes pecked out in my sleep."

Talie laughed and Molly hesitated, her hand hovering over her coat. She couldn't remember if she'd ever heard Talie laugh before, but it was the most amazing sound for it being freely given. Given the clearing of her throat a moment after, Talie wasn't used to it either.

Molly left her coat on the back of her chair. It would be cold outside but she could come back for it if their plans changed. She wanted to avoid whatever mental training meant and talk to Talie properly.

She locked the workshop door and led the way up onto the beams, tracing the familiar path to her cushion. Heaping down onto it, she left enough space for Talie to budge up next to her.

"So, what does mental training entail?" she asked once Talie was seated, close enough for their arms to brush.

"I figured we could talk freely up here. Well, freer than down there."

Molly smiled as Talie pulled two bottles of *Beast Lite* from her pocket and handed one over without a word.

"So, what did you want to talk about?" she asked, adding extra sugar to the innocence in her voice.

Talie shrugged. "What we found. What we plan to do about it."

"We? Is there a specific we now? I'm not exactly on the side of your enemy, or your enemy's enemy either, but I'm not exactly sure where you stand on it all."

"I want safety for Sammy. If I'm lucky enough to secure that, I guess safety and freedom for myself as well."

"We all want that for ourselves and those we love," Molly agreed. "if you're seriously telling me you have no plans of citadel domination or wanting to be in charge, then you're the closest to my own stance as I'm going to get."

"That's flattering, Princess," Talie said drily.

Molly shrugged. "It is what it is. What happens if we find out what we need to though? You take it to Phoenix and I have to take it to the Menagerie and what, we let them fight it out?"

"They'd use us as pawns to fight it out. They're already doing it."

"I know." Molly sighed. "Nothing we can do to change that though, short of leave, and whoever heard of anyone other than nobility leaving the citadel?"

Celeste had gotten her and Ru out of the citadel to spy on the Oak Queen, but she still didn't have a clue how. Then May had offered her a route back there after everything went wrong at the Kayla Crane concert, an offer she hadn't taken.

"We can't trust anyone but ourselves," Talie said.

"And Sammy, I'm guessing. I don't have many friends other than that, not that aren't tied to places I want to be free from. Neighbours, people I do work for, sure, but not actual friends."

"You have your admirer hanging about though."

"Admirer?" Molly frowned. "You mean Ru? He's not-we're definitely not-"

"No, Daisy, walking around smiling at you, all... smiley."

Molly grinned. "Still grouchy about that?"

"What do you mean?"

"You threw a sparring pad at my head for talking to her before. That's grouchy."

"You were wasting time."

"Sammy dragged me over there!" she protested, unable to hide her smile. "I wasn't going to be rude, and it was all of two minutes. Why do you care who I talk to anyway?"

Talie drained half her bottle and wiped the corners of her mouth with her forefinger and thumb.

"We don't know anything about her. For all we know, she's one if your lot sent in as like a double super spy."

Molly huffed a laugh and swigged a mouthful.

"Doubt it. Do you suspect everyone then?"

"Don't you?"

"Fair. You can't truly trust anyone beyond what they need you for. She sounds like she's friendly with Sammy though, so maybe you should be bugging her about Daisy instead of me."

"She wouldn't listen. She wants to see the good in everyone, even when she knows they're anything but."

"It must be nice to believe the best in everyone, but dangerous. I'm starting to doubt everything after the recent evenings I've had."

She left it dangling, as if waiting, maybe even hoping that Talie would bite.

"Your hands hurting from the climb?" Talie asked instead.

Molly rolled her eyes. "Not that."

"Something happened after the guild?"

"I didn't- Orbs alive, you're annoying. I got dragged in to report to the Menagerie. I'm beginning to fear that what you say about them is true."

Talie shrugged, draining her bottle and slipping it into her coat pocket.

"I know there's still a lot of stuff I can't tell you," she said. "Stuff I would if I could."

"Helpful."

Talie smiled. "You're welcome. Ask yourself this, if the Menagerie are the good guys, why hide in gilded halls? Why all the sneaking around? Why not own the boots outright and admit it?"

"They say it's because it helps keep on top of their enemies."

"If they're not harming people, why do they have so many enemies then? The nobles I'll give you, but aren't the Menagerie all over them? Fawning in low places while the higher up levels rot."

"They say the wealth will rise bit by bit, like all things, 'rising smoke finances' I think they call it."

Talie arched an eyebrow. "And has it?"

"No, and I'm beginning to think it was never meant to."

"Don't need outright lies to mislead people, Princess. Just the hope of fools and the promise of basic necessities that are tightly controlled. If we could only figure out how far along they are with this whole stealing the fairies for gifts thing."

"There is something…" Molly hesitated.

"Well, you're either going to tell me or you're not. I won't beg."

"I'd never expect you to. When I was away for a bit, before the Kayla Crane concert, I found something out."

Talie leaned back on her elbows with a sigh.

"And?"

"I shouldn't really tell you how, but I came across some information about gift extraction."

Talie sat up again. "What do you mean?"

"Remember I told you a while back that I found a scrap of paper you dropped. It had some kind of potion on it. Well, Celeste wanted to know the details, then she sent me where she sent me to get that specific information."

Talie sighed. "Which is only more proof that the Menagerie are looking to steal gifts. Phoenix says it would take mass power to sever a given gift from a Fae though."

"Yes, and at the guild they mentioned needing a great power."

"And the Menagerie is built around the core of the citadel," Talie added, her tone turning sharp.

"And the citadel is built over a well of power of sorts."

"So perhaps that's what Celeste is after, finding this well of power."

"Or she's already found it and is using it to strip Fae and fairies of their gifts." Molly shuddered.

"Either way, ask yourself how they managed to find and choose the fairies in the first place? Who outside helped them?"

"That's a scary thought. It might explain the missing artificers though. If they refused to do what part of the craft they were told to, or threatened to expose the project, then perhaps outsiders are needed instead."

Talie tapped her fingers gently over the beam by her knee, the light from the nearby lamps catching the black and silver rings she wore.

"They need to be stopped," she said. "Before they start using more people as resources for whatever mad schemes they have planned, like those fairies."

Molly bit her lip. "Speaking of mad plans… what if someone were to force the two sides together? Get them to talk and reach a compromise?"

"How in the name of Faerie would anyone do that?"

"Say they could." Molly hesitated. "How would it be possible to get both sides in a room without a crowd?"

"Not sure it'd be possible. We don't know how high up the Menagerie goes. As for Phoenix, if he's truly the absolute head of the resistance then you're a long lost princess of Faerie."

Molly smiled. "Can't see either of us in a fancy dress and a crown somehow."

"You've seen me in a dress," Talie reminded her quietly.

Molly's insides flipped at the memory, her skin growing warm. It felt like ages ago that she and Talie had stood on opposing sides, all dressed up for a ball but hiding between the levels beneath it. Talie asked her to dance as a way of getting information, but in that moment the lines blurred irretrievably for her.

"No crown though," she countered.

"Don't need a crown to be royal blood." Talie shrugged.

"It really is a mad plan though. Even if you could get whoever is really in charge together, how would you convince them to play nice?"

Molly thought of her compulsion gift and how she'd always shied away from using it. The few times at the queen's court had been minor slips to get her out of trouble with the courtiers, like a leering eye resistant to charm in a deserted hallway sent packing, or once when one of the kitchen maids had cut her finger deeply and needed calming so the healer could work on her. They were tiny little dents in whatever fate Faerie and the nether had planned for everyone, but changing the fortune of the entire citadel might not even be possible for any amount of gift power.

"I'm sure there are ways. I did say it was a mad plan."

Talie nodded. "Nice idea in theory, but unless you've somehow got a mighty compulsion gift hiding- oh, what now?"

She reached into her pocket and pulled out a pale green orb. As she scanned the surface of it, no doubt reading a message, Molly grabbed her bottle and took a sip.

Then Talie scrambled to her feet with a gasp, and Molly knocked the lip of the bottle against her chin as she scrambled to get out of the way.

"What's wrong?"

Talie grimaced. "I thought we'd have more time."

"For what? What's going on?"

Molly dropped her bottle beside the cushion and stood as Talie pushed the orb back into her pocket.

"The resistance are storming the Menagerie."

Molly gasped. "Why?!"

"Why do you think? The Menagerie stole fairies and brought them in from outside the citadel, they've been stealing artificers, and even if they're all-powerful around here, they can't lie about it if forced to answer."

"What does that have to do with anything? Is Phoenix planning to force a public confession or something? Marcus is too well protected, they'll never even get in."

Talie glanced over her shoulder as a loud bang echoed, enough to vibrate the citadel glass.

"You need to keep their attention," she announced.

Molly folded her arms across her chest. "Excuse me? How do you think I'm going to do that?"

The 'why me' was implied, but Talie answered before she could voice it for emphasis.

"Phoenix won't be looking to get those fairies out. He wants the Menagerie taken down. I… might have forgotten to tell you something I overheard, something about his family being the ruling dynasty before the Menagerie arrived."

Molly froze. "Phoenix is… this is all about revenge?"

"I don't think so, not entirely. But he's determined to bring them down, and considering they're the ones stealing fairies it's about time he did."

Molly couldn't argue with that, but she couldn't risk trusting Phoenix, not that she'd assumed she ever could before.

"So, what's your plan then?" she asked.

"You distract them. Go to the Menagerie, call for peace or something, ask your lot to stand down."

"And while I'm doing that?"

"I'll sneak into the core and find out what I can."

"What about setting the fairies free?"

Talie nodded. "All of that. If I can set them free, I will, I promise."

"And you'll share whatever you find out with me?"

"Of course. I can't trust you won't take this all back to them, but at least buy me time to get in and free the fairies. Anything I find out, I'll tell you and you can get it out to your fancy friends outside the citadel."

Molly knew that was as good a promise as she would get. Ignoring the fact she didn't exactly know how to get word out of the citadel, not now Celeste had taken her original orb with the citadel permission settings programmed into it, she nodded.

"Okay. But what do I do if nobody listens? Does Phoenix even have enough people to bring a proper fight?"

"The resistance has enough secrets to make an impact." Talie held a hand out. "Are you coming with me or what?"

Molly stared at the hand. The urge to whirl straight into the fight nipped at her heels, and she raised a hand to clasp Talie's fingers tight.

"There's a less chaotic way in," she announced as Talie hauled her to her feet.

They raced across the beams together, and along the levels toward the Menagerie window. Sounds of fighting echoed out and Molly's heart squeezed tight in her chest, but she had to hope whoever was doing the most damage could be persuaded to stand down. She hurried through the window and waited for Talie to slither in behind her.

"Which way?" Talie asked.

Molly eyed the doors, all closed, then pressed a finger to her lips and listened.

"No sounds of voices up here," she murmured. "Marcus is many things but a coward isn't one of them. He'll be wherever the fight is. Celeste might be around, but I doubt she does the fighting."

A loud rumble quaked through the building and Molly set off toward the far end of the hall, dragging Talie with her to the stairwell. She leaned over the banister, then veered back as a puff of purple smoke floated up past her face.

"Fight's down there."

Talie pulled a face. "Yeah, I figured that out."

Molly started forward but Talie tightened her grip and pulled her back.

"If I tell you to hide, you hide, got it? If I tell you to run, do it."

Molly blinked. "Excuse me?"

"Orbs alive, Molly, it's not difficult. Distract them if you can but don't put yourself in any danger. If-"

"I know what you said, but you don't dictate what I do." She pulled her arm free. "I can look after myself fine."

She set off down the stairs before Talie could grab her again.

"Wait! You don't understand what's really going on here."

Molly dredged up a warding around herself, grabbed the banister and increased her pace, the thud of Talie thundering after her echoing behind.

"I know, because nobody will tell me anything," she snapped back over her shoulder. "But it's fine, I can figure it out myself."

Talie cursed under her breath, and Molly's adrenalin spiked as they rounded the corner of the staircase and saw the absolute chaos in the entrance hall.

The sizzle and bang of gifts exploding on wardings filled the air, smoke and what looked like glitter mingling above a yawning pit of Fae fighting each other. The main doors were open, or so she thought until she realised one had been broken clean off its hinges, the fringes of the battle echoing back in from the street.

"We need to find people we know, not go attacking people we don't," Talie shouted above the din.

Molly pointed. "There's Phoenix."

She hurried down the remaining steps without waiting. Talie shot after her, ducking as something on fire sailed over her head. She skidded to a halt at Molly's side, her face set in grim determination as someone came flying toward them.

"You don't have any offensive gifts," she announced, bodily shoving the person aside.

Molly scowled. "Tell everyone that why don't you?"

"How are you going to keep yourself safe then, Princess?"

Molly ducked a punch, swinging her arm into the assailant's stomach before retreating back under her warding.

"If you want me to trust you, then trust me when I say I can handle myself."

Talie grimaced. "Fine, but any sign of proper trouble, I mean it…"

Molly almost smiled to see her struggling with the words, a fleeting moment of amusement in the pit of mayhem around them. Then she squeaked in horror as Talie's face loomed in front of hers.

The softest brush of lips against her own, firm and utterly claiming, sent her head spinning. Talie didn't even look at her the moment they broke apart, but Molly felt the sudden chill as Talie pulled her hand free and charged into the fray.

Molly dodged someone approaching her and held her warding firm with her nerves pounding fast. Her gifts would be better placed to creep through the Menagerie while Talie fought up front, but she hadn't even considered suggesting they go together. It wasn't as if the Menagerie weren't already suitably distracted either.

The icy fingers of doubt crept around her chest.

If she's doing something under-handed after all, maybe I should follow her.

Clinging to the fringe of the hall, she spied Celeste holding court behind a dome of protection on top of the raised stage at the far end of the hall. Framed by a stained glass window, the lamps behind the glass cast her in an ethereal glow of pinks and greens. Menagerie guards and a collection of the boots fought a straggled line of resistance men and women, but one person broke through the fringes and charged.

Molly firmed her warding tighter as Ru skidded to a halt in front of her. The domineering push of his protection batted against hers, but she wouldn't merge hers with his, not now.

"Which side does Celeste want me on then?" she asked sarcastically.

"Molly, enough. You shouldn't be here."

She frowned. "I'm part of the Menagerie, aren't I? DUCK."

Ru obeyed without hesitation, without question, sinking low alongside her as an enormous swarm of bees roared overhead.

"Come behind the line," he insisted.

"Molly!" Phoenix hollered. "Where is she? What are you doing here?"

Torn between both sides, she dodged the hand Ru put against her warding and took a step back as Phoenix approached.

She couldn't see Talie in the mess and one of the ominous double doors at the far end of the hall was ajar.

She knows so much I don't. Maybe this is what she expected me to do, keep both sides talking.

Molly folded her arms and backed up against the bottom of the staircase as Ru and Phoenix stopped in front of her while eying each other warily.

She glanced from one to the other and hoped with everything she had that Talie knew what she was doing.

"Well?" she demanded. "I'm listening."

CHAPTER SEVENTEEN

TALIE

The vast inner doors of the Menagerie's entrance hall loomed in the far corner of the room, imposing black wood studded and adorned with metal. Talie grimaced as she ducked and crept through the fighting groups toward them. The guards were occupied but she had to hope Celeste was arrogant enough to assume nobody was after the Menagerie's big secret.

Molly would have been better for this with her stealth.

Talie shook the thought from her head. Molly would be safe enough in the crush. Phoenix would make sure of it because however much he knew that he wasn't telling, he needed Molly safe.

She glanced over her shoulder as she reached the doors and eased one open. Dim light flickered on the other side, but most of whatever lay beyond was shrouded in gloom.

I should have done more research on the maps, or asked Molly where all these magic vents she keeps finding are.

She slipped through the gap and started down the bare stone corridor. The absence of guards wasn't a good sign.

Phoenix was testing the boundaries, she knew that much, but not why. He didn't have a full group of fighters with him either given the numbers in the hall. She couldn't rule out him having a side mission going on elsewhere, but she would have bet what little she had that he wasn't too worried about freeing random fairies.

She hurried toward the single door at the end of the corridor, non-descript wood with no sign or marking. With the dulled sound of the battle raging behind her she couldn't hear if there were any sounds beyond. She eased the door open a crack and peered into the fire lit gloom beyond.

No guards still.

She bit her lip and opened the door further, squeezing through. Two steps in and she stopped.

Corridors branched off, several going in every direction. Down some of them she could make out more paths and corridors. Some of the nearest doors had small hatches in at face height, horizontal metal bars blocking any chance of much reaching in or out.

It's a labyrinth. She'd heard of fae-tales and rumour of one, but thought they were just that. *I can't risk going any further.*

They would need maps and failsafe plans to avoid getting lost, something she couldn't do alone.

As she turned to go back to the fight, a pained groan echoed from one of the nearby doors. Sense screamed at her to leave while she could, but the sound was drowning in agony. She inched toward the door and risked a quick peek through the bars.

Her heart twisted in her chest, and she lifted a hand to cover her mouth as a gasp escaped. Behind the door was a bare cell, and inside a woman lay on the stone floor. She looked thin to the bone, her skin sunken and pallid with patches of hair missing from her head. Her skeletal fingers twitching was the only sign of life betraying the otherwise death-like state.

"Orbs alive," Talie muttered.

"They drained her." A feeble voice echoed behind her. "Failed, but they kept trying anyway."

Talie whirled around. Another door stood opposite the woman's, the pinched face of a man looking through.

"What happened?" she demanded. "How did you get in here?"

"We were travelling by cart. Got set upon. It's meant to be a safe road. When we woke again, we were here. Seen many come through since."

He coughed several times before he managed to finish speaking, and Talie struggled to hear some of it.

"They kidnapped you? From where? Outside the citadel?"

"The citadel, that's where we are?" He shook his head. "Too far from home to make it back then."

"Maybe I can get some of you out, maybe-"

"Cells are metirin iron. You can't use gifts on them."

Molly. Talie glanced back at the door to the hall. *She can pick locks, hinges.*

"I can come back with someone who can get you out. Maybe we can get her some help or something."

She gestured to the woman in the cell, but he shook his

head again.

"She's gone." His voice broke. "She doesn't even recognise me anymore. Doubt she'd even recognise her own kids. Sometimes... sometimes death's a kindness."

Talie clenched her fists as he disappeared from view.

"How are they doing it? What happens?"

Silence screamed back at her and the man's face disappeared. She scanned the numerous hallways branching off again, but she had no way to get any of the cell doors open, and no gifts to defend herself with if found.

Defeat clawed at her insides as she stormed back toward the exit. She closed the middle door behind her and started down the hallway toward the entrance hall. The clash and clang of fighting greeted her as she approached the vast black doors, but a man and a woman in boots uniforms hurried through before she could make it.

Crud.

Talie grabbed the first glamour she could think of and donned the pretence of the woman from the guild.

"There's one!" the man shouted.

Talie saw a gap beside them and charged before either could lunge for her.

The woman dodged to block her path, but Talie slammed her heel into the woman's ankle and threw a punch to her shoulder.

The woman crashed into the wall as Talie ducked low and swung her hand out again. The man grunted as she made contact, and she didn't even have time to cringe as she swirled past and left him clutching between his legs with a pained whimper.

She swapped her glamour for a protection warding and slipped back into the melee, searching the crowd for Molly.

Phoenix and the Menagerie boy had her flanked against the base of the staircase. With a battle ground between them, Talie ducked and dodged the gifts flying everywhere as they bounced off wardings and plumed through the air. She fought with shoves and jabs aimed at anyone coming near, her gaze fixed on the trio at the far end of the room.

Molly had her arms folded, fury blazing in her stormy eyes like one of the fabled spirits of old. With the light shining over her golden hair, haloing her face, she looked like a Fae princess, one that Talie would have knelt for given the chance.

But Phoenix and Ru weren't kneeling, and Molly wasn't safe around any of them.

Across the room, Celeste stood on a platform with one hand raised, a constant pulsating wave of pale blue powder scattering from her fingertips. The moment it hit wardings it became water, sloshing to the ground ready for people to trip on it.

Talie struggled past the fractured groups still fighting, her heart spasming as she saw familiar faces in the mix, those she trained with at the gym. She hooked away from someone racing for her and dashed past Phoenix. He gave her a grim nod but she didn't stop to dwell on how disappointed he'd be once it was all over. She had failed to keep Molly away from the Menagerie, the one instruction he'd given her.

Ru had his hands up in front of Molly, but as Talie skidded past him and twisted into the momentum to put herself alongside Molly, she realised that he had his hands against Molly's warding.

The warding Talie had breezed straight through.

Hope and a scary dash of delight flickered in her gut, giving her the boldness to reach down and clasp Molly's hand.

"Anything?" Molly asked.

Talie gave Ru a dismissive look. "Some, not all. We need to get out of here."

"That's what I've been trying to tell her," Ru snapped. "Maybe you'll listen to her, Molly. Go."

Talie lifted her head in time to see Celeste look their way, then down at their hands still clasped together.

"I tried to spare you this, Molly," Phoenix announced. "Remember that."

Before Talie could ask him what he was going on about, foreboding cutting right through her chest, Phoenix strode forward. His warding domed like granite, gifts and Fae bouncing right off the moment they tried to attack.

Talie stared as Phoenix approached the stage, Molly's hand now tight around her fingers.

"What did he mean?" Molly asked.

Ru grimaced. "I will literally drag you out myself if you don't go right now."

"Touch her and die." Talie snapped automatically. "Literally or figuratively, I don't care."

All eyes turned to Phoenix as he reached the stage.

"Why are you attacking us?" Celeste asked, her tone

ringing out across the hall.

The fringes continued fighting but several closest to the stage slowed their attacks and pulled their gifts back. Groups formed on both sides of the hall but Talie didn't dare move to one or the other. She knew what side she was meant to be on but she stood firm at Molly's side. The least she could do was keep her hand firm around Molly's clammy, shaking one.

"If you need me to remind you of all the chaos you've caused, I can," Phoenix said, his stance easy, confident. "The Menagerie has controlled the citadel by force and by siphoning off our resources to benefit the nobles for two decades now. There are those of us who remember what it used to be like before."

"Only twenty years?" Molly frowned. "The Menagerie is far older."

Talie scoffed quietly. "Is that what they tell you?"

"The Menagerie's rule may be more focused around the nobility, but what came before was a worse kind of chaos." Celeste said. "Besides, most Fae don't know the Menagerie exists so how can all the failures of the citadel be levelled at our door? Everything we do is for the continued safety and improvement of the citadel."

"Safety? How is it safe to keep Fae going hungry in the upper levels? To take so much of what they produce they can barely afford to heat their homes? Why have the Menagerie been allowing the guilds to charge more for fuel yet turning the citadel's atmosphere colder and colder each time winter is simulated?"

Celeste smiled, her hands clasping in front of her like a

mother placating a child. Talie eyed the uncertain faces on both sides, wondering how many of them had been misled with empty promises.

"The seasons have proved important for regulating people," Celeste insisted. "Monotony is not good, and celebrations of seasons must be observed."

Phoenix scoffed and took a firm step forward, his arms relaxed at his sides even as his fingers flexed in preparation.

"Pretty words. But none of that answers why fuel costs have risen, or why the resources we produce are taken from us, often quicker than we can produce them. Is that it? We work ever harder to fund a growing debt we'll never end up repaying?"

Molly lifted a hand to her chest. Talie glanced at her in time to see her fingers graze the necklace she wore, the acorn Talie had given her lying next to her workshop key.

Celeste sighed. "The citadel is self-sustaining. We need to ensure that everything continues to function without outside assistance, and sometimes the cost of fuel is not comparative to the cost of water, or heating, or food."

None of this is getting them to stop fighting.

Talie glanced at the two groups eying each other warily. One inflammatory word and the whole thing would spill over again.

"I understand the financials better than most," Phoenix scoffed. "My father taught me well. What can you say about your family? What exactly did they teach you, I wonder?"

He smiled at Celeste, who matched his expression with

one of unfailing confidence.

He knows. Talie's insides chilled. *He knows everything, and he's going to use it.*

She tightened her grip on Molly's hand.

"I can't tell you, but I want to, remember that," she muttered. "Connect the dots, Princess."

"My family is of no concern here," Celeste said, the pause only slightly too long to be comfortable.

Phoenix splayed his arms out.

"I disagree. I believe your family is of every concern here. The citadel has always been self-sustaining, outside of royal control. Until you turned up twenty years ago."

A gasp wavered through the crowd, a fierce murmur picking up. Molly stared, catching the slightest twitch of Celeste's eyes narrowing before she laughed, reclaiming the hall's attention.

"Is that so?" she asked.

Phoenix laughed too, the noise a note too loud in its eagerness.

"Celestial, that is your full name, yes? Celestial Elverhill, the firstborn and now abdicated princess of the royal oak line. Rumour had it that you fled here after abdicating, but nobody believed it. Now we have proof."

A shocked murmur rippled across the room as Talie's pulse raced. Molly's hand tightened around hers as Celeste's smile widened.

"I have no need to deny it, but who I was before the citadel is irrelevant. Everything I am now is what I've built since then. The Menagerie is what I have built since, and it thrives because of me. Who needs to pander to inheritance when you can build your own kingdom?"

"We're going to walk out of here very slowly," Talie murmured, tugging gently on Molly's fingers. "Now. Trust me. Take a step back, nice and steady."

Molly didn't move.

"You're ruining my plans before I'm ready," Celeste continued. "But I am nothing if not amenable to change. Do you not think I've been aware of your little resistance since you formed against us? All those fanciful notions about freedom, self-government. How is that to work exactly, when you can't even work cohesively with us as it is? If you only asked, we would have given."

"Oh, we've asked-"

"You've demanded." She shook her head. "You haven't asked. Respect is so important."

"Respect?" Phoenix spluttered, his body going rigid. "You came to the citadel, overthrew several of the groups governing already, killed several, including *my* family."

"Losses are unfortunate, but we cannot allow protests to wage war on what we're trying to build here."

"How compassionate. Don't bother with the honeyed words. My gift is to see truth, and I can see that you are a killer."

Celeste shrugged and surveyed the crowd.

"You may think so. I believe you have also done what you have to do in the name of what you think is right. Are you utterly blameless? Are your hands entirely clean?"

Talie moved her shoulder in front of Molly's chest, slowly using it to shunt her backwards while still clinging to her hand. Molly took the first step backward, and another.

"You stole my family, but I'm fully aware that you have a child of your own," Phoenix announced.

Molly's grip turned from firm to painful and she refused to move another step, putting her weight against Talie's attempt to move her backwards instead.

Celeste tilted her head. "Are you now? How clever of you."

"When I can prove who it is, I will take them from you like you've taken my family from me."

Celeste smiled and lifted a delicate hand.

Talie froze as Celeste's finger landed directly on them.

"Go ahead. She's right over there."

CHAPTER EIGHTEEN

MOLLY

Molly's mind waged a war of its own, doubt and realisation swirling until she felt dizzy.

Celeste had shown her kindness since she joined the Menagerie, even given her the stealth gift after sending her into the queen's court.

She sent me there as a spy. Did May know? Was it all fixed?

She couldn't believe the oak queen would have known, but she couldn't trust what anyone told her now. Celeste didn't owe her any honesties, but the shock had struck her motionless all the same. Even Phoenix seemed stunned into silence.

Neither of them care about the Fae or the citadel. It's the war ground for Celeste's ego and Phoenix's vendetta.

She wasn't close to either of them but the realisation still hit her deep enough to steal her breath away.

As Celeste claimed a daughter and pointed their way, Molly stared at Talie. All her mentions about royal blood, about not being able to tell her things, knowing more about the death of Molly's guardians than she should. Her insides washed icy.

Phoenix frowned, his head turned to look at them while still keeping Celeste in view.

"I take it you don't mean Talie," he said.

Celeste snorted. "Of course not."

Molly shook as Celeste's gaze softened and turned her way next.

"You can't mean me." She waited for another scathing dismissal but none came. "That's ridiculous. I might be indebted to the Menagerie, but how can I be related to you?"

Her legs wobbled, her pulse pounding until it was all she could hear. She had a vague awareness of Talie's arm sliding around her waist and holding her steady.

"This wasn't how I wanted you to find out," Celeste said, her voice softening.

Molly shook her head. "No. This is some kind of joke. My parents were nobodies, Basil and Lily told me so."

"Your guardians had no idea who I really was. You were still a baby when I left you with them, and I made sure to cloak myself appropriately. Your name is Molinia, because the grass often grows stronger than any flower, but I told them it was Molly to be safe."

Molinia. All this time, even my name isn't really my own.

Her fingers anchored on the charms around her neck, until realisation trickled in. She looked up to find Talie's jaw clenched, her gaze fixed ahead.

"Did you know?" she asked.

"Molly…"

She pushed herself away from Talie and forced her legs to hold her up without support.

"You knew this? You knew who I was? Who she was?"

"It's-"

"Don't you dare say it's complicated!"

Talie grimaced and pain slanted across her face, but Molly could barely focus on that as rising panic clawed at her limbs. As Celeste descended the stage and strode toward her, Molly stumbled back a step and lifted a hand.

"DON'T."

Her compulsion gift flooded out of her, spasming along with the pounding in her veins and the rushing in her ears.

Celeste slowed. "Oh, my dear, do you honestly think I'd gift you with compulsion and not make myself immune to it? I expected some tantrums when you found out. I understand."

Molly shook her head and caught the surprise on Talie's face at the mention of her compulsion gift.

"It took some planning," Celeste continued. "Whether I abdicated or not, children of the royal family aren't allowed to gift others. Court Fae however are nobles, which was maddening growing up."

Growing up. With May, and the king consort, and the oak queen. Oh orbs, did I clear out her old bin while I was at the court?

Sickness bubbled up, the acid tang of it sharpening her mind as she choked it back down. Talie had told her to trust nobody and she'd meant it literally. But while Molly couldn't compel Celeste, she could still compel any others who came near.

A woman darted forward from the crowd with a whip of fire that lashed toward her. She scrambled to get her warding firm in time even as Ru surged forward and Talie's arms anchored around her waist to haul her back.

Celeste lifted a hand and the fire halted, frozen in midair. With a mere twitch of her fingers, she sent the flames zooming back to their wielder and wrapped them around the woman's neck.

"Stop it!" Molly hissed.

Celeste sighed even as her hand lowered. The woman dropped to her knees and pressed her fingers to her neck as the fire receded.

"It's pointless to try fighting against me," Celeste announced, loud enough for all to hear. "That goes for you too, Molinia."

"Threats already?"

"I won't have you harmed, but you must know I expect you to respect me. You may question some of my methods, but I've built the citadel into what it is now. Orbs alive, by all accounts you see this as your home and now you're heir apparent to it. You should be thanking me!"

Molly took a step back, but she had no friends left to run to, no safe place to seek sanctuary.

"Why? Why do all this?" she asked. "Why bring me into it now? Why not, I don't know, acknowledge me before now?"

Celeste chuckled as though they were having a leisurely chat and Molly fought the rising fury inside. Even in her current state taking on Celeste was impossible, and she had no hope now of Phoenix not using her as a pawn in the wider game of 'who gets to rule the citadel'.

"You are my daughter, Molinia. Heir apparent to the citadel and a princess of Faerie by blood. I admit, it has amused me to see how you've developed over the years. The citadel has been the perfect playground to toughen you up. With you beside me as heir apparent, one day we can even challenge the queens for our birthright, and take the entire throne of Faerie, united under one banner."

"I don't want the entire throne of Faerie!"

Celeste sighed. "You need some time to adjust. So did I before I decided to abdicate. The moment Oakthorn was born and became crown prince, I was passed over. I knew I had to bide my time. It's our crown, my dear, and we will take it the traditional way.

"What, through war and death and conquest?"

"If we must. Ideally, it won't come to that. War is a waste, Molinia."

"My name is Molly."

"It is," Phoenix spoke up. "Molly's one of us now."

Celeste laughed. "Before she was yours, she was mine, in all ways."

"She's not an orbing toy for you to fight over," Talie growled.

Even as the three of them eyed each other, Molly caught Ru moving out of the corner of her eye, coming from the left. She started backing away again, desperate to get outside before the mob threw off their shock and saw just how valuable a toy she'd become.

"Molly, stay here," Ru murmured, closer than she could possibly handle. "I know it's a shock, but now everyone knows who you are the Menagerie is the safest place for you. With family."

Even as Phoenix raised a hand and Celeste copied him, ready to attack, Talie was past them and bearing down on Ru. Wrapping the full extent of her compulsion gift around her, Molly glared at both of them.

"Stay where you are right now."

She didn't have time to think about the practicalities. Too vague an instruction and she would weld them to the spot. Thoughts of them stuck in the entrance hall forever while she went into hiding, not around to release them again, sent a bark of hysteria flying from her lips.

Talie and Ru both stumbled to a halt in front of her, Talie stilling while Ru's arms jerked at his sides as though he was trying to fight the compulsion.

As Phoenix attacked first, the hall exploded into absolute mayhem, gifts flying again with renewed force. Several pairs of eyes were drifting toward her mid-fight and she had nowhere to go, nowhere left to hide where they wouldn't find her.

"Molly, be sensible," Ru cajoled, eyes wide and tone deceptively pleading. "Celeste might be your mother, but she's watched over you all this time."

"You knew," Molly spat.

He grimaced. "Only since we went to the queen's court. She trusted me to watch over you there and protect you, and I did."

"Only because you're Celeste's puppet," Talie

countered. "She had to put a swear-block on me to keep me quiet."

Molly hesitated. Talie couldn't lie and it didn't sound like she was trying to word-tangle either, her cheeks pink with frustration and her eyes wide enough to look wild.

"You gave me clues," Molly said as she inched backwards.

Talie nodded. "I tried to. You wear half of them around your neck. Acorn is-"

"The symbol of the oak queen's family, I know."

"Not her whole family, just her direct descendants."

"And you called me Princess. I thought you were just being snarky."

Talie's lips twitched the slightest amount. "That too. Honestly, if I could have told you, I would. In a heartbeat."

"What does she have over you?"

"What does it matter?" Ru snapped. "This is irrelevant. You can't hide from this, Molly. Dig your head in the sand and she'll still be your mother. There's no way out of the citadel either. Do the right thing and listen to her."

Molly caught Talie's eye instead.

"What does she have over you?" she repeated.

Talie's gaze fixed on Ru before she mouthed the answer.

"*Sammy.*"

Molly understood it then. One day, she would find a way to ask Talie the whole truth, to get her story. She might even be able to forgive her.

I can't risk being her friend if it puts her and Sammy in the firing line.

She pulled her compulsion gift to the fore, calculating how much time she'd need.

"Once I'm out of sight, don't follow me. Don't tell anyone where you think I've gone. Don't come looking for me until I'm ready."

"How will I know when you're ready?" Talie asked.

Molly eyed Ru, glowering at her as he fought the new compulsion she'd set on him. He would be furious she'd never shared knowledge of the gift with him, perhaps even upset Celeste hadn't either. As she turned her gaze away, she disowned any remnant of knowing him and focused on Talie instead. She lifted her necklace with one finger.

"When I'm ready, you'll know. Until then, if you want to tell me the truth, you can leave word where I'll find it."

She turned on her heel, Ru's frantic shouts and Talie's deafening silence echoing behind her. Someone barrelled toward her but she dodged and slid into stealth mode without daring to look back. Passing through the fighting crowd, she bounced off wardings and into the lane.

The moment she found a side-alley, she dashed into it and scaled the nearest pillar, running as fast as she dared between the levels toward her workshop. She needed Aurora. If there was any hope of getting a message out, she'd have to try now. She was almost definitely convinced she could manage to at least ask without Aurora pecking her eyes out.

She slid down into the alley and pressed a shaking hand to her doorframe as she fumbled with the key.

"Molly!"

She groaned under her breath. Now was not Beryl-in-full-maternal-mode time. She forced a smile across her face.

"Hi Beryl, now's really not a good- ouch!"

She squeaked as Beryl grabbed her hand and started pulling.

"If you know what's good for you, you'll get inside before your Menagerie and whoever else comes looking for you. First place they're going to look is your workshop."

So stunned Beryl had mentioned the Menagerie, let alone seemed to know something was going on, Molly found herself stumbling behind Beryl toward her home. Struggling with the weirdness of it, she said the only thing she could focus on in the whole barrel of weird that had landed on top of her.

"What did you say?!"

CHAPTER NINETEEN

TALIE

The chaos of the fight was crumbling fast. In the sizzle and slash of gifts flying again as Phoenix backed the bedraggled lines of the resistance out of the hall, Talie stumbled away from them. From all of it.

Her heaving breaths didn't hit her chest properly, her knees like jelly as she left the lines and set off along the lane. She couldn't see Molly anywhere, no doubt she'd gone straight up between levels to escape, but Molly had told her, compelled her somehow, not to approach until she was ready.

She wasn't looking at Ru when she said about being ready eventually, but perhaps the whole restriction wasn't intended for him at all.

She choked a sob down, almost catching her shoulder on the back of a waiting cart as she careened past it. Ignoring the indignant holler echoing behind her, she dodged and stumbled up the lane until the familiar dirty stones of her alley wavered beneath her feet. She pushed open her door, not daring to look as Sammy gasped in alarm, and threw herself face down onto her bed.

"What happened?"

The bed creaked as Sammy sat beside her, knowing better than to touch, just the edge of her hip against Talie's to anchor her in.

"There was a fight. Molly… she's… she won't ever want to speak to me again now."

Sammy sighed. "Can I ask? I know you keep all this from me, but I'm not a child, not anymore. I know you're involved with some kind of control group, not the boots but higher up. I know you always have been."

"It's not safe-"

"Nothing's safe anymore. It hasn't been for a while. I'm your sister. Trust me."

Talie clung to her ragged pillow, pressing it as hard to her face as she could, like that would erase some of the thundering pain inside. She sniffed and wiped her eyes on the fabric. She didn't cry, ever. She couldn't remember a single moment where Sammy would have been her cry before, but then Sammy was the only person she could trust. She turned her face to the wall.

"There are several units of power," she began. "The boots aren't really in control of anything. The Menagerie, they control the boots, make the decisions. They all but kneel to the nobles further down. The guilds hold their own power, much like the nobles do, but they don't coordinate like the Menagerie do. Then there's the resistance. Phoenix leads it."

"And that's who you're allied with?"

Talie stared at the wall, the little chips and marks made

over the years familiar enough to focus on while the rest of her chaotic mind whirled.

"I thought so. I- yes, but it's complicated."

"Because of Molly, who she is?"

Talie tensed. "Who exactly do you think she is?"

"Someone important. Come on, a princess of Faerie walks through a citadel she's never visited to check on a maid she's known a couple of weeks. Molly sneaks about even more than you do, and suddenly she's in the gym as part of your skulduggery club that you barely let me into. Is she on the other side? She secretly one of the nobles or something?"

Talie choked over a laugh, shaking her head.

"You could say that. It's a long story, but there's a reason all of this started with her, revolves around her even. The Menagerie want her, the resistance want her, the powers outside the citadel will want her once they find out who she is."

Sammy sighed. "I won't pretend I get all of it, but Molly's not a bad person. Neither are you. Both of you have been used as pawns by warring factions and that's horrible. Will Molly decide to join the resistance, or is she loyal to this Menagerie?"

"I don't think she wants to be on any side now. Phoenix will want to use her as his poster girl if she strays his way. The Menagerie will have their own big plans for her. I want to protect her, and I can't. I'm useless."

She curled back into her pillow as Sammy stood, her feet tapping across the floor to the kitchenette. The familiar clunk of the mugs and tins filled the quiet space.

"You're not useless, but you won't believe it from me. Why not go talk to her? Or do we need to rescue her?"

Talie might have smiled at that any other time. Sammy would absolutely have marched into the Menagerie and pulled Molly out, warring factions or not.

"She got away during the fight, but I can't go and talk to her. She forbade it. Compelled me, I think, Faerie knows how she got that gift."

"Oh. She mad at you?"

"You could say that." Talie wiped her damp cheeks with a hand. "I ruin everything."

"Stop it. You saved me, remember? You took me from being tormented after Birch died in that awful home to here."

"I promised him I'd keep you safe," Talie sniffed.

"And you have. I get to go to school, and I know I don't know everything about how you make that happen, but don't tell me you ruin everything because you make a huge difference to me."

Talie pressed her eyes to the pillow. "It's not enough. I don't know how long I can keep anyone safe now."

"Then start trusting me to keep myself safe. You're barely a year older than I am but you took on responsibility for me so you wouldn't have to face yourself. I get it, you wanted to atone for all this supposed darkness you see in yourself, but I'm not your responsibility. I'm mine. Don't avoid your life because you're too busy pretending to defend mine."

When Talie didn't answer, Sammy huffed.

"Trust Molly too," she added. "She's smart,

resourceful."

"She'll never forgive me."

"She will. I'll make her. I don't even need a charm gift to be persuasive."

Talie took a deep breath, letting Sammy's strong voice calm her. She didn't think Molly would be forgiving her anytime soon, but she had been wanting to ask something else for a long time.

"Do you remember him? Birch?"

Sammy sighed. "I do, but it's only bits. Like breakfast when he used to pretend he was sick of bread to give me his. You did that too."

"For a while, yeah. You wised up quick enough. I just didn't want you to lose anymore than him."

"Well, I haven't, but I couldn't bear it if I lost you too. Friends come and go sometimes, living their own lives, but we're family. That's deeper. After Birch died, you became my sister, and I need you to be safe too."

Talie nodded. She couldn't say crying and sulking forever. Phoenix would expect her to show up. He would expect her to have followed Molly, to have worked on convincing her to join them instead.

"She said I'm not to approach her until she's ready," she muttered.

Sammy thunked back down beside her, extending an arm until a mug appeared in front of Talie's face. She took it, guessing it would end up thrown over her if she didn't.

"Well there you go then," Sammy said cheerfully. "Approach isn't exactly a finite term. She doesn't want you to walk up to her without an invitation, but that doesn't mean you can't leave her a letter."

Talie frowned. "What good would that do?"

"Explain your side. Let her know you're as much of a pawn as she is. She probably already knows this but at least it'll let her know you're thinking of her. She might choose to end your exile early."

There was some merit in it. They had some scraps of paper left from making Yuletide cards, and Sammy would have a pen somewhere.

Talie balanced her mug and eased herself up to sitting with her legs crossed. Before she could even lift her head, a bit of paper and a pen dropped into her lap, along with a ridiculously heavy school book to lean on. Then a single pesana.

"What's that for?"

Sammy grinned. "Buy her something nice, a peace offering."

"What do I even say though?"

"The truth. Tell her what happened, your side of it, everything you can. Then tell her how you feel. I'm going to the shop. I want it done by time I get back."

Talie drained her mug and winced over the burn of the still hot liquid. It sharpened her resolve though. Molly might never speak to her again, but she had to try.

Then I'm going to Phoenix to demand answers.

"The attack didn't even achieve anything," she muttered.

Sammy paused, halfway through putting her coat on.

"When you say attack…"

Talie frowned at the blank page, distracted.

"The Menagerie has a base. The resistance attacked it tonight, but I don't know why. We didn't even make a dent in their main hall. If it was a distraction of some kind, then it means Phoenix knows more than he's telling anyone. If it wasn't, it means he wanted to force Celeste's hand so she revealed who she really was. But even then, what does that achieve?"

Sammy hovered for a moment before quietly slipping out and closing the door behind her. Talie continued to stare at the paper, her mind dancing through the clutter of information.

"Unless, this is all about Molly. Phoenix wants to chase her to his side because of who she is. What she can do."

She can compel and I had no idea of that. What else is she capable of?

Talie wiped a hand over her face and picked up the pen.

She needed answers first, and Phoenix would be the person to answer them, assuming he even trusted her after her running away. Slipping the pen, paper and coin into her pocket, she left the room and locked the door behind her. A few minutes later, she strode into the gym and eyed the deserted space until she saw Phoenix seated on a pile of mats.

He watched as she approached, gauging her reaction, but she kept her face neutral.

"Random chaos tonight," she announced.

He nodded slowly. "What happened to you?"

She folded her arms across her chest, banking her anger. One show of emotion and Phoenix would use it to end the conversation.

"I was with Molly when you messaged me. I was with her when all was revealed. She forbade me from following her and left."

"And you obeyed?" he asked, one eyebrow arching.

She nodded. "Molly's stubborn. If she doesn't want me around, forcing the issue only pushes her further away. I've learned that much."

Truth without the whole truth. In that moment, she knew she would hide Molly's compulsion, and anything else she could get away with, from all the realms of Faerie if she had to.

When Phoenix didn't answer, she pushed.

"What was the point of that anyway?"

He hesitated. "We forced their hand. Celeste is grooming Molly for obvious reasons and if the rumours about them being close to absorbing the gifts of others is correct, we had to show our hand."

"What is our hand exactly? We stop them from stealing gifts?"

She thought about the artificers' guild, and what she and Molly had overheard.

If Phoenix is after this well of power like the Menagerie, that makes him almost as bad as they are.

She wouldn't mention it, wouldn't report it, not unless forced to. If she was any side now it was Molly's, even if Molly didn't accept her as part of it.

"We need more information before we make any decisions," he insisted.

Talie held in the derisive huff with valiant effort.

"Right. And forcing their hand got us what information

exactly? I'm guessing you already knew who Molly is?"

"I had a hunch." He shrugged. "I asked you to train her because you were already in touch with her, but it's vital we bring her to our cause now more than ever. If she supports us, grows stronger with time, the nobles may well turn to our side over Celeste's."

Talie clenched every muscle, her body tightening with rage. She sucked in a sharp breath to keep any sign of it away from her face, holding Phoenix's gaze.

"Like I said, she's stubborn. I'm probably the last person she wants to see right now. She thinks I lied to her, or kept stuff from her anyway. She doesn't deserve to be a pawn in any of this either."

"She can't change her destiny, Talie. She was born royal and she can't change her bloodline. She can, however, make it work to her advantage, and everyone else's."

"You treat her like a resource," she muttered.

Phoenix sighed. "I do care for Molly as much as I care for everyone in the citadel. Perhaps you need to take a day to yourself, get your head clear. If you do see Molly, tell her we'll happily offer her sanctuary."

"Okay." Talie nodded, dropping her arms to her sides and taking a step back. "It might be a while, orbs, it might be never, but if I do get to see her I'll tell her."

"Good. She would do well supporting us now her true identity is out. Who knows what it could grow into? She could be the saviour of the citadel. Has a nice ring to it."

Talie nodded again. *Keep everything calm, repetitive.*

She'd learned early on that Phoenix could sometimes be

distracted by repetition, his mind instantly twisting elsewhere. She managed a few more backwards steps before turning around and heading for the door, left with absolutely no doubt that Phoenix was no better than Molly's mother after all.

Not much I can do if Molly won't talk to me.

She dodged down the nearest side-alley and clambered up onto a window ledge in order to reach the nearest pillar. The possibility of accidentally coming across Molly on the beams was an enticing one, but Talie only had one plan now. Finding a spot out of the gusty drafts being sent out from the vents, she crouched down and slid to sitting, her back against a pillar and her legs dangling over the lane below.

As she pulled the paper and pen out of her pocket, her gaze drifted to the lights still on at Butch's shop. He would have something suitable for her to spend her pesana on.

Pen in hand, she grimaced down at the blank page.

Sammy had told her to write the truth, then what she felt. She could do that.

'There's not much I can say.'

CHAPTER TWENTY

<u>MOLLY</u>

Beryl shut the door behind them and Molly grimaced a greeting at Harvey sitting in the rocking chair with baby Aurora on his lap.

Oh orbs, they middle-named their daughter after… what even am I?

"Right, no more secrets," Beryl announced. "You're more than a workshop owner and we're not a squabbling couple from a few levels up."

"We do squabble a fair bit," Harvey said.

Beryl rolled her eyes. "Are you going to do this the whole way through?"

He mimed pinning his lips together. Molly stood in the centre of the messy room, surrounded by several unnameable piles of baby paraphernalia, and wrapped her arms around her middle.

"Who are you then?" she asked.

Beryl sighed and moved past her to sit on the sofa. When she patted the cushion beside her, Molly hesitated.

"I'll stand, thanks."

Beryl nodded. "Wise, you don't know us. Okay, so we're FDPs."

"Um… what are FDPs?"

Beryl's eyes widened. She looked at Harvey, who shrugged.

"You've never heard of us? But… you went to Arcanium right?"

Molly nodded. "That's where the queen and king consort- how did you know I went to Arcanium?"

Beryl sighed and held her arms out to Harvey. He groaned out of his seat and gave baby Aurora to her, then slouched off toward the kitchenette at the back.

"FDPs work for Arcanium, we take on assignments and charges throughout Faerie. We're kind of like peacekeepers, of a sort." She paused as Harvey's loud snort echoed over. "Demi, that's the queen but you met her already, she's worried about mutterings that have drifted out from the citadel for a while now. There's barely a word, but when there is, it isn't good. She's also worried about Taz's eldest sister being here, biding her time."

Molly thought of May, of the brief meeting she'd had with the queen and king consort, the royals who'd been casual enough to insist she call them Demi and Taz rather than by their titles.

She crossed the room and sank onto the sofa beside Beryl.

"You can get word out to the queen? To May even?"

Beryl grimaced. "Not by orb, not safely. We have to wait for a visit and we never know when it's coming."

"Really inconvenient," Harvey added. "The last time

they arrived right in the middle of-"

"Am I telling this or are you?" Beryl huffed.

Molly glanced at baby Aurora, but apparently she was already used to her parents enough to sleep through their bickering.

"Sorry, I really don't want to be rude, but nobody's going to be telling anything if we don't get to it quick," Molly prompted. "They'll come to the workshop looking for me, and then here."

She hadn't even admitted she was in any trouble yet, but panic was taking hold again.

If I have to climb into their rubbish chute and cling onto the ledge, I can do. Or I can hope my stealth gift holds.

"Oh, they won't find you, don't worry," Beryl said. "Where was I?"

Molly fought the urge to scream. "You can get a message out to the queen."

"Oh! Right, yeah. Kind of. We need to wait until someone visits, and we don't know when that'll happen next."

"Okay, I can try to keep myself hidden until then. I won't be able to stay in the workshop and all my friends have let me down, but I'll try."

"Ah don't be daft," Beryl scoffed. "We'll glamour you up until then. Stay here. Pretend you're the hired nanny."

"You don't think anyone's going to ask how you conveniently ended up with a nanny on the day I disappeared?"

Beryl grinned, the slow spread of wickedness over her face almost frightening in the gloom and shadows of the lamplight.

"We've had a nanny for a while now. She's been meeting the locals, flitting about town, that sort of thing. Trust me, nobody will know it's you."

Molly hunched over her knees with tears welling in her eyes.

"Why are you helping me?" she mumbled.

Seconds later, a steaming mug of *offke* appeared in front of her face. She looked up to find Harvey holding it out to her with a kind smile. Beneath the shock of bright purple hair that matched Beryl's, he looked almost as tired as she felt.

"Would it make you feel better if we told you we were following orders?" he asked.

Molly took the mug, eying the liquid.

How do I know who I can trust though? They can't lie but even so...

Harvey held his hand out. "Want a bottle of *Beast Lite* instead? Cap still on?"

"Yes please. Sorry."

"No need to be sorry," Beryl insisted. "It's sensible. You don't know us that well yet, but you will. We're Demi's friends, Taz's too, when he's not being dim. Demi asked us to come here and keep an eye on things."

"Do you know who I am?"

Beryl nodded. "We do. Wayfinders are strange things."

"What's a wayfinder?"

"It's this weird star thing, and you can use it to find stuff. Turns out you can use it to find people too."

"I can't tell you the amount of research we had to do,"

Harvey said. "Getting ourselves in under aliases was one thing, but then we came up the levels enough for who we are to be inconsequential anyway. Nobody here seems to know a thing about the realms outside."

He handed Molly a bottle with the cap still sealed. She managed a weak smile for him and cracked the cap, downing half of the bottle in one go.

"So, why not look for… you say you know who I am, but do you know… I mean, she…"

Beryl's hand landed on her arm but retreated when she flinched.

"We know who the leader of the Menagerie is. We know who she is to you as well. We couldn't be sure when we moved in here, but we've figured out that much."

"Are you part of the resistance?"

Beryl shook her head. "Nope. Don't know them. Don't know the Menagerie either, and they don't know us, and we need to keep it that way."

"Well, I'm not going to tell them. Can't the queens just come in like they did for the show and do something?"

Beryl sighed. "Demi's having to abide by ancient laws and not get involved. She's allowed to visit of course, but there's an ancient covenant that was set in place when the citadel was built absolute ages ago that ensures it stays free from royal interference. Demi's already towing that line by having us here."

"But… surely if Celeste is royal, she shouldn't be interfering either?"

Harvey sank onto the floor in front of them, his forearms on his knees.

"She abdicated so she's no longer officially a legitimate line of the royal family." He gave her a rueful nod. "Not sure about you as her daughter though."

"Did May know? When I went to the queen's court, did she know who I was?"

Beryl shook her head. "Nope. From our last intel, she went absolutely mental when she found out. She and Taz are very alike actually, both insisting you need to be extracted immediately because you're family, and both agreeing that having a niece is really weird."

"Being a niece is weird enough," Molly muttered. "I can't process any of this. It's mad. What if I'm not who everyone thinks I am? What if I was, I don't know, switched at birth or something?"

"You look like the rest of them to me." Beryl shrugged. "I'm guessing royals know things we don't, but they're certain it's you."

Molly nodded. "So is Celeste. And now the resistance knows too so I can't go there or they'll use me to get back at her."

She sniffed a couple of times to suck the burn of tears back in. Halfway through an inhale, she almost choked as the shadows in one corner of the room started to ripple.

"Oh that's convenient timing," Beryl announced.

Harvey twisted around with a grin on his face.

"I doubt it's convenience. Hiya, come on in. I've got pants on this time."

Molly stared as the shadows began to wriggle, darker patches forming outlines until they took on subtle colours and a man and a woman stepped into being.

"Is that a realm-skip?" she asked, astonished.

The man glanced her way, an irritable frown stuck on a handsome face under artfully ruffled brown hair.

"Not exactly," he said.

The woman beside him rolled her eyes and tucked her blonde hair behind her ear as she tugged him by the hand into the room.

"Ignore him. He's just grouchy because the gift sharing is a lot harder on him than it is on me."

"That's because the court likes you better than me," he grumbled.

"Does not."

"It so does."

"Yeah well." Beryl gave them both a look. "This is Molly. Things have kicked off, which I'm guessing is why you're here. Molly, this is Kainen and Reyan, Lord and Lady of the Court of Illusions."

"Surprised it's not Lady and Lord these days," Kainen muttered, not quite managing to hide a smile.

Molly bowed her head, unsure if she was meant to greet them the same as she might if she ever saw a noble, not that any would ever venture up as far as her level to be seen.

"We met before," she reminded them. "At the Kayla Crane concert."

Beryl nudged her arm. "They should be bowing to you technically. But not to worry, you'll get the hang of it."

"Bowing is for courts and none of you are sworn to ours," Reyan said. "Hi, Molly. Is your brain exploding?"

Molly nodded. "Kind of."

"Thought so. I wasn't originally a lady of anything, then suddenly this idiot gets ideas-"

"Hey!"

"-and here I am. I used to do the laundry."

Molly managed a tiny smile. "I used to clean bins for a while at the oak queen's court."

"There we go then. We need to do this formally otherwise it doesn't stick, but if you want to leave the citadel then you're welcome to take sanctuary at our court. It'll take a while to get you out, but the offer is there."

"Taz threw a tantrum?" Harvey asked.

Reyan laughed. "Big one. He threatened to overthrow his mother. To her face."

Molly tried to imagine the king consort squaring up to the oak queen, and memories of May doing the same thing surfaced. She choked over an unexpected sob, the sound drowned out by Beryl's cackling.

"Please tell me someone got an orb recording of that," she begged.

Kainen grinned. "No, but the tales will be legendary I'm sure. Makes a change from him threatening to abdicate."

Molly sucked in a breath, willing her volatile emotions to calm down. She had so much to sort out in her mind, but she needed space and quiet, none of which she'd get if she stayed with Beryl.

I don't have any choice either, unless I trust these friends of Beryl's to get me out of here.

"I need to think about this," she muttered.

Harvey nodded. "Of course you do. Let me glamour you into our nanny, who is even as we speak going from holding down two personas to only one. Could say you're doing her a favour, really."

He held a hand out and waved it in front of Molly's face, continuing down until he reached her shoes. She glanced at her clothes, still the same, but her hands were paler, the nails no longer chewed to oblivion.

"Is there a mirror?" she asked.

Beryl nodded as Harvey hurried to fetch one. She lifted a hand to find loose chestnut hair cascading around her shoulders, so she twisted back and forth until she found the hair ribbon Talie had given her on the cushion. Scooping it up, she tied her hair back again and took the small mirror Harvey held out to her.

She almost dropped it.

"I'm… this is…" She stared in horror, one thought surfacing above the chaos of the others.

Talie's going to hate me on sight if she sees me.

"I'm Daisy."

Beryl grinned. "You've met her, have you? Good. We did say she should ingratiate herself with your friends, especially the loud one. The taller one looks like she might bite."

Molly choked over an incredulous laugh as she stared at the glossy chestnut hair, pert nose and the shining green eyes that were nothing like her own.

"This is going to take some getting used to. I'm going to… yeah, I need to go outside for a bit."

"No going to the workshop," Harvey warned. "No old haunts. You can go to the gym though. Daisy was very insistent she'd be going back to the gym."

Molly handed the mirror back and stood, her sense of balance woolly from a combined cocktail of shock and standing at a height she wasn't used to. Daisy was half a head taller and a slight bit slimmer, but deep to the core it was just a glamour, and Molly could still feel her real, exhausted body groaning to accommodate the change.

"We'll be here when you get back," Reyan said. "The offer will stand if you need it, to come to our court as a guest. I imagine if we get you out May will want to take you back to the oak court with her, but they know who you are now. We can offer you anonymity."

Molly nodded. "Thanks. I just need some space to think."

She headed toward the door and peered out. The alley was suspiciously empty of people. Not too unusual for the locals, but she'd expected Ru skulking by her doorstep or some of the boots at the very least.

Closing the door behind her, she hauled herself up onto the beam between levels and traced her steps back to the cushion where she'd sat with Talie only hours ago.

It was the only secret she'd ever taken pains to hide from Ru, that and her compulsion gift. Somehow, knowing she had one hiding place he wasn't aware of had been her failsafe at protecting herself, even from him.

Not from Talie though.

She looked down at something sticking out from underneath the sheet covering her cushion. A folded scrap of paper, tied with a bit of purple ribbon. Lowering herself to sit on the cushion, she glanced around before grabbing the paper and pulling the ribbon off.

Something dropped into her lap, but she eyed the hurried scrawl first.

There's nothing much I can say. I doubt you'll forgive me but I promise I couldn't tell you even though I wanted to. I'm not even sure how much I'm able to tell you now, but you of all people deserve the truth.

Sammy and I were in the same children's home a fair few levels up. I looked out for her and when I was eight, she was seven, Celeste came to visit the home. I don't know what she saw in me, but she gave me my mind-wipe gift and told me I could keep it as long as I did a few favours for her with it. When she realised how protective I was of Sammy, she told me if I continued helping her, she'd help me keep Sammy safe. When she suggested I start ingratiating myself with Phoenix and she'd be stepping back from my training, I did it. Phoenix gave us a roof over our head away from the children's home, and helped put Sammy in school. Celeste started it but it's been a long time since she's been in touch, several years, and when I saw her in the office with you, I started wondering how deep everything really goes.

I've done things I'll never forgive myself for but Sammy's safety always comes first. I promised her brother that when he died, and I'm keeping to it.

When Celeste brought me to wipe your mind the night your guardians died

Molly squinted at several blotchy squiggles before the words resumed on the next line.

My hand cramps every time I try to write certain things, so the swear-block is still there. I wiped your mind at her request, it lets me tell you that at least. I knew then that there was something about you she wanted to keep control of, and figuring out why wasn't exactly difficult. You have similar eyebrows.

Then after your guardians were gone, I walked past your workshop sometimes. There's a second where you pass the corner and you can see your door still open at night. Not safe, by the way. But the light spilled out. I used to wonder what you were doing, what you were like, how much you knew. Then there you were, falling out of the rafters at the warehouse, and we kept chancing on each other after. I never believed in Fate, barely believed in Faerie as anything more than a sodden landmass I'd never see. But there you were. Defensive, smiling, confusing. I started wondering when I'd see you next, knowing nothing could ever happen.

I guessed there was a possibility you were another version of me, another one of her child puppets, but then I saw the way she looked at you in the office that day and I knew. She's not a good person but neither is Phoenix. No matter what happens, don't trust either of them. He would have taken you to spite her and used you just as she wants to use you.

I don't know if you'll take warnings from me now, or whether you'll ever even speak to me again. You said once that we weren't friends but I've never not liked you, even when you had no idea who I was. That night at the ball was the first thing I'd ever done for myself, selfishly keeping you between the levels dancing. It's the moment I cling to in the dark.

Get yourself out while you can. If my eternal debt is worth anything to you, even now, please try to get Sammy out too, if not now then one day.

It's probably pointless, but the Akiai is from me to you for nothing, and the Beast bottle is so you can one last drink on me. I really wish things had been different.

Molly nudged the bottle of *Beast* aside and held up the tiny item tucked with it, her face flushing hot. The dried threads from the *Akiai* tree were easy enough to get but tricky to dry correctly. Too fast and they shredded into dust, too slow and you ended up with pulp. For anyone that did manage to dry it, or more likely buy it dried, the red threads could be woven into fabric, bracelets, all sorts of things. It wasn't the threads that had Molly blushing, but what they'd been made into. The small ring, barely big enough to fit over her finger, had been dried and lacquered into a small heart. Fae often gave them as a symbol of interest, like a small kiss before an invitation to a date. To wear it was to say you felt the same.

Molly reached behind her neck and unclipped her necklace. She wouldn't be able to be seen wearing it or Talie would know who she was immediately.

Or she'd accuse me as Daisy of stealing it and try to fight me. Her lips lifted.

She couldn't risk telling Talie who she was either because Talie's situation with both the Menagerie and the resistance were dangerous enough, not to mention Sammy might be used to control her.

She slid the charm onto the chain and did up the clasp.

Rookie mistake number one – going out in my own clothes.

She slid the necklace into her pocket and folded up Talie's letter. No more mistakes. A soft crooning had her flinching, but Aurora hopped straight past her and dropped a small pebble by her boot.

"Thanks?"

Not sure what to do with the pebble, Molly picked it up and pocketed it alongside her necklace.

"If you can in any way understand me, things are going to get tough. If you want to fly out and go back to May, or anywhere, you can."

Aurora tilted her head and clicked her beak firmly.

No to that then. Molly sighed.

"On your head be it. I guess you can sense who I am without needing to see through the glamour, but you can't be flying around me out in the open or everyone will be suspicious."

Aurora cawed, the sound bouncing off the glass, her wings lifting as she hopped toward Molly.

"Okay, okay, I'm going," she grumbled. "Talie must have run straight here to write this so it's probably best I go back."

Aurora's wings furled again, her cawing turning to crooning. Refusing to contemplate that she was being herded by a bird, as if that was the weirdest thing that had happened to her recently, Molly got to her feet and walked along the beam to the barrels. She checked the coast was clear then dropped down and hurried back to Beryl and Harvey's. She knocked on the door and glanced over her shoulder until Harvey opened up, and they both ducked automatically as bird Aurora sailed over her head to perch next to baby Aurora.

"That's a bird," Kainen announced.

"That's Aurora," Harvey said. "She's a Greater Spotted Hump Warbler."

Kainen pressed his fist to his mouth to hide a laugh.

"A what?"

"I thought the baby was Aurora?" Reyan asked.

Molly wiped a hand over her face.

"Bird Aurora, baby Aurora. She's decided I'm her keeper, for some reason, even though birds freak me out." She eyed Aurora just in case. "No offense."

"Fair enough."

Kainen grabbed one of the bottles of *Beast Lite* now on the coffee table, handing one to Reyan then holding one out to Molly. She took it and sat on the sofa beside Beryl.

"I appreciate the escape offer, but I can't take it," she announced. "We don't choose our family but mine is… well, my moth- nope, can't do it. Celeste and the resistance both need stopping. Not sure how, but if what she said about me being heir apparent to the entire citadel is actually thing, I might as well put my pillar on the level and fight for it."

Four pairs of eyes blinked at her, and a genteel snuffle from baby Aurora.

"It doesn't have to be our court, or the Oak Queen's,"

Reyan said gently. "If you'd rather go to Arcanium, they'd be happy to have you."

Molly shook her head. "If it was a case of life or death then I'd take it, but I have to think of everyone I grew up around, locals and neighbours, people like my friend who's just trying to exist and live."

"Your family is disgustingly noble," Kainen said cheerfully.

"Well yours is opening your big mouth," Beryl added, glancing not-so-discreetly at Molly. "She's only known they're her family for about half a second."

Harvey gave Molly a sympathetic look and she opened her bottle, draining it until she was light-headed. Word would spread that she was missing, that she wasn't who they all thought she was. The workshop would have to stay shut and her commissions would need to go unfinished.

As everyone tried to look at her without looking at her, she forced herself to think of the future. The sooner she figured out a way to best her mother and stop a potential war, the quicker she could get the workshop back. Sammy would be safe, Talie could relax, all debts would be nullified and there would be ways to ensure everyone got a fair enough chance at life.

"The citadel is my home, and it's… we don't choose our family but I'm part of this whether I like it or not." She took a deep breath. "She's announced plans to train me up to one day take over the whole of Faerie, and I have no intention of helping her do it."

A worried look passed between Kainen and Reyan.

"It's not going to be safe for you," Reyan said after a

pause. "Demi's been concerned for a while about the citadel, but you don't have to take this on. It doesn't have to be your fight just because your family started it. We could find you a place in whatever court suits you best-"

"I really do appreciate it, but I'm not going to any court to be made to speak nice and drink tea while my friends are suffering."

Kainen snorted. "Speak nice and drink tea? That definitely isn't something you have to worry about, not at our court at least."

Reyan rolled her eyes and exchanged a weary look with Beryl.

"If you're sure, but the offer stands. We've got a few things going on at the moment, so Kainen will be your go-between while I manage the court."

"She's better at it than I am," Kainen announced, sounding far too happy about it. "And you're welcome any time you change your mind, Molly, even if you are related to Taz."

Molly sensed some kind of scandalous story lurking there, but Beryl's eyes picked up a decidedly worrying gleam.

"I never thought of it like that. So if your Taz's sister's daughter, Molly, that makes you like my great second niece."

Harvey stared at her. "I- even I can't decode that."

He reached forward from his seat on the floor and took baby Aurora as Beryl huffed in irritation.

"My sister is Meryl, who is dating Tira, who is Lady to the Word Court. Now, Tira's mother was a distant cousin to Queen Tavania, that's the Oak Queen, which makes her like my great second cousin in law, or something. Then of course you're the Oak Queen's granddaughter, so maybe it's like great niece twice removed. Either way, you're family."

Molly opened her mouth without any hope of finding suitable words, or any words, not sure if she was more bewildered about having the queens of Faerie as family or Beryl.

"I still don't believe it," she muttered. "That makes May my aunt. First I was her maid, now she's my aunt. And the actual Holly Queen of Faerie is like my aunt-in-law."

She looked up, her mind finally landing on the one thing she'd forgotten in all the upheaval.

"Can you get a message to May?" she asked.

Kainen nodded. "Sure. Not sure when I'll be able to come back again, and I can't focus enough yet to carry things that aren't attached to me or conveniently in my pocket, but I can take a letter if you want to scribble one."

"We should be getting back soon," Reyan added.

Beryl got up and grabbed a sheet of paper and a pen, and Molly sat while their talk turned to updates that didn't involve her. Something about an explosion, a hutch, a lolly, and someone threatening to stick a greenhouse up someone's behind.

She kept the letter short. While she was grateful for Kainen and Reyan taking a message for her, she couldn't be totally sure they wouldn't read it first. She asked May to send her any information she had on Celeste from when they were children, weaknesses, gifts, memories, anything that might help her plan. She guessed May would likely have told the others everything already, but they weren't on the inside like she was.

Kainen stood to take the letter and slid it into the pocket of his jeans without looking at it.

"Nobody will see it until she gets it, I promise."

He held out a hand to help Reyan to her feet and she gave Molly a wry smile.

"Welcome to the aristocracy. It doesn't entirely suck."

She winked as shadows rolled from the corners of the room, wraithing around them until they faded from view.

"Very show-offy court," Beryl said with a grin. "Still, they're decent where it counts. Now, we only have the one bedroom, but Harvey's going to block off that bare corner over there for you."

Molly eyed the corner. It was a deceptively large room, with more than enough space for her to put up a couple of stud walls and block herself off a room.

"I can do it," she offered. "It'll give me something to focus on. I think I need that. I just need to get my…"

She couldn't bear the sympathy on Harvey's face as she almost mentioned the workshop, but he rallied quickly.

"You can assist me," he said. "I'll be lazy, I promise. There's a wood merchant a level down where I can pick up everything we need."

"Don't go to down Off Cuts, they'll overcharge you. Go one up instead to Root's place. He'll give you everything you need. Tell him… tell him that Molly recommended him and you need everything to put in a box room. Say she said he'd see you right and he will."

Harvey nodded. "Gotcha. Kip on the sofa until then. We were planning to take a dawn walk with Aurora anyway."

"We were?" Beryl frowned until he eyeballed her meaningfully. "Oh! Right, sure. A dawn walk? Really? We're not that old yet."

Molly let the wash of their bickering flow over her as they bundled up Aurora in Harvey's arms and Beryl got herself a coat and shoes.

"Wait." Molly called out as they were almost out the door. "What happened to Daisy? Who was she?"

Beryl grinned. "An FDP like us, someone we'd trust as much as we would each other. They've taken on another role nearby going forward. Not any of your friends you know or anything, don't worry. You wouldn't recognise them."

Molly stared at the back of the door long after it had closed. She hadn't asked them about a change of clothes either, but as long as nobody came barging in, it wouldn't matter for now.

She couldn't even consider sleeping yet and snagged another *Beast Lite* bottle, cracking the cap. No doubt in the coming days she would look after Aurora, but instinct told her Beryl and Harvey would give her a few days grace first to let the chaos settle.

Daisy can go to the gym. She smiled slightly. *Talie's not going to be happy to see me.*

She would take that leap another day, after she worked out a way to overthrow Celeste and the Menagerie, and make sure Phoenix and the resistance weren't going to be a different type of evil.

Sipping her drink, she thought about the artificers still missing, the ones now dead, the stolen fairies petrified away from their families and the lives they knew. She thought about Talie no doubt back with Sammy, and then the mysterious 'no-longer-Daisy' who was still out in the citadel somewhere as someone entirely different.

Above all, Celeste was still out there, and Molly was beginning to realise she couldn't escape a war if there was one.

She lifted the bottle to her lips and let the deadly calm of resolve settle over her.

"Game on."

CHAPTER TWENTY ONE

MOLLY

"No, you can't eat that. Okay, that hurts."

Molly pulled her hair out of baby Aurora's fist and settled her into the wooden rocking crib. After she almost lost her favourite hair ribbon the day before, she didn't want to risk it again. Even though she was glamoured as someone else, her usually blonde hair now shining auburn and her body still much less sturdy than she was used to, the hair pulling still hurt.

Three days and I want to be anywhere else.

She couldn't fathom how she was meant to go on indefinitely masquerading as Daisy the nanny if three days were enough to drive her up the wall.

Before she could dive any deeper into self-pity, a subtle shift in the shadows at the corner of the room caught her eye, coiling into Fae form and solidifying into the Lord of the Court of Illusions.

"Hey Molly." Kainen eyed the crib warily. "Baby Aurora." He glanced sideways at the sound of beak clicking. "Bird Aurora."

Greetings done without threat of wailing or impromptu eye-pecking, he stepped into the room.

"Wow, you got that extra room up quick."

Molly nodded. "Had to. Gave me something to focus on that didn't involve spit or… well, you get the idea."

She'd managed to build a tiny box room big enough for a bed and a shelf nailed to the wall in the far corner, but with Beryl and Harvey arguing often, she spent as much time hiding up on the beams outside as she did holed up in the room.

"Do you want anything to drink or eat?" she offered.

"No thanks. Demi wanted me to come and check in as the orb-waves have gone completely silent."

Molly nodded. "We expected that. Celeste has been sending out flyers calling for people to turn me in. People have been watching the workshop. Beryl's also now forbidden me from going to the gym."

That last one hurt. It was the only place she might see Talie, not that she could risk blowing her glamour cover by saying who she was. To all the eyes of the citadel, she was Daisy, Beryl and Harvey's nanny, and with the Menagerie and Celeste no doubt hunting every corner for her, she had to keep up appearances.

"You don't like being cooped up," Kainen guessed.

Molly sighed. "I'm not. I can go to the shop, I can take Aurora for walks. I just can't do any of my old life things when that's all I want to do."

"What about practicing your gifts? Surely Beryl of all people hasn't outlawed that?"

Molly sighed. "If they're here, it's too cramped and

chaotic to practice anything. If they're not, I can't risk it around Aurora while we're alone. I have charm and stealth, and I do fine with those."

Kainen arched one eyebrow. "Those are all the gifts you have?"

Molly eyed him back, wondering if she should tell him.

"What gifts do you have then?" she countered.

"Speed, charm, and a bunch that came unexpectedly with both leading a court and leading it with Reyan. I can shadow-merge badly now. Oh, and compulsions."

Molly tensed and he noticed, a grin crossing his face.

"So, charm and stealth are your only gifts?" he asked, ever so innocently.

He already knows.

"I can compel people."

There. Someone knew her secret. In all her life, she hadn't told anyone else but her guardians, not until Celeste's big reveal to half the citadel. Now the lord of an entire Faerie court knew.

"Want me to teach you how to wield it properly?" he offered.

No sudden gleam of anticipation in his eyes, no flashing hints of opportunistic interest. Just a casual flick of his hands through his brown hair and that subtle smile pointed in her direction as he stood waiting.

Molly nodded. "Please."

"Good. Okay, the first thing about compulsions is you have to think literally. If they're compelling you to stand on one leg, that doesn't stop you using your hands. Anyone with any training knows that."

"I've not had any training."

He grimaced. "Okay, that sucks. How did you manage it then?"

"I refused to use it, told nobody, hid it away. Only my guardians knew."

He wiped a hand over his face.

"So we're starting from scratch. Compulsions are literal. Tell a man not to sing, he won't, ever, until you release him. Unless you add conditions. That's the skill to it. Compulsions can break with distance, weaken with time, but around the caster, they will always linger. You could have accidentally compelled people without realising it in anger."

"Oh orbs!"

"You probably haven't, don't worry. You just have to learn to set conditions, 'no singing until I leave' sets a time condition. 'No singing while I'm around' sets a permanent location condition."

She nodded, determined. "Got it."

"The more conviction you hold inside you when casting a compulsion, the stronger the power." He started pacing the small stretch of floor, brow furrowed.

"Plan ahead as best you can and think what kind of wording you may need in advance."

Molly nodded. "I've had more than enough overthinking time to prepare me for practice. Wait, if I tell someone to 'move left', will they just keep going until they hit a wall?"

Kainen stopped pacing and looked her way with a devilish grin.

"If it's strong enough, they'll find a way around or through the walls right to the very ends of Faerie. Exactly that, be specific. Move two steps left is much clearer. I don't have too much time left as I need to get back to court, but next time I visit we can practice properly. Until then, try it on tiny things. Compel the baby to raise a fist, or the bird to flap its wings."

Aurora uttered a threatening caw and Kainen flinched.

"Okay, maybe just the baby. Use your conditions and it will be fine, 'raise your arm for one second', things like that. Or practice on Harvey, he probably won't even notice."

Molly stifled a smile. "Not Beryl though?"

"Orbs no, she scares me. Oh, that reminds me, talking of scary women." He sank onto the sofa and pulled a small pouch from his pocket with a grin. "Maybe a present from your dear old auntie May will cheer you up."

"Don't let her hear you call her that. She's not much older than I am."

She took the purple velvet pouch and peered inside, bemused to find two percats and a small scroll of paper tied with a long, golden ribbon.

"She insisted that it's not what's in it that's the gift, but what it is," he said.

Molly frowned, looking for some kind of emblem or indication on the fabric.

"It's a privy purse," he added. "Only you can see or access what's inside it. Unless you choose to re-gift it."

"Wow. Seriously?" She stared from the pouch to him in amazement.

He laughed. "Yes. It doesn't take extra-large items or anything, but for small trinkets or secrets, it will keep them safe."

"Can you thank her for me please? I have nothing to send back in return."

"Good. Carrying things through the shadow is an absolute pain. She wasn't impressed either that I couldn't bring the entire wardrobe she wanted to send you."

"Yeah, please don't worry about bringing that." She trailed a forefinger over the soft velvet. "The citadel does have clothes shops, tailors, all of that. Not that she's likely seen much of it."

"I also asked her about Celeste's past."

Molly checked on Aurora then sat down next to him.

"Great, anything useful?"

"Not as spiteful as Belladonna, not as vindictive as Blossom. Quiet, reserved, dutiful. Amused by long games and ongoing intrigues rather than petty sleights." He shifted his weight with a sigh. "She attended society less after Taz was born and abdicated shortly after. There was a huge row apparently between her and Queen Tavania, but nobody knows what was said."

Molly wiped a hand over her mouth. It wasn't much more to go on than she'd assumed already.

"What about gifts?" she asked.

"Speed, charm, and water-wielding. I imagine she will have amassed others since though."

The water was a problem, but speed and charm were fairly common among the nobles.

"Demi also asked me to pass on a gift for you, but I said

we can wait for Reyan to visit," he added. "A gift is usually given-"

"By a kiss, yeah. Although…"

She hesitated, unsure if to admit the whole truth. Telling Talie what she knew was one thing, but as nice as Kainen and the rest were being, they worked for the Holly Queen.

"Although?" he prompted.

She bit her lip.

They've given me no reasons to doubt them yet.

"Celeste gave me a stealth gift for Yuletide," she admitted. "Not with a kiss, but with a vial. She had me open it, put it to my head and in the gift went. No kiss necessary."

Kainen's eyes widened. "Oh, wow. That's… Okay."

Molly waited for him to gather himself. Somehow, she sensed he wasn't at a loss for words often.

"Yeah. As for the new gift, if you're worried about the whole kissing thing, your lady's more my type than you are. No offense."

That wiped his shock away fast enough. His brow lifted and amusement played across his face again.

"You have exquisite taste then. Demi was worried your gifts seem mostly persuasive, and compulsion can be tricky to wield. She's suggested the ability to quench water."

Molly blinked. The queen of Faerie clearly knew from May what gifts Celeste had, but she was offering to arm Molly against one of them.

"It will take some getting used to," he warned. "Too much and you could dry out someone's blood or something mad, I don't know, but Beryl is good with elemental gifts. You want it?"

Molly hesitated. "It's curious."

"What is?"

"I know Fae without gifts. So many of my neighbours just go about their lives only able to ward, and that's enough. They don't get offered fancy gifts. Suddenly, all because I'm meant to be of royal blood or whatever, everyone wants to give me gifts."

Kainen grimaced. "Orbs, Reyan would handle this conversation so much better than I can. She didn't start off noble. Neither did Demi. Trust me, if they didn't think you deserved it, earned it, they wouldn't be so quick to trust you with it."

"Maybe. But what about all the other Fae who don't have noble friends?"

"Believe it or not, that was the first thing Taz fought for as king consort," he insisted. "Every Fae or fairy kid gets a gift when they turn sixteen. Takes a long time to roll these things out though. Laws would need to be changed if anyone other than nobility were able to gift, and the nobility will fight losing that exclusivity. Most wouldn't want the job of doing it either to keep said exclusivity."

Molly frowned, thoughts of the recently kidnapped fairies brought in from outside the citadel, and the missing artificers being used to trial extracting people's gifts to be sold, filling her head.

She hadn't had a chance to ask Talie if she managed to free any, and there were still several stuck inside the Menagerie being tested on.

Levelling the field had its merits, but who could be trusted to distribute gifts fairly? It would take laws, and clarity, something the citadel had been lacking for a long time, even before Celeste took over the Menagerie and made the citadel into her personal training playground.

"That's a start," she said grudgingly.

Kainen snorted. "You remind me of Taz when you glower like that. Okay, want it or not? On the promise that you don't use it until Beryl shows you how."

"Go on then."

Molly leaned forward with her eyes shut and flinched when he took her hand in his. As he pressed a chaste kiss to the back of it and let the contact drop, she waited.

For a moment, she felt nothing. Then a warm tingle started in her fingertips, heating through her hand and up her arm until her whole body radiated, like basking in the pure sunlight she missed so much from her brief time at the oak Queen's court.

"It feels... wow."

Kainen nodded. "It's powerful. Use it sparingly. Demi's put great trust in you. You're up against it here and there's only so much she can do without interfering."

"I know she can't. I'll do my best to only use it on Celeste, and only when it's absolutely necessary."

Kainen grinned. "Well, have a little fun with it, but not until Beryl's trained you. I should be getting back. I'll try to check in soon. Keep testing the orb-waves too, just in case the block goes down."

Molly nodded, her insides still rippling with rolling heat that eased lingering aches in her muscles. She wanted to stretch out in it like a cat, to close her eyes and bask forever.

"I will. Thank May for me, and Demi, and thank you."

Kainen stood, his easy smile fading.

"You're not alone, Molly. Remember that, and not because of your family or your blood either."

He faded into the shadows until she was alone again, or as alone as she could be with both baby and bird Auroras in the room. Bird Aurora ruffled her wings, crooning softly, and baby Aurora slept on, but it was only her promise to Kainen that stopped Molly from digging deeply into the blissful heat and seeing how far the gift could go.

She still had the scroll inside the privy pouch May had given her, but the front door swung open before she could take it out.

Beryl looked up and her jaw dropped as she halted Harvey, who struggled in behind her under a mountain of bags.

"Molly, you're *glowing*."

CHAPTER TWENTY TWO

MOLLY

"Sunlight. The orbing idiot gifted you with sunlight. How are we going to explain that?"

Beryl paced back and forth across the room. Harvey wisely hid himself behind the shopping bags and pretended to put things away.

"He said it was a gift to quench water," Molly muttered. "Celeste can-"

"Oh it'll quench water alright, dry it right up. It'll also give sunburn if you lose control of it, or you'll catch the right angle of the citadel glass and set the pillars on fire."

Alarmed, Molly reached deep inside herself and tried to find some sense that she could summon her inner cloud before Beryl woke Aurora.

Harvey popped his head up from behind the bags.

"You're not trying to cover it or hide it. You're wielding it. At your will, it can lie dormant, appear as invisible warmth, appear as a heatless glow, or burn brighter than the morning sky. Don't see it as separate from you."

For once, Beryl was silent. Astonished, Molly focused

on the sensation of sunlight warming her to the bone. Willing it to cool, to dim, she let the reassurance flow through her mind.

It's not forever. We'll find a safe place to shine. Time for night now.

The sudden chill iced through her limbs like a wave. She gasped, fighting the urge to flare bright again, to find peace in the irresistible heat.

"Good, let it settle inside you. It's not going anywhere." Beryl said.

Molly shivered. "I hope not."

Harvey emerged from his bag fort and held out a thick sweatshirt of soft, dark blue fabric.

"You'll need some fresh clothes," he said. "You might find your new normal is colder now, but we can get more."

Molly bit her lip as she pulled the sweatshirt over her head.

"You don't have to."

Harvey rolled his eyes. "Least we can do to help. What did Kainen say?"

Molly explained the information from May, the privy pouch and that the sunshine gift was an idea from Demi.

Beryl sighed. "Of course it was. Always thinking ahead that girl."

Molly eased to her feet. "It's time for Aurora's walk."

"You can't go outside! What if the sun starts shining, if you get me?"

"I can't stay in here forever. Worst case, I'll say it's new and word-tangle, but I'm in control of it."

Beryl gave her a doubtful look.

"How about I chaperone?" Harvey offered. "A quick stroll without fear of any more bags would be nice."

Molly opened her mouth to argue, but given the eager look on his face she wondered if he needed the escape as much as she did.

He's seeing his future when Aurora grows up and starts having a mind of her own.

Harvey strode to the crib before Beryl could refuse and bundled Aurora into his arms, ferrying her across to the pram. Molly grabbed the coat Beryl had given her.

"Not too far then," Beryl grumbled. "The first hint of any gifts splurging, straight back home."

Harvey swung the door open with a grin, the pram already ahead of him through the doorway.

"We'll be no trouble at all."

Beryl's disbelieving snort echoed behind them as Molly scarpered, pulling the door shut behind her.

She glanced at the workshop door as they passed and the familiar gloom swept through her chest. She yearned to go in, but even sneaking in the dead of night had been forbidden.

Harvey gave her a sympathetic look and paused with the pram as they hit the main lane.

"Up or down?" he asked.

"Up." It wasn't even a consideration.

If they walked up a few levels, they couldn't avoid passing the gym. She couldn't go in of course, Beryl had seen to that, but even a glimpse of her friends would do.

As Harvey dutifully turned left and started up the lane, Molly let her mind wander. Her pulse picked up the closer they got to the gym. Just knowing Talie and Sammy were okay would be enough.

"Daisy!"

Molly frowned at Harvey as he slowed their pace to a dawdle.

He knows I want to stop at the gym. Beryl is going to go mad if she finds out.

"Daisy!"

Molly eyed the gym doors but she couldn't see anyone she recognised standing outside. Then she caught sight of herself and Harvey in the reflection of the window.

"Orbs alive, DAISY!"

Oh, right. I'm Daisy.

She turned around a moment before Sammy slammed into her. Staggering backwards, she caught Harvey's outstretched arm and steadied herself.

"Hi Sammy."

She stepped back and focused on keeping the sunlight dormant, even as it heated delightfully across her skin. Seeing Sammy safe made everything seem brighter somehow.

Sammy beamed. "I haven't seen you in weeks, where have you been?"

"That one's keeping me busy." She pointed at the pram. "How are you?"

Sammy's smile dimmed. "I'm okay. I don't know if you heard what happened with Molly, but I'm so worried about her."

Molly hesitated as guilt gnawed at her insides, but before she could find some non-committal answer, footsteps thudded close by.

"Sammy, enough. People don't need to hear about all that."

Molly sucked in a sharp breath and lifted her head, her heart going from glum to galloping as she faced Talie, magnificent scowl and all.

I'm Daisy, and she hates Daisy for some reason.

The thought brought a smile to her face and a tremor of wickedness with it.

"Hi, Talie isn't it?" She smiled extra annoyingly.

Talie grunted in reply as Sammy rolled her eyes.

"I'm sure wherever she is, Molly is fine," she added. "She seems the resourceful type."

Harvey laughed. "She is. I'll take a slow stroll back down, but don't be too far behind okay? All this motherhood has made Beryl even more delightful than usual."

Molly nodded. She didn't often find herself in a position where she knew something Talie didn't, and the urge to make the most of it was too strong.

"How's the baby?" Sammy asked.

Molly grinned. "Loud. Fussy. She likes the bird though."

Talie's head snapped up.

"What bird?"

Beryl had agreed to the cover that they were looking after Aurora in Molly's absence, just in case anyone asked. Talie clearly hadn't considered that and Molly leaned into referring to herself in third person, delighting in having something to laugh at later when she saw the sharp-eyed suspicion on Talie's face.

"Molly's bird. She flies in and out now and then. Baby Aurora loves her, giggles like anything."

"Aurora's still here? She hasn't gone-" Talie frowned. "You barely know Molly anyway. You met what, once? Twice?"

Molly smiled. "The odd brief meeting. Might have been more but you threw a sparring pad at her head."

Sammy snorted over a laugh as Molly eyed the lane. One parting shot, just a tiny hint of rebellion. The thought of Talie leaving her the heartfelt letter after the fight, along with the *Akiai* charm which was still on the necklace in her pocket, made her reckless.

"Who knows? Maybe she's closer than anyone thinks."

She gave Sammy a smile and Talie the tiniest hint of a wink, then turned on her heel and started walking back down the lane.

The moment she was around the turn out of sight, she glanced over her shoulder. Even though she didn't really expect Talie to come after her, she'd hoped just a little.

Remembering May's gift, she pulled the privy pouch out and slid her necklace into it. On the silver chain was her key to the workshop, the acorn and moor-grass Talie had given her both cast in resin for safekeeping, and then the hard ring of the *Akiai* charm curved into a heart.

A heart.

Molly slipped the pouch back into her pocket and the loop of the charm onto her finger like a ring.

We spent so long spatting each other and now I can't do anything about it because of my stupid family that I didn't even know I had until a few weeks ago.

So wrapped in her thoughts, she almost missed the subtle tap of footsteps behind her. Intuition flared and she slowed her pace. Whoever was behind her slowed theirs.

She smiled. Talie was light on her feet but not enough to go undetected when Molly was expecting her.

I shouldn't stray off the main lane, she thought, then veered left into the nearest alley.

She slowed to a halt, amused at the thought of Talie creeping up to interrogate her. A shadow fell over her, a large, bulky shadow. The scent of oia berry wafted forward and her insides chilled with realisation.

"Molly, you have to come with me."

She froze at the sound of Ru's voice, firm with determination. Shock and a wash of humiliation at being so arrogant with her safety pulled any hope of word-tangling from her mind.

"I don't have to go anywhere with you." She folded her arms and turned to face him. "Who are you anyway?"

Ru rolled his eyes. "I've known you years, Molly, a glamour can't hide you from me."

With her pulse thudding, Molly mentally assessed the alleyway. The pillar to her right was the quickest route out. She was a fast climber and Ru was likely clutching at straws. He wouldn't risk grabbing her in public.

Beryl is going to kill me.

"Whoever you are, I need to get back to work," she tried.

She stepped forward as if to brush past him, her arms dropping to her sides ready. Even as he reached sideways to block her path, she dodged the other way and leapt.

Her fingers found the necessary grooves on the pillar and she scrambled upward. Top of the pillar, run left and drop down next to the grocer's awning, then he wouldn't be able to grab her without causing a fuss.

Her fingers snagged the top of the pillar as his hand grabbed her shoe. She tilted her foot, letting it slip off as she kicked out. Using the momentum, she hauled herself up. Her hips hit the beam and her arms screamed under the strain. A strong hold anchored round her middle before she could scramble her legs up, so she kicked out again. Ru clung on, one arm firm on the pillar and the other tugging her back against his chest.

"Let me go," she snarled.

With a feral grunt, Ru set all his strength against her. She didn't even have time to scream as her hold on the pillar broke, both of them tumbling downward. She jack-knifed her elbow into Ru's gut moments before they hit the ground, but he wasn't letting go for an ill-placed jab.

They jolted not onto the hard cobbles, but something softer, and Molly wriggled, fighting and clawing as his hand came over her mouth. She screamed, the sensation burning her throat, but no sound came out. Darkness swept over both of them, a hood being lifted over what she realised was an open-topped cart.

She tried to scream again but no sound came out, and her struggling gave Ru something to curse over but it wasn't enough to best him.

"Stop fighting me," he hissed. "Celeste gave me the ability to take your voice, but I don't want to. You need to hear her out."

Fear tore through Molly's limbs, panic overriding all sense. She sank her nails into his cheek but of course, she'd cut them to nothing to avoid hurting baby Aurora.

She sought for her sunlight, frantically trying to pull it, or something, anything to the fore, but the terror was cutting off her focus.

Stupid, stupid, stupid. If I'd only listened to Beryl, not been so arrogant about Talie.

She stopped struggling, her breath coming in shallow pants. There wasn't going to be any bearing Ru for strength in a straight fight, but she knew the citadel well enough. When he got her out at whatever end they reached, she could kick him and run.

"That's better. When we get back to Celeste, I'll return your voice. I just can't risk you screaming. I've waited for weeks to get you alone."

Molly held herself tense on top of him, unable to even roll to the side as he held her tight. Revulsion crawled across her skin but she forced it aside.

Calm. Find your focus. She imagined Talie's training voice in her head, demanding and devoid of emotion. *If you don't have your voice, he can't make you talk. The moment he lets you go, even for a second, ward yourself.*

She fell entirely still. Leaving Ru before she got her voice back wasn't ideal, but unless she got a hold on her sunlight gift before they arrived and threatened him with it, somehow, she might have to.

"Did you really think hiding on your own doorstep was a good idea?" he huffed.

She couldn't speak but she let her lack of any responsive body language answer for her. After a moment, she opened her mouth to ask where they were going, or at least how far, more willing to sit in a corner and glower at him than be pressed up against him. Of course no sound came out.

A lock of hair fell across her forehead and she jerked aside as soft fingertips brushed it away.

"I'm not your enemy, Molly," he said.

She lifted an arm and flicked a pointed hand at the cart, then made a defined jab at her throat.

"You'll understand when we get there. Celeste has been worried about you. We both have. There's so much going on you don't understand."

Molly snorted, the action merely a weird convulsion without the accompanying sound.

"She can explain better than I can," he added. "She's had a really nice room prepared for you, and she's said I can help her train you for what's to come."

Like a doll, or a pet. Like what I believe or want doesn't even exist.

She focused her gaze on the thick fabric covering the cart, digging deep inside to drum up her sunshine gift. Ru knew about her compulsion gift after the last battle, and while Celeste was immune to it, he wasn't. Without her voice she had no way of wielding her compulsion or charm gifts against him either, short of using hand signals.

I didn't even bother using stealth back in that alley, so convinced Talie was coming after me.

Ru didn't venture any further hazy reassurances and she

did her best to ignore him holding her tight. By time the rumble of the cart ceased, she was prepared. If Ru slipped up enough for her to ward, she'd take the chance to run. If not, she would ward the moment she was inside Celeste's domain and fight her way out from the inside.

Ru rolled her to the side and sat up, one hand curling tight around her wrist as the cart's covering was whisked away.

Molly recognised the entrance to the Menagerie with her heart sinking. Even if the others figured out where she was, there was no way they'd be getting in.

Ru held out his free hand to help her down but she ignored it and willed the awkward angle to trick him into letting her go instead. He clung on, towing her eagerly by the wrist toward the Menagerie doors.

The guard lowered his head as they passed, whether to her now they knew who she was or in recognition of Ru, she couldn't be sure.

As they entered the dim light of the main hall, Molly saw the scene of their last battle and her nerves seized. Ru noticed her shaking and slowed their pace.

"It's okay, she's not angry with you," he soothed.

Molly shot him an acidic look and settled for mouthing a curse at him. He only sighed and turned his gaze toward the staircase.

"Well done, Ru. I'm extremely pleased with you."

Celeste swept into view, gliding down the stairs in a long black skirt topped with a fighting corset layered with tiny chains.

Ru bowed his head and Molly scoffed silently.

"I imagine you're still not sure which side the truth lies on," Celste added as she glanced at Molly. "We'll have time to disabuse you of all the rot and rumour flying around, but you look tired. I've had a lovely room prepared for you."

Molly didn't answer which drew Ru's attention back to her. When she mouthed another curse at him, his eyes widened.

"Oops."

He reached a hand toward her neck but she batted it away.

"I need to restore your voice, hold still," he muttered.

Molly didn't trust herself to start shouting if he returned it, but she was already inside Celeste's bountiful protection so escaping wasn't likely anymore. Her only option now was to compel someone to let her out, and she definitely needed her voice for that.

She held still, glaring at him the whole time. A needling sting filled her throat and she coughed the moment Ru lowered his hand.

"Better?" he asked.

She faked a smile. "Oh you have no idea how much. I will never, ever forgive you for any of this. Three hundred years could pass and I will still see you as the worst, most spineless-"

"Now Molinia, don't say anything you'll regret," Celeste warned, her smile widening. "Ru has been a true friend to you. Our secrecy has kept you safe all these years, let you grow untouched by the tiresome gauntlet of Fae politics. Do you think someone like Phoenix won't use you for his own ends against us now he knows who you are?"

Molly tore her wrist away from Ru's grip, surprised when he let her. She wrapped her warding tight around her and put all her strength behind it.

"Why send me into the citadel at all then?" she demanded. "You can't have cared that much."

"To test you. To prove that you were tough enough, mature enough to do what needs to be done. You may still be acclimatising to who you really are, but one day you'll rule after me and you need to be prepared."

"So I'm a resource? A pet heir for you to mould and toy around with? And don't you dare give me the crud about family honour. You clearly have none."

She expected some kind of retaliation but Celeste laughed, her hands clasping together in delight.

"You're tired. Ru will get you settled in. I do hope you like your room, we spent time designing it to suit you. Now that you're home, we can work on building your future properly."

Molly stared in horror as Celeste swept up the stairs and left them in the entrance hall unguarded.

"This is madness," she muttered.

"It's not. Celeste built the citadel up into what it is today for you. She gave you freedom to grow up away from the nobility. She gave you me as a friend to keep you safe. And we are friends, Molly, even if you don't believe it right now. I'll always be your friend."

Molly flicked a glare at him.

"You may as well be dead to me."

He flinched and his cheeks turned pink. Molly held firm

as his lips pressed thin and forced herself to ignore the sweep of guilt at the undisguised hurt in his eyes.

"Well you can't sleep here in the hall," he said. "Follow me. I really did try to convince her to make the room something you'd like."

"Tools?" she asked, having to follow him up the stairs.

He slowed a step. "No, not exactly."

"Dresses and gems and hair ribbons?" She faked an excited gasp.

He wisely chose not to answer that one and led her along the long balcony that surrounded the upper floor overlooking the entrance hall. The first corridor was lined with large paintings and endless vases of flowers, and Ru opened a door at the far end. He stood aside to let her go ahead of him, and she stepped through the doorway with a feral glare in his direction.

Beneath a high white ceiling, the bedroom had two tall, wide windows that overlooked something green. The furniture was all unvarnished wood and a muted green carpet lay thick underfoot. The room was as natural in terms of décor as Molly could have imagined, similar to what she would have chosen for herself given funds and time. But she wasn't going to tell Ru that.

"I won't hang around for a verdict," he said, his tone subdued. "Celeste will come see you soon. The windows can stay open as the wards won't let you out, but the door will have to be locked for now."

Molly glowered extra hard at him until he shut the door behind him, and she listened to the lock turning in the door.

The moment he was gone, she started to pace. Beryl had

taken her orb Phoenix had given her. She only had the privy pouch with her necklace, key and charms in, plus a couple of pesanas on her, none of which would work for what she had planned.

As she placed the floor, she assessed the opulence of the room. The collection of books wouldn't help her pick the lock, and neither would the huge collection of clothes in the walk-in closet. Getting the door open wouldn't get her outside the Menagerie either, but if she could find someone wandering around then she could compel them to get her out.

Or I could hide in laundry or something, that works in those human tales Beryl has.

She moved to the writing desk and pulled the tiny drawers on the top open. Extravagant pens, inks, nothing she could use.

She opened the next drawer.

Aha.

She picked up a couple of paper clips with a grin. Grabbing one of the pens, she used it to straighten the paper clips and wind them around each other.

Halfway to the door, she halted. They knew so little about Celeste and what she was planning, or how much strength she truly had behind her.

If I play along, see what a few routines are, I've got a better shot of escaping. Then I can take something concrete back to Kainen to give to Demi.

She slid the paperclip pick into her privy pouch and eyed the room again.

Such a fur-lined cage, full of useless trinkets adorning

the fireplace, enough to melt down or sell onto some unsuspecting noble for enough money to feed an entire level for a week. Molly marched to the window and peered out as best she could without aggravating the subtle zing of the wards that kept her in. There was a garden below, vibrant flowers bursting into bloom amid luscious green hedges and softly trickling fountains of stone.

Molly had never once seen any sign of a garden in her previous trips to the Menagerie, another gem Celeste kept for herself. It was a subtle 'look what you could have if only you submit to me', and Molly hated such beauty being abused. It reminded her somewhat of the oak queen's court, the gardens and wilds of the land beyond, locked in tight so only the queen and her chosen court could experience it.

Molly lifted her gaze and craned her neck to peer through the towers beyond the Menagerie, just able to glimpse the tiniest slip of citadel glass. Beyond the walls of glass was the real wilds of Faerie, the land outside the citadel. But then even the oak queen's court wasn't truly free, locked in to the queen's whim as much as the citadel seemed to be to Celeste's.

The sound the door being unlocked echoed through the silent room, but she refused to turn away from the window. She stared instead at that slip of glass, and at what she now thought of as the real Faerie beyond.

"Celeste asked me to bring you some food personally, something you'd really like," Ru announced.

The scent of whatever he had, rich and aromatic, hit Molly's nose and her stomach growled disobediently. Still she didn't turn around.

"I know you're angry and confused, but we really do want what's best for you," he tried.

Confused. Like I'm somehow skipping around with nothing between my ears and no idea of what's been going on.

She folded her arms across her chest to tamp down on the urge to start throwing fists. She could compel him, but it wouldn't get her far until she knew for certain that he would be able to get her out without being caught.

"And of course everyone else knows what's best for me," she muttered. "Celeste barely knows me, and you betrayed me. Were we ever truly friends, or has she been pulling your strings the whole time?"

"It wasn't like that. Yes, technically she asked me to befriend you, but it was a long time before she gave me any specific instructions. Before that we were just friends. People get thrown together by circumstances all the time."

"They don't lie to each other about them though. You could have told me any time. What, did she have a swear-block on you?"

She did turn around this time, fighting to keep the urge to burn bright and angry down.

Ru grimaced. "Well, no… but-"

"She had to swear-block Talie. Even then, Talie managed to let things slip. She tried to tell me the truth. She at least treated me like a person."

"Talie isn't the vision of purity you seem to think she is," he muttered.

Molly laughed, the sound sour as she pulled a face.

"No, she definitely has her secrets, but at least she tried. At least she's only running around after people like Celeste or Marcus or Phoenix because she literally has no other choice. You screwed me over willingly."

"I don't see it as screwing you over. You think you've had a hard time, and you have what with losing Lily and Basil, but at least you had them for a while. I owe Celeste my life."

Molly hesitated. Nothing he could tell her would excuse what he'd done, but if she let him think she was softening, she might be able to tease some information out of him.

"Explain."

He sighed. "There's no harm in telling you now."

"You mean your mistress said you could," Molly scoffed.

"If you want. Celeste picked me up from a children's home when I was seven. It was several levels further up and trust me, you've never seen trouble or danger like it. There are people willing to sell their kids for food, all sorts. The home made us work for our board as well."

Molly clenched her folded arms tighter around her. She resolved not to be taken in, but Ru couldn't lie and he'd never admitted anything like this before.

He never admitted anything about himself before because we were never truly friends.

"Celeste saw promise in me," he continued. "She took me out of the home, gave me purpose and a family in the Menagerie. I've lived here since then. It's my home. For what it's worth, you are my friend, whether you believe me or not."

Molly shrugged, unwilling to let his past influence her.

Talie had a rough time growing up and she at least has some decency.

"You don't behave like it," she countered. "Friends don't keep those kind of secrets by choice. Friends don't choose your mother over you. Friends don't pretend to fancy you to get you onside."

Ru sighed. "That... it wasn't pretending. Come on, Molly, you have to know that at least was real? I know you weren't interested in the end, but I was. I am."

"Nope, not happening," she spat. "Forget it."

"I expected as much. But Celeste does have your best interests at heart. She only wants you to be strong for your future, the future we could all have together."

Molly looked at him then, really looked at him. Utter sincerity mingled with hope shone from his eyes and radiated in his voice.

He really is indoctrinated into this happy clappy Menagerie fan-club Celeste has created for herself.

"Well, you do sound like the perfect puppet for her," she said. "Perhaps she should let me go and adopt you instead. I wouldn't even be needed then."

Ru set the tray of food he was still holding down on the table at the end of her bed.

"You're heir to the oak line, Molly. With the king consort taking himself out of the running by marrying the Holly Queen, after your grandmother dies, your mother will be reinstated as the next oak queen. Then you. There's no avoiding that."

Molly shook her head. "No, that's impossible. Celeste

abdicated and became all but a ghost in royal stories. She hasn't had anything to do with the royals since then."

Ru's expression turned pitiful as he walked back to the door. Molly stared as he opened it and stood framed in the doorway.

"How do you think we managed to get into the Oak Queen's court in the first place?"

CHAPTER TWENTY THREE

TALIE

Talie eyed Daisy's departing back. She had half a mind to go and rattle her until she spilled whatever the cryptic parting comment meant, but Sammy was frowning at her.

"You don't need to be so rude," Sammy said. "I know you're worried about Molly, but you should be happy. If Aurora's around then Molly probably is too. Maybe she's hiding up on the beams or something."

Talie grunted, wishing she hadn't succumbed quite so easily to telling Sammy tales about what she and Molly had been up to. She hadn't mentioned that she'd spent far more times walking up on the beams though, wobbly knees and all, in the hope of coming across Molly by chance.

Phoenix hadn't called on her for anything since the fight, but she'd turned up to train in the gym since so he hadn't banished her. Nia was as chatty as ever too but Talie didn't care. Phoenix neglecting her gave her more time to look for Molly, something she guessed he was counting on.

"I'm going to walk a bit," she announced. "You'll go straight home?"

Sammy rolled her eyes. "If I must. School finishes soon and then you'll have to spend all day every day with me. Or you know, trust me to do my own thing."

Talie couldn't bear that idea and stuffed it deep down with the other repressed worries as Sammy set off up the levels in the direction of home.

The moment the milling crowd swallowed Sammy from view, Talie set off after Daisy. She'd already lost sight of her but no doubt Daisy was going back to Molly's neighbours. If she didn't manage to catch her, she would get her daily check of the workshop out of the way. One day, she might return to find the door open with Molly inside.

She turned the curve of the lane but the clatter of cart wheels had her darting sideways. She scowled at the back of the cart as it rushed past her and swung into a side alley. The moment the noise halted, the faintest hint of muffled shouting drifted down to her, and the tip of a boot swung out around the edge of the building.

Talie cloaked herself in her protection warding and peered around the corner into the alley. Movement drew her attention upward and she choked back a gasp as Daisy let go of the beam she was clinging to.

The man clutching at her waist, Molly's Menagerie friend, twisted as they fell so that he took the brunt of the impact. He clung to Daisy with his arms and legs wrapped around her, but as they hit the back of the cart waiting beneath them, Daisy angled an elbow into his gut.

Talie had no gifts to fight with, but she'd trained in combat long enough to recognise she wouldn't be able to take Ru and the driver on her own. Daisy was mouthing things without any sound coming out but Talie couldn't do anything to help her. Ru was Celeste's puppet, so any altercation in public would get them dragged in by the boots, then Talie would become the captive instantly.

She dodged behind a pillar as the driver yanked a cover over the struggling pair and urged the Arumpii to reverse with a jerk of the reins. The animal tossed its silver-spined neck with a snort and veered backward in a clatter of huge hooves.

Talie held herself in place as the cart reversed in an arc and rumbled down the lane at a deceptively sedate pace. Then she broke into a jog with her pulse pounding, the urge to dash warring with the knowledge she couldn't draw attention to herself.

She twisted into Molly's alleyway, barely sparing a glance for the closed workshop, and hammered on Molly's neighbour's door instead. A loud wail started up followed by a feral string of cursing as the door swung open to reveal a feral looking woman with mad purple hair.

"I *just* got her to sleep- who are you?" the woman demanded.

Talie couldn't remember her name, or that of the man who appeared behind her. He was the one who'd been walking along with Daisy, but further inside their home she spotted the shining white feathers and green plumage of Aurora, Molly's bird, who was hopping around on the coffee table.

"Your nanny, she's been taken. I..." she hesitated. "I saw her trying to climb up to the beams and someone tackled her into a cart, threw a cover over it and off they went with her held down."

"Orbs, I knew she shouldn't have been let out," the woman muttered.

As she moved from the doorway, Talie noticed a man she didn't know sitting on the sofa.

"Come inside, quickly," the woman snapped, but Talie flinched away before anyone could grab her. "Orbs alive, you're Molly's friend, aren't you?"

Talie nodded. "I am, yeah. What's Molly got to do with this?"

Wild thoughts of Daisy being somehow in league with Molly's family filled her head, and she wrapped a warding around herself, ready to fight if she had to.

"Inside, seriously. We're friends of Molly's too."

"Is this wise?" the man on the sofa asked.

Talie took a deep breath and stepped inside. The woman was Fae and couldn't lie, but whether they were the kind of friends who were looking after Molly's best interests, or the sort who saw her as a commodity, Talie wouldn't know without going inside.

"I'd say take a seat, but we don't have any left," the woman mumbled. "Right, quick introductions. I'm Beryl. That over there is Harvey and baby Aurora. Bird Aurora you probably already know. And that there is Kainen of the Illusion Court."

Talie stared around the room. "I'm Talie. Molly's my friend. Daisy isn't, but I figured you'd want to know what happened."

The man on the sofa, Kainen, snorted. "Do you know

much about Molly's family, her past?"

The question left a bitter taste in Talie's mouth but she found the truth burbling from her lips all the same.

"I know enough. We got thrown together due to circumstance but I'd never do anything to hurt her."

"What do you know about her?"

Talie frowned. "She's kind, annoyingly so. She's a princess too technically, not that she behaves like one. She only just found that out though."

She froze as the secrets leapt out.

"How did you-"

"Compulsion gift." He shrugged. "Had to make sure we could trust you. Can we?"

Again that sour taste filled her mouth, familiar now. She'd only experienced it once before when Molly compelled her to stay away.

"I don't know," she answered honestly. "Right now, I'm on Molly's side. The Menagerie, the resistance, they're all acting as bad as each other. Where is she, is she safe?"

He sighed. "She was."

"If you hadn't gifted her orbing sunlight, she might still be," Beryl snapped.

"Sunlight?" Talie's jaw dropped. "Wow. That'll suit her."

"Thanks, I thought so." Kainen gave Beryl a bratty look. "Um… are we telling her?"

Beryl nodded. "Might as well. We managed to get to Molly before her mother did, glamoured her up right nice. But of course, she had to go and get herself caught. Did you see who took her?"

"You mean Daisy? His name is Ru. He works for Molly's mother." Talie's brain glitched. "Wait... you don't mean... Molly was glamouring as Daisy? But... they were in the same room..."

"We've had Daisy here for a while as a failsafe option in case we needed to bring Molly into our protection. It worked until *someone* decided to leave her on her own."

Harvey held up both hands. "I literally left her for two minutes. She was under strict instructions to come straight back. You can't lock her up forever."

"Yeah, she doesn't listen to orders well," Talie muttered. "They have her, Ru and Celeste. What do we do? Who's going in to get her?"

Kainen grimaced. "Things are tricky. Because of who we hold allegiance to, even unofficially, we can't just go charging in to the Menagerie to haul her out."

Talie folded her arms across her chest and took a long step back to the doorway.

"Well, someone needs to do something," she snapped. "I know people who might try."

Phoenix wouldn't want to risk a second charge on the Menagerie for a rescue, but Molly had shown her ways in. If Phoenix gave her a couple of people to take with her, she could risk it.

For Molly, she would risk it.

When nobody answered immediately, she headed toward the door. She would need to make sure Sammy was safe first, but if she could get Molly out...

"She's really important to you, isn't she?" Kainen

asked, his tone soft.

Talie turned in the doorway. "Yeah. You have no idea how much."

A communal look rippled around the group. Talie tensed as Kainen stood, his shadowed gaze fixed on her.

"How far would you be willing to go?"

CHAPTER TWENTY FOUR

MOLLY

Molly stood frozen in the middle of the room after Ru left, her mind racing. If the Oak Queen knew who Celeste was, and where she was, then they must have planned the whole thing between them.

Why send me in for the book though, why not just ask?

Celeste wouldn't trust anyone blindly. She was smart enough to recognise other people's arrogance, and the Oak Queen seemed more focused on besting Queen Demerara than seeing her own daughter as a foe.

Orbs, is May in on it too?

She didn't want to believe it, but until she heard the words from May's lips she couldn't trust based on her own foolish hope.

Anger rose as she slipped her boots and socks off and threw them aside. The brush of the plush carpet underfoot anchored her as she paced back and forth, a reminder of the opulent incarceration she was now so desperate to break free from, if only to warn Demi and the others of the truth.

"What if this has all been some massive master plan?" she muttered to herself.

Her memories of Faerie's past were hazy, mostly glib tales Beryl and Harvey had been filling her head with over the past few evenings, but she knew that Demi had once been a normal fairy, crowned by the nether after fighting the Apocalyptians in the Battle of Queens.

Did the Oak Queen know she might need her true heir hidden away when the king consort was born? Was he named crown prince solely to take attention away from Celeste?

The multitude of questions and possibilities made her head spin, but one thought rose above all the rest.

Demi was fighting for a fairer Faerie. Celeste, the Oak Queen, and the resistance were all fighting for power, for themselves. Phoenix maybe had more stake in seeing the citadel Fae treated equally, but she wouldn't have chosen him to rule anyone.

Even if she didn't manage to get herself out of the Menagerie, she needed to get a message to Demi somehow, which would take some thinking.

"There's no way I can get out of this immediately," she murmured. "Not without risking being locked in here forever. I can't concede to easily either, or she'll know I don't mean it."

She scanned the bookshelves for something that might give her an idea but none of the titles jumped out with anything useful, no sign of 'how to escape a warding for beginners'.

Next time Ru came in, she would compel him to tell her

everything. Then she'd pick the lock, sneak out with her stealth gift and find a way to get a message out.

They must send mail out from somewhere. I can slip a letter in with the rest, or hide in the laundry, or throw a note out of one of the windows.

She grabbed a blank sheet of paper from the pad on the desk, folded it into a crude paper bird and strode to the window. Winding her arm back, she threw it as far as she could and ducked in case the warding caught it.

The paper sailed through the window and across the garden, embedding itself in a hedge. Satisfied, Molly crossed the room to the food tray.

She'd need her strength up for whatever 'delights' Celeste decided to test her with next, and to be ready in case a chance to get a message or escape came up unexpectedly.

The key rattled in the lock and door flew open while she was still finishing the last few mouthfuls. Her heart picked up as Celeste swept in, but she turned and faced her with as much fake attitude as she could dredge up.

"Don't bother knocking then," she muttered.

If she channelled her inner Talie, she might even get herself kicked out.

Or get pulverised.

"Let's take a walk."

Molly frowned. "Why? I thought you told me to rest."

"Well, things change."

"Only if people choose to change them. Got someone pulling your strings? Marcus perhaps?"

Celeste scoffed delicately. "Marcus is extremely useful,

but he is the figurehead of the Menagerie, not the orchestrator."

"That wasn't an outright no."

Celeste tilted her head, eying Molly for several excruciating seconds.

"I have some people I want you to meet."

"No thanks."

She laughed. "I wasn't asking. We can do this the easy way or the painful way. You might be my daughter but let there be no confusion between us. I will not let anyone undermine my plans, not even you."

"I *might* be your daughter? Are you not sure?"

It was a lame attempt at a dig, but Molly couldn't hide her flinch as Celeste powered toward her and wrapped pinching fingers tight around her wrist.

"I am your mother. No word-tangling needed. I've kept track of you your whole life and there are no mistakes."

"Ru kept track of me, you mean."

Celeste sighed and started towing. Unable to resist without falling over, Molly had to hurry along behind her.

"Ru is a loyal servant to our family. He's proved himself over and over again. I found and raised him, in a way, as a companion to you."

Molly scowled. "Does he know that you're probably going to marry me off to some random noble? Am I what you promised him as a prize for obedience?"

"I have no need to trade for that boy's obedience. He gives it oh so willingly. Now, I expect you to be polite to our guests."

"Who are they?"

They reached the stairs and Celeste paused at the top of the stairs, casting a critical eye over Molly's clothes.

"Citadel nobles. They're intrigued by your existence, but it's beyond time to introduce you to society, and to acclimatise you to a more noble life at my side."

"Is this where you tell me the whole nefarious plan then?" she asked, without any hope.

Celeste chuckled. "So you can run to your neighbours and pass it all over to the Holly Queen?"

"How-"

"Do you not think I keep myself informed of the queen's entourage? No idea how they managed to get into the citadel but we have what we need now."

"Like what?"

She put the tiniest hint of her charm gift behind the question, widening her eyes and keeping her tone soft. Celeste might have made herself immune to compulsions, but Molly had to hope she was arrogant enough to assume herself above common gifts like charm.

"All these questions, Molinia. No doubt you've discovered already that we've been borrowing fairies from other realms."

"Borrowing? They looked petrified. I'm betting you don't 'give them back' in any acceptable condition either."

Celeste slowed to a halt.

"How do you know what they looked like?"

Molly shrugged. "I get around."

"I hope you mean that figuratively."

"Why, not able to sell me on if I'm not pure?"

Celeste closed her eyes in momentary frustration.

"You have our family's quick temper, and disagreeable nature."

"The only family I'm willing to recognise is Taz and May. The rest of you can burn in the deepest depths of-"

"The nobles are getting restless." Ru hurried up the stairs toward them.

Celeste nodded. "Yes, of course they are. Insufferable but necessary. Come along, Molinia. Just remember that all actions have consequences, so you'd do well to mind yours."

She frowned again at Molly's sweatshirt and jeans, her nose wrinkling.

"You should really change into something less, *that*," she added.

Ru glanced between them, a charming smile lighting on his face before Molly could snap back.

"You could always do a before and after," he suggested.

Like I'm nothing more than another device for them to use in the mad dash for ultimate power.

Celeste nodded. "That will work."

She swept down the stairs and Molly stormed after her. Better that than risk spending a second lingering with Ru. As they turned the curve of the staircase, a gaggle of finely dressed nobles watched their progress. Molly thought of Talie and Sammy, and how they would have laughed at her plan.

I can try to beat Celeste at her own game. Turn the nobles against her.

She relaxed her shoulders and levelled her chin in what she hoped was some kind of graceful pose, trying to embody a well-bred noble lady.

Trouble is, I've only had a few brief meetings with the queens and a short time with people like May and Kainen, and none of them are remotely ladylike.

"Lords, Ladies, esteemed guests, it's my delight to present my daughter, Molinia Elverhill, to you," Celeste announced.

Molly eyed the gathered group, seven of them assessing her like an unexpected commodity. She held herself tall and said nothing.

Celeste laughed. "As you can see, she's inherited the Elverhill bearing. Say hello, Molinia."

Molly held her tongue instead of speaking immediately. Something about Celeste, her tone or perhaps her overly friendly behaviour, suggested she wanted the audience to go well. She tilted her head the way she'd seen May do often, looking each one in the face until she managed a dismissive smile.

"Hello."

It was exactly what Celeste had told her to do, no more, no less. None of these nobles would dare assist her in any way; she couldn't consider asking them to help her escape, but they might know more than she did about what Celeste was up to.

"We weren't sure if you were a myth or not, Princess," one woman said.

A smattering of laughter circled the group. Molly thought about her friends and found the fake smile a little easier to wear.

"Even the best myths have at least a grain of truth in

them." She held the woman's gaze, favouring her with attention until someone else earned it instead. "So here I am at Celeste's demand."

A ripple of soft inhalations passed around the group, but Molly didn't languish long enough to let it affect her nerves.

"I take it you're supposed to be the elite of the elite then, if she's called you here?" she added. "I believe there are meant to be many of the nobility scattered about the citadel."

"We aren't as ubiquitous as some might think, Princess," one man said, his tone entirely arch at her audacity. "It's true there are some recent stains on the description but I assure you, those are outside of our great walls."

Molly smiled. "You mean the Holly Queen's more innovative promotions to rank and title? Inheriting is more traditional than earning, for sure. Easier too for those who luck into it."

She had no idea where the performance was coming from, but there was a riotous thrill along with it, the idea that she could speak her mind and Celeste most likely wouldn't blast her to tiny pieces.

She needs me. Not sure what for, but if she didn't she would have gotten rid of me long before now.

Before the group could school their scandalised expressions, one of the ladies broke the line and stepped forward.

"We understand you've spent some time outside the citadel," she said more gently. "That must have been exciting for you."

She joined Molly's side and turned so that they were in a position to walk away from the group together. Molly followed her but kept her warding firm as they set off on a lap of the hall.

"I'm not sure exciting is the word. Novel yes, eye-opening certainly. The queen's court is fine in every respect, right down to the colour-changing uniforms we were given. I'm afraid I don't know your name."

The woman chuckled. "Lady Featherdown, Princess. The names and titles can be tiresome, the lineages even more so."

"But you benefit so richly from it."

"As do we all, Princess."

Molly snorted. "I haven't seen much benefitting. I spent the first sixteen years of my life believing I was a normal Fae, then suddenly I'm a princess and being given absolutely no say in my own life. Do you know, she has me locked in here? Won't let me leave or see my friends?"

"Parents can be querulous at times."

"I wouldn't know. I've never known mine. They never bothered to keep in touch."

Lady Featherdown sighed and slowed their pace to a halt.

"Your mother has been focused on her great work, and with increasing success. I mean, the fairies in the core have yielded amazing results."

Molly tensed. "The fairies that came from outside the citadel?"

"Yes! Oh she's already told you?"

Molly couldn't lie, but she could smile and play along.

"She has told me some, but I imagine not as much as she could. As you say, she's been busy my whole life."

Lady Featherdown frowned. "Well, she's very close to achieving it now, or so she says. We nobles must keep the status quo balanced, enable the ongoing support. We'll all reap the profits when the time comes."

Molly kept the fake smile pinned to her face with great effort.

"The status quo is important apparently."

Lady Featherdown nodded and patted her arm softly. Molly eyed the clinking rings adorning her fingers over the elbow-length satin gloves.

"The status quo is everything. There will always be nobility, no matter what it's called. Noble Fae ruling normal Fae is what keeps Faerie thriving."

"Well, I'm sure the fairies in the chamber won't see it like that, but what good are they if not sacrificial lambs for our great work?"

Molly couldn't keep the mockery out of her tone. Lady Featherdown's eyes widened and her gaze passed over Molly's shoulder.

"Ru, I think it's bedtime," Celeste announced. "Molinia looks tired from her first audience and is in dire need of proper clothes, and a long bath. Get something sorted about the awful state of that hair too."

Molly's insides flushed icy even as her cheeks burned. The slightest tightness to Celeste's expression should have been a victory, but the scathing assessment still carved itself down deep. Fury seesawed against the embarrassment and her mouth opened before she could obey.

"I'm in the middle of a conversation right now," she said, her tone loud enough to fill the hall. "You're being extremely rude."

Silence.

Even Celeste looked visibly stunned as the nobles stepped back, some of them with expectant glee lighting in their eyes.

"Children can be very stubborn." Celeste laughed and lifted a hand. "Molinia has much to learn about the nobility and hierarchy."

Molly reinforced her warding to prepare for some kind of attack. Celeste twitched her fingers, a stream of water flying from her palm. It became a maelstrom around Molly's warding, pressuring from all sides until she didn't even know which way to focus her energy. She grimaced as one of the marble tiles cracked next to her shoe, the gap giving the water a way through before she could ward into it.

It splashed through, whirling upward and drenching her before focusing around her hands, icy cold as it began to bite. She fought the pain but the rest of her skin burned as panic snatched at her ability to breathe.

Even if I use my sunshine gift, I might burn everyone to a crisp.

Revealing her gifts too early wouldn't give her anything in reserve either.

"Let this be your first lesson, Molinia," Celeste said. "You will learn to obey me or I will make you."

The vice around her hands lessened and the ice turned back to water, splatting onto the floor. Molly panted through the pain, knowing it was showing all too clearly on her face. Without being able to ward, she was only one step up from a puppet. If she refused to obey, she had no doubt Celeste would do whatever it took to make her.

My only option is to try and get a message out somehow. Beryl and Harvey will be missing me by now. They'll guess that this means danger's coming soon and will tell Kainen.

Aware of all the eyes on her, Molly straightened and forced her stinging hands to her sides. Without a second look at any of them, she walked toward Ru standing at the base of the stairs. He didn't give her any sign of comfort but she didn't expect any. He knew her enough to remember that mentioning her humiliation would push her even further away.

With each step up the stairs, she cleared her mind. Celeste was using the fairies as conduits to steal their gifts, either for replication or to bottle for further use. Molly had no doubts about what happened to the fairies after they were no longer useful either.

The moment they were up the stairs and walking along the hall to her room, Ru dodged close enough for their arms to brush. Molly grimaced at the pain in her hands and stepped clean away from him, dredging up her warding again as he opened her door for her.

She strode in and turned to face him.

"Don't," she snapped. "You chose your side and it's not the same as mine."

Ru sighed. She thought he might go for some kind of

heartbreaking spiel given the doleful look in his eyes, but he only shut the door behind him and left her alone.

"Idiot," she muttered.

She shook sodden strands of hair out of her eyes, unable to use her fingers. Then she realised what was missing.

"No, please no," she groaned, gingerly patting down her hair with her wrists.

She flinched away from the door as it opened, her arms still raised in search of her missing hair ribbon as a young woman entered carrying a tray.

"I'm warded, Princess," the woman warned.

She might have even been a relative, so similar were her honey blonde curls to Molly's own, but Molly caught the title and glared.

"Don't call me that."

The woman hesitated, already halfway across the room with the tray.

"It's your title, Princess, I have to."

She set the tray down and turned to leave, but her eyes blew wide when she saw Molly's hands.

"What happened?!"

Her hand flew to her mouth immediately after, but Molly waved away the outburst.

"My mother decided to punish me for speaking out of turn. I don't suppose I can convince you to take a message out of the Menagerie for me?"

The woman grimaced. "I..."

"No, don't trouble yourself. If this is how she punishes her daughter and heir, I don't want anyone else suffering worse because of me. Thank you for whatever the tray is."

The woman stared at her, eyes still wide orbs of green that flashed momentarily gold. Molly sighed, turning away.

Not only was she in pain from the freezing effect, but she'd lost her hair ribbon. She patted the back of her head just in case, her heart sinking.

"There will be many pins and ribbons in your closet I'm sure," the woman suggested. "Towels too. I've also heard *liquin* essence is good for burns."

Molly smiled. "Thank you. I'm sure there are countless ribbons in there, but the one I lost is important to me."

"Is it magic?" the woman asked, a note of almost amusement in her tone.

"No, just a gift from someone special."

The realisation hit her square in the gut, forcing a sharp breath from her lips.

Insane, we've barely even kissed each other.

She thought of the *Akiai* charm still secure on her finger, the supposed preamble to a kiss that Talie never had the chance to follow up on.

"I'm sure wherever they are, they're thinking of you too," the woman offered.

Molly sighed. "She has no idea. Not about me being trapped here, how I feel, none of it. At least she's safe though. That's what matters."

"What about you?"

"I survive, or I don't. Not sure why Celeste doesn't just get rid of me and raise a more amenable child in my place, but apparently she and the Oak Queen have been planning this for ages- sorry, I'm sure you don't need me rambling on."

The woman bowed her head in gratitude and retreated to the door.

"Food's best while it's hot, Princess."

"Thank you." Molly hesitated. "What's your name?"

"Lia, Princess. I'll find some *liquin* for your hands, if I can. The mistress has told everyone you're not to be given a healer, but most won't think of *liquin*. It's usually used as orb polish."

She opened the door and scurried out before Molly could dredge up any kind of thank you, the sound of the key being turned in the lock echoing behind her.

Molly picked up the spoon and winced at the feel of it against her skin. Using her fingertips instead, she balanced the bowl of soup between them and gulped it down. The bread went next, followed by a hot mug of *offke*.

Not a meat pocket, but it'll do. She sank onto her bed with a sigh. *At least I know one thing now. Tonight I'm breaking out and going to see what they're doing with the fairies.*

CHAPTER TWENTY FIVE

MOLLY

Molly barely had time to come up with a plan for breaking out before the key rattled in the lock. Cross-legged on her bed, she wrapped her warding around herself and prepared for Ru, or perhaps Lia, to come bowling in.

She tensed as Celeste breezed through and closed the door behind her.

"Before you begin cursing me, remember you brought that on yourself." Celeste nodded to her upturned palms, still red and raw. "I had to use strength in return. I am pleased though that you are able to show suitable spirit. In time that can be harnessed the right way."

Molly tracked Celeste's path to the window and looked for some sign of familial resemblance she might have missed before. They shared a similar-ish hair colour, but where hers was wavy Celeste's either wasn't or had been straightened. They had the same sea-blue eyes too, and Talie had mentioned similar eyebrows, but Molly couldn't imagine looking in a mirror and seeing much more than that between them.

Kainen's words came back to her then, *"you look like Taz when you glower like that"* and she stifled an ill-timed smile. Taz, king consort of Faerie and likely a very important political and social figure in Faerie, probably didn't even know or remember what she looked like.

"I don't want us to be enemies," Celeste announced. "I understand you find this difficult, and perhaps emotionally I could have kept you with me, but for your own safety I decided it was best to give you a normal childhood."

Molly shrugged. "It was normal until the Menagerie showed up. Were you the ones to kill my guardians?"

"Let's not dwell on the past. What's done is done, and there's no undoing it. There must be something you want that this new life can give you."

"You can't give me anything I want. You've eviscerated my old life, exposed people I thought were my friends as disloyal fakes, and now you refuse to let me leave the Menagerie. Do you really think trinkets or fancy clothes or promises of dominion over people I care about is going to sway me?"

Celeste sighed, drifting from the window toward the bed to sit down. Even though it was pointless, Molly firmed her warding around herself while inching as far across to the edge of the bed as she could without making it obvious.

"I'm not a monster, Molinia, despite what you might think."

"It's not safe for me to think, you've proven that," Molly muttered.

"Of course it is. I can't read minds. That was more a trait

of the Illusion Court from what I remember, but of course you won't be aware of the courts outside of the citadel. No, you can think freely, and I want you to talk freely too, but I won't tolerate disrespect."

Molly held her tongue. She had no hope of getting out of the Menagerie and no chance of beating Celeste in a fight, but perhaps if she played clever instead, she might get some answers.

"I've built the Menagerie up over the years on my own merit," Celeste continued. "I didn't use my mother's title or my own to do it either. The citadel was all but crumbling when I arrived, and it took several rounds of persuasion and some less than acceptable dealings to get the nobles on side."

"I won't ask."

Celeste chuckled. "Perhaps for the best. The nobles need someone to lead them as much as they need pandering to. They're simple enough to mould. The Fae of the citadel itself were more intransigent."

Molly thought of Phoenix, and of what Talie had mentioned about his family being the previous rulers of the citadel. It was a war of egos, a vendetta of entitlement on both sides, and she was trapped between the two.

"So you built the Menagerie," she prompted. "Then took control of the boots and left me to grow up unaware, I get that. But why did Lily and Basil have to die? To get me indebted to the Menagerie?"

Celeste's mouth thinned, a momentary flash of true emotion before the placating smile returned.

"The old you was indebted for the workshop. You have

no need of it now, so there's no debt. Besides, you're my daughter. The entire citadel is yours, if you'd only agree to take it."

Molly's heart lurched as temptation rose strong. She could pretend for a few years, lull Celeste into letting her guard down and save the citadel that way. Perhaps even reform-

Too good to be true. There'll never be any leeway, just the pretence of it.

Asking about her guardians also seemed to be a sore point, one she would have to tread carefully around.

"What about Marcus?" she asked.

Celeste frowned. "What about him?"

"Well, he's the head of the Menagerie. Does he report to you or you to him?"

"He's the figurehead as you say, and very helpful. I never intended to rule the Menagerie. It takes a lot of tedious work. No, I'm best placed placating the nobles and ensuring the guilds stay on our side. It's a symbiotic relationship that serves our family's goal."

Molly hesitated. "And Ru?"

"Well now, he's been very good to you. I appreciate you need to keep him in his place, and he did technically betray you, but it was for your own good in the long run. Don't torment the poor boy for too long. He's quite smitten with you."

"Smitten the moment we went to the queen's court when he found out who I was."

"Perhaps even before then."

Molly shrugged. Even if Ru did actually have feelings

for her, he would be waiting forever if he had any delusions about her forgiving him, let alone anything else.

I have to deal with Celeste before anything else though.

"So how does this work?" she asked. "I'm a captive here but I'm expected to play nice? Beg for my freedom drip by drop?"

Celeste sighed. "I'd prefer it to see you earning my trust through good behaviour, the foundation of every good parent child relationship."

"Good parents wouldn't abandon their kid."

Celeste stood swiftly and Molly flinched, her insides twisting at the narrow-eyed fury beaming back at her.

"I've explained my reasoning," Celeste snapped. "I don't expect to have to explain myself again. How am I to trust you if you refuse to behave? You ask about having your freedom but I can't guarantee you won't go running straight to Phoenix and your resistance friends, or those miscreants the Holly Queen has planted here. If it weren't too much of a risk to attack openly, I'd-"

Celeste inhaled sharply and her smile returned as Molly fought to keep the fear off her face. She wouldn't give up her friends for anything but Celeste knew about Beryl and Harvey, which meant they were also in danger.

"Like it or not, Molinia, Faerie has a tradition of hierarchy," Celeste continued, her tone now drastically calm. "I am above you in every sense. Familial standing, socially, politically, and even in terms of my gift strength. You will accept that or you will be made to."

Molly bit her lips together between her teeth and fought the words surging to burst out as Celeste swept toward the door.

"We have a dinner tonight with the nobility and I expect you to be polite and charming. Be ready and downstairs in twenty minutes. Above all else, let them see our family is united."

She didn't wait for an answer but the 'or else' hung in the air as she swung the door shut behind her. A second later, the sound of the key clanged in the lock.

Molly waited a few moments before collapsing back on the bed, letting the tension tumble out of her limbs.

Do I go downstairs as me and make a stand, or play nice and try to get on her good side?

Belligerence suggested she go downstairs as herself, mucky clothes and all. Talie would have done the same. Kainen might have even agreed, but everyone else would have counselled caution.

She sat up and eyed the door to the walk-in wardrobe. No doubt there would be bountiful dresses waiting for her to try them on, all a perfect fit. She could almost visualise Celeste spending her downtime ascertaining the necessary measurements.

Twenty minutes later, her compromise was her own clothes but with brushed hair, washed face and the kind of attitude that could charm the deepest, darkest secrets from the most guarded of minds.

She was halfway to the door when it swung open. Ru eyed her up and down, then grimaced.

"No time, although I suppose you could be fashionably late," he said.

She shrugged. "I washed my face and hands. Even

brushed my hair. What more do they need?"

"A dress would be a start. Even a pantsuit. When was the last time you changed your-" He pinched the bridge of his nose. "You know what? Never mind. She's been extolling your virtues for the last ten minutes so please be amenable. No more backchatting."

"Or what?" she challenged.

"She'll hurt you. Please Molly, she's not someone to antagonise. Just play nice and then we can look at getting you some more freedom."

Molly stomped past him. "You should be careful. She'll think you're on my side not hers and punish you if you try to help me."

She didn't wait to see his reaction, striding along the hall to the stairs. The sound of chatter echoed up, but she vaguely remembered Celeste telling her long ago that there was a dining hall for the more esteemed visitors.

The entrance hall was empty and her gaze drifted across the vast space, past the stage and the stained glass window of a night-time sky sparkling with multi-coloured stars, onto the ornately carved black doors lined with steel. Enormous doors with two Menagerie guards cloaked in grey uniforms standing in front of them.

The fairies have to be down there, and I bet the supposed well of power is too.

She moved her attention quickly to the high archway the noise was emanating from, not wanting anyone to see her staring. Given time and space to roam, she would get beyond those doors and free as many fairies and collect as much information as she could, but first she needed Celeste on side enough to loosen the reins a little.

As she approached the archway, Celeste's gaze lifted to her. A thin line of disapproval flickered across her face, but the nobles were busy talking and didn't notice.

Molly sucked in a breath.

Here goes nothing. If I ever see Talie and Sammy again, the tale will give them a good laugh.

She squared her shoulders, levelled her chin and softened her pace to a glide.

"Excuse my lateness," she announced, loud enough to silence the entire table. "I couldn't find anything I liked to wear."

She eyed those assembled, several turning their noses up immediately, and found Lady Featherdown seated on the other side of the empty seat beside Celeste.

Lady Featherdown recovered from her shock first.

"Fashion is subject to change amongst the young, I suppose," she said with a fluttery laugh. "I once paired linen pants with a leather waistcoat. I was almost laughed out of court."

Celeste lifted a glass goblet, one eyebrow lifting.

"As I understand it, your court is subject to oddities."

Lady Featherdown inclined her head. "As you say. The recent changes aren't suitable for everyone, but I'm fond of any rule that allows me to oust my enemies."

Molly slid into the seat between Lady Featherdown and Celeste.

"You have enemies?" she asked.

Lady Featherdown nodded. "Oh absolutely. The court I'm from has an absolutely odious man who used to occupy the top nobility spot. There have been managerial changes in the last year however that I've turned to my advantage. Evolve or perish, that's the way of Faerie."

Molly smothered her smile with a sip of the wine that appeared in front of her. Lady Featherdown gave her a twinkling smile, utterly at odds with the snooty behaviour she'd expected. Some of the other nobles exchanged glances. She had no doubt Lady Featherdown was doing exactly what she'd said, turning things to her advantage, but she could take a lesson from that.

"Evolution is definitely the way forward," she agreed. "But tradition has its merits. The steel of the soul, the depth of the gift, nether and Faerie intertwined. The vital things never change."

Silence rounded the group, but again Lady Featherdown recovered first. She lifted her goblet in Molly's direction.

"How true that is. We are all stuck in our various entitlements, Princess, me as much as anyone here, but from what I understand you've not grown up with any nobility."

"Proud of it," Molly agreed. "I learned the true cost of hard work. If you didn't have servants, or money, how would you survive? If you were a child ungifted, how would you manage? Sometimes learning to be very not-noble is what keeps you safe."

"And yet you joined the Menagerie," a man reminded her.

She nodded. "I did because it was that or lose the workshop I inherited. Funny how manipulations come for us all, whether we ask to be part of the game or not."

"Molinia still hasn't quite forgiven me for that," Celeste said with a laugh. "Heritage comes for us all, sooner or later."

Unlike her own lame quips, all the nobles laughed at that one, although Lady Featherdown gave Molly the slightest hint of an eye roll.

I favoured her when we spoke earlier and she's honouring it. She wants to know if staking a social claim on me early will benefit her, but she won't ever go openly against Celeste.

Molly frowned at the empty cup in front of her. She didn't realise she'd drank the whole lot already, but someone was already at her side to refill it. Celeste nodded her approval.

"You might find our wine a tad refined for your normal tastes, Molinia," she announced.

Molly shrugged. "I'm used to a bottle of *Beast Lite* or two off the carts. You can get three for five if you know who to go to."

"Three for, five?" A woman asked. "Three crates for the cost of five? How is that prudent?"

Molly's jaw dropped. "Three bottles for five pesanas."

"Oh." The woman frowned. "But why would you only buy three bottles?"

"Some can only afford three. A pesana doesn't go a long way up the levels."

"Nonsense. Pesanas are exactly what they are. True, when you're among the nobility we're more likely to deal in percats, but currency is still currency."

"Maybe, but it still doesn't go too far up here."

He scoffed. "Here we go, another bleeding heart. Do you think noble children are given freebies when they come of age, Princess? No, they have to work like any other, take over parts of the family heritage, make appearances of their own, gain contacts. It's no free ride."

"And who puts them in touch with those contacts?" Molly countered. "Who gives them a piece of the family heritage to take over in the first place? So many families don't have anything to hand down. Noble kids are given opportunities that normal Fae aren't."

"What rot. Fae just don't want to put in the work to earn them nowadays."

Molly froze, revulsion rippling over her skin.

"How much do you pay your citadel servants then?" she demanded.

"Enough." The man sniffed. "They get thirty pesanas as standard."

"A week?" she asked in disbelief.

"Of course not! A month."

"Thirty pesanas a month will barely pay for a room and the associated fees this far up the levels," she snapped. "Then they have travel down which most carts charge above the odds for, because they can. Then food, any medicine, school fees if they have children."

The man drew his shoulders up tall, but Molly had forgotten the situation she was in and faced him just as fiercely.

"Well, surely they can do without a few luxuries if that's the life they've chosen," he suggested.

"How is it a life they've chosen?" she exploded. "Being

born into relative poverty, barely able to live, let alone have luxuries. They don't choose their parents, like some weird, garish flip of how I definitely didn't choose mine!"

A brief moment of silence hung over the table as several scandalised faces gawped at her. Then Celeste laughed, the delicate trill hiding a vein of venom beneath it.

"Such a progressive," she said. "It's true there are news ways and methods that can be useful. Evolutions of a sort. Think about the traditional days of old Faerie, after all. You had the royalty lording over all. Then the nobility provided themselves as useful fans, ebbing and flowing in and out of favour, and finally the common Fae forming the obedient serving masses."

"Yeah, not a big fan of that myself," Molly muttered.

"It had it's benefits but also a lot of downfalls," Celeste added. "Nowadays, the royalty and the nobility are seen as symbiotic, usually judged by the level of fear they impose."

Molly scowled. "The Holly Queen doesn't rule that way, or so I've heard."

"The Holly Queen may have cultivated her friends into those head spots, but the nobles beneath them remain the same. Power is currency, and it pays to be rich, either in money or skill or desire."

"So that's the end goal? Get as powerful as you can and slay anyone in your way to get it?"

Celeste lifted her drink and took a sip, a vision of calm.

"Not always. More often than not, what goes up must come down."

"But what about those that have always been up from

the beginning?" Molly demanded. "Are you saying they're where they 'should' be? Is this some antiquated notion that heritage is everything and bloodlines win out in the end?"

"Heritage can be important, especially when mundane Fae respect it. It is a tool though, and nothing more."

Someone swiped Molly's wine glass out of her hand and another glass thudded in front of her, full of water. She swiped it up and drained the liquid inside. It tanged against her tongue but she was already failing in her intention to play the game, no doubt due to the strong Fae wine and minimal food intake. She blinked as the room twisted in front of her, the sudden blur of the table and faces disorientating.

"I think Molinia has had far too much excitement recently," Celeste announced. "You, maid, take her back to her room."

Through groggy, unfocused eyes, Molly saw the misshapen lump of Ru grow closer.

"I'll do it." His voice sounded, distant, garbled.

"Stay where you are," Celeste snapped. "I think we need to revisit who your allegiance is to, her or me."

Molly fought the lurching sensation of pity for him, even though she was sure she was meant to be mad at him for something instead. Then the lurching span her toward the stairs, and she got a fleeting flash in a passing mirror of Lia hauling her up.

"You don't do anything by halves, Princess," Lia muttered. "I'll get you to bed and fetch you some water."

Molly shook her entire body in reply, the carpet swaying perilously close before strength anchored back around her waist.

"Nooo, she's in the water."

"She's not, she just wields it. From the tap is safe."

"Double pinky promise?"

"Er... yeah. Here's the room."

Molly swayed as Lia shuffled her against the door frame to open the door. The moment Lia reclaimed her weight, Molly wrapped her arms around Lia's neck and snuggled into her shoulder.

"I like someone else," she muttered with her eyes closing. "This doesn't mean anything."

Moments later, the world tilted and she crashed onto something soft.

"Never said it did. Here, drink this."

Molly cracked one bleary eye open.

"What is it?"

"Only water." Lia held out the glass in her hand and hesitated. "Double pinky promise."

Molly sighed and reached out a sluggish hand, missing the glass by several inches. Lia sat on the bed and brought the glass to Molly's lips, and Molly managed to gulp the contents down.

"Don't tell Talie," she mumbled.

Lia stood and disappeared from view. Molly let her head drop onto the bed, eyes closing to the sway of dizziness.

"Who's Talie?"

Warning flickered in Molly's head but she couldn't make sense of it.

"A girl I know."

"She give you that ring you wear?"

Molly couldn't lift her head again, but she ran her thumb over the *Akiai* charm on her forefinger.

"Don't tell Celeste about her, please. She's very important to me."

"I won't, Princess, don't worry." Lia's voice faded along with Molly's consciousness. "I've got everything I need already."

CHAPTER TWENTY SIX

TALIE

"I still don't understand," Sammy insisted. "Why did I have to bring my stuff? What's going on?"

Talie continued towing her by the hand, wishing she had some calm, grown-up way of explaining why Sammy was being forced out of her bed and into the lanes with all her belongings.

"Molly's got some friends. Ones that can get you out of the citadel. It's not safe."

Sammy tried to slow down but Talie charged on along the lane.

"I don't want to leave! I'm so close to finishing school, I need to do that. Besides, maybe I can help."

Talie turned into Molly's alleyway, her gaze fixed on the door at the end.

"You can finish school outside the citadel, at an even better school I'll bet. I'm not risking keeping you here."

"I'm almost sixteen," Sammy argued. "You can't tell me what to do."

Talie ignored the logic in that and marched them up to

Beryl's front door. She knocked three times.

"These people will keep you safe, that's what matters."

The door swung open and Beryl hurried them inside before Sammy could argue.

"This is my sister, Sammy," Talie announced.

Sammy nodded coyly to those assembled. Harvey waved half a bagel from behind the kitchenette counter and Kainen stood from his seat on the sofa. Beryl grabbed baby Aurora and gave them what she probably thought was a reassuring smile.

"Welcome, Sammy. Talie's not had time to tell us much about you."

Sammy folded her arms and Talie groaned, recognising the stubborn set of Sammy's chin.

"I'm not leaving the citadel," she announced. "I have to finish school."

The others exchanged various looks as Talie pressed a hand to her forehead.

"It's not going to be safe for you here. They know you're linked to me and they know I'm linked to Molly."

Sammy frowned. "Who's 'they'? Phoenix?"

"No- well, I hope not. It's a long story, too long and I have things I need to go and do, but I need you to be safe, Sam."

"She's only trying to look out for you," Beryl added.

"We could take her to the Illusion Court," Kainen suggested. "That'd be safe and we do have links to some great Fae schools. Birchwood, or even Arcanium-"

Sammy stamped her foot. "I'm not going to any court, or any school. I'm staying right here."

Talie groaned. "Sammy, please be reasonable."

"I'm not a child! If I choose to stay, you literally can't stop me."

"What about Molly's room?" Harvey stunned them all into silence.

Beryl frowned. "What are you blathering about?"

"Molly's room, here. Sammy could stay and help with Aurora like Molly did. It'd still be in the citadel and I can walk her to school in the mornings, low-key of course."

Talie bit her lip. It would solve all her problems, including the ones Sammy was currently causing.

"If everything went completely wrong though, would you still take her with you?" she asked.

"I am here you know," Sammy muttered.

Talie ignored that and looked past the others to Kainen. She got the feeling when it all came down to it, despite appearances, he would be the final decision maker.

"You both have a place at our court for as long as the citadel is a danger to you, I'm not rescinding that," he said firmly. "If there's a delay to getting there, it makes no difference to us. If Sammy wants to stay here and help with baby Aurora until we sort Molly out, there shouldn't be a problem."

Talie sagged, relief making her momentarily dizzy.

"Right then, let's get you set up." Beryl grinned. "The room's nothing fancy but we'll feed you three square meals, and Aurora isn't exactly a troublesome baby either."

Talie eyed the bright brown baby eyes that were peering suspiciously at them from Beryl's shoulder, glad it would be Sammy on baby duty while she went for espionage.

Sammy crossed the room with her tiny bag of belongings swinging from her shoulder. She held up a finger to the baby, who reached out and dribbled over it.

"She's cute."

That seemed to be that. Beryl shuffled Sammy toward the wooden walled box in the far corner of the room, the corner of a bed visible through the doorway, and they shut the door behind them.

"She'll be safe here, I promise," Harvey said. "I may have ballsed up with Molly, but we won't make the same mistake."

Talie wiped a hand over her face. "Nobody can keep tabs on Molly if she doesn't want them to. She's ridiculously stubborn."

Kainen chuckled. "Family trait. She reminds me a lot of Taz. Anyway, we need to make sure you're prepared for what may come."

Talie nodded. "I'm ready. As long as Sammy's safe, I'll do whatever needs to be done."

Kainen glanced at the shut bedroom door and lowered his voice.

"If I know anything about anything, Molly will be testing the boundaries. She'll try to escape and Celeste will likely lock the place down. You need to be prepared for that in case you can't get back out."

He held something out to her and she crossed the room to take it. The gold orb lay in her palm, a soft weight.

"Hide that and make sure both you and Molly know where it is. Don't reveal who you really are, not to her or anyone. If your identity is compromised, hide yourself. No heroics. If it's life or death, use the orb."

Talie nodded. "I'll do what needs to be done."

"That tells me absolutely nothing," he retorted. "We don't have the numbers to charge in and get her out, but we're not going to put anyone at risk more than we have to."

"If she's hurting her, I'm not going to allow it," Talie warned.

Kainen's expression darkened and Talie could have sworn the shadows swelled in answer.

"If she's seriously hurting her, you find a way to get her out," he said.

"After we've found out where the core is and how to get down there and how many guards she's got-"

"No." His voice went deep and the shadows roiled toward him from the corners of the room. "Molly's safety comes first, and yours. If we find a way to free the fairies, then we need time to get enough people into the citadel to match her numbers."

Surprised, Talie stared at him. He really sounded as though he meant it.

"As long as I can get Molly out, and Sammy's safe, I'll do whatever it takes," she insisted. "If... if something happens to me though, you need to look after both of them."

Kainen sighed. "I meant what I said. They'll have a place in my court, and so will you if you want it, with or without helping us. Well, Molly technically gets to choose her court, but we've offered ours and I like to think she'd choose ours over Demi's."

Talie had no idea who Demi was, but she guessed another noble with a court. It was more than she could ever have dreamed of being offered for Sammy though, so she nodded.

"Sammy might not go quietly," she muttered.

"Yeah, she obviously takes after you."

Talie took that as a compliment. "I've not managed to get much information yet, but I took a job in the Menagerie laundry from someone who was sick."

"I won't ask how." He frowned. "Have you seen her?"

"Yeah, she's hanging on from what I've gathered so far, causing trouble."

"Good, as long as she doesn't antagonise Celeste too much. Try to dissuade her from that when you get in there."

"This will be tough," Harvey said gently.

Talie shrugged. "It's going to be difficult holding a glamour for long periods but I've managed it before, and I can handle odd slips easily enough. It's just about making the right jokes in the right guards' ears. I'm not good at it or anything, but I'll try."

Kainen glanced at Harvey. "You doing the honours then?"

Harvey snorted. "I think it'd better be a gift. Safer for control if anything happens to me. Not that anything ever does. Parenthood is all baby spit, poop and getting shouted at with slightly lower decibels than before."

Talie glanced between them and stepped back as Kainen stalked toward her. In that moment, with wickedness shining in his eyes, she could see the powerful lord of a far-flung court approaching.

He held his hand out to her and she extended hers, tensing as he grabbed it and lifted it to his lips. Then he dropped a featherlight kiss to the back of her hand and she resisted the swelling urge to punch him.

"*Eww.* What was that for?"

Even the mere touch of it sent uncomfortable ripples over her skin.

"Okay, the eww was uncalled for," he grumbled. "It's a gift. I gift you with the ability to glamour whenever you choose, for as long as you choose, into whatever Fae form takes your fancy. It will be immune to any glamour lifts, and removable only by rulers of my court or the Holly Queen's. We'll also see through it too, Demi, Taz, Reyan and I."

Talie's jaw dropped. "I- that's-how- *what?*"

Kainen grinned. "It's a gift. Nobility can gift other Fae when they choose to. A gift is-"

"I know what a gift is!" She fought to rein in the bewilderment because it was having a very ungrateful effect on her temper. "Sorry. Thank you. I'm not used to… I don't often… we don't get gifted here."

"I figured as much. Find yourself a glamour and get used to holding it. No blue eyes one day, green eyes the next. It'll be different to mentally holding a glamour, so you might get into a habit of forgetting what you look like because your focus isn't on it."

"I'll manage. Any more idea what protections Celeste has on the outside?"

Kainen grimaced. "We're not entirely sure. Wards to stop Molly getting out most definitely. Guards on the doors. We can't rule out glamour lifts, but they take a lot of effort so she won't be able to keep doing them."

"Getting Molly out is the first priority," Harvey insisted. "Until then, watch and learn and above all find her a way out."

Talie nodded. "I will. I'll say goodbye to Sammy then go."

"Choose your glamour first," Kainen said.

Talie looked down at her front. She'd not wasted much time wishing to be different because she didn't have the money or time to make it happen even if she'd wanted to.

She focused on the new tingle of magic bubbling through her limbs, the surge of it tingling near her elbows. She made her nose a bit smaller and slimmed down her muscles without losing too much strength. Thinking of Molly, she turned her dark hair blonde but changed herself to match Sammy's skin tone. As she visualised her new self, fully expecting it not to work, Harvey pointed to a mirror. She turned, pleased to have mastered her new gift so easily.

I actually look like I could be Sammy's sister by birth now.

She didn't wait for approval from Kainen or Harvey. The only person she wanted to show was Sammy while she had the chance. As she knocked on the bedroom door, she wondered what Molly would think. A shiver of anticipation curled in her chest as she realised she would hopefully be seeing Molly again soon, maybe even rescuing her this time.

The door opened to reveal the frightening sight of Sammy with the baby snoozing happily on her shoulder.

"Who are you?" Sammy asked.

Talie smiled. "You don't recognise me already? Kainen gave me a glamour gift."

"Wow! Really? That's amazing! You're so lucky."

"Yeah but I have something I need to do now with it, so I might not be able to be back for dinner."

Sammy nodded. "This is something to do with Molly disappearing, right?"

"Yeah."

"Good. Bring her home. We can yell at her for leaving us then."

"You'll have to get in line," Beryl said.

"Nobody is yelling at Molly," Talie muttered. "She's been through enough."

"Beryl sighed. "Fair. Okay, Sammy, it's time to give Aurora her bottle, then I'll show you how to use your warding to repel out in the lane."

Talie headed for the door, her heart settling the tiniest amount at knowing Sammy was safe and apparently already endearing herself to her new hosts enough for them to offer more than the bare minimum.

She was out in the lane when footsteps echoed behind her.

"Talie?" Kainen's voice turned her around. "I mean it when I say no heroics."

"Sure." She shrugged, keen to get on her way.

He folded his arms as sternness fell over his face.

"You're used to making sacrifices and I get that. You've always put your sister first, your cause, the people paying your bills in case they won't anymore."

She matched his folded arms. "You think you know me?"

"Maybe not, but I see you've given up a lot for others and you don't put much value on yourself. Molly's important, but so are you."

"Why?" The discomfort writhed through her limbs and she fought the urge to cringe away. "I'm nobody special."

"Nobody is and everyone is. I used to think the same. Strapped on a court mask to hide what I thought I lacked. I had a mask, and you have this charmingly prickly attitude. Do with that what you will, but if you value the lives of normal Fae here in the citadel, well, you're one of them, aren't you? Same restrictions, same allowances. Same value. Anyway, I figured nobody had ever said it to you. Maybe I'm wrong."

Talie stepped back. "Molly has, kind of. Sammy does all the time but she's my sister, she's unstoppable."

"Yeah, I don't envy Beryl now to be honest." He smiled. "Go, do what you have to do. Bring Molly home. We'll be busy trying to find a way through Celeste's wards in the meantime."

Talie nodded and set off down the lane. She would lock away his words to be reviewed in private later, because even if he meant them, he had no idea who she really was. Her only focus now had to be getting back into the Menagerie and getting Molly out.

CHAPTER TWENTY SEVEN

MOLLY

Molly opened her eyes to dim half-light coming through the parted curtains, the first rays of dawn casting the room in shadows. She lay still until a subtle noise from outside the door caught her attention.

She didn't have anything in her room that would be useable as a weapon, unless she wanted to smother someone with a bunch of over-priced dresses, and wrapped her warding tight around her as she sat up.

The blankets brushed against her hands and she seethed as the skin twinged with pain, but the door inched open before she could figure out a suitable place to hide.

Light filtered in from the hall and her jaw dropped even as she swung her legs out of bed.

"What are you doing here?" she whispered.

She fought the urge to cry as Talie hurried across the floor toward her. Her dark hair was tucked roughly behind her ears and her face twisted with anxiety as she glanced over her shoulder.

"We need to be quick, come on."

Molly nodded. "Okay, but how do we get out? The whole place is warded."

"Never mind that, I've got it covered."

Molly tensed as Talie reached forward to grab her hand, strong fingers sliding between hers.

"But how? There are guards on the entrance, and Celeste has warded all the windows."

She squeaked as Talie's free hand landed on her hip. Deep brown eyes, darker by several shades in the pre-morning gloom, stared back at her, snaring her protests until she fell silent.

"Come on, Molly, trust me. We need to be quick."

"Wow, you never call me Molly, it must be serious." The quip slipped past her lips before she could get her senses straight. "But-"

Her words died as Talie leaned forward and pressed a kiss to her mouth, firm and brief. As Talie stepped back, Molly blinked in bewilderment.

"You need to stop doing that when I'm not ready for it," she muttered.

"Sorry." Talie didn't sound sorry at all, her voice oddly deep as she tried to keep it hushed. "I have to take the chances when I can get them."

Molly choked over a laugh. "If you say so."

"We should go," Talie insisted, but she didn't move away.

Molly nodded. "We should." She inched closer. "But you've caught me unaware a few times now and that's hardly fair."

Molly leaned forward, amused to find Talie frozen as

she kissed her softly. It wasn't like the times before, the wild fluttering of unexpected contact absent, but when Talie kissed her back she let herself sink into it. Breaking apart soon after, Molly wiped a hand over her face.

"Is this what you came here for?" she asked.

"No, of course not." Talie clenched her hand firmly and towed her toward the door. "We need to go. There's time everything after."

"How did you get in?"

Molly kept her voice low as they started down the corridor toward the main stairs and the entrance hall.

"Doesn't matter," Talie insisted. "Hurry up."

Molly stumbled behind her to the top of the stairs and almost ran into the back of her as they peered over the banister.

She frowned. "Not a single guard. Something's not right."

"Stop thinking and start moving, come on."

I'll snap back later. She is technically rescuing me right now.

Their shoes made barely a sound on the stairs, the thick carpet runner muffling their steps. One of the main entrance doors was open and Molly had no idea how Talie had managed it, whether with Phoenix's help or not, but it didn't matter. She just had to assume Talie knew how to get her through the wards or Celeste would be waking up in a fearsome mood any second.

"Do we take the beams or do I need to use my stealth gift?" she asked.

The door was mere inches away when Talie's hand

slipped from hers. She slid to a halt as a delighted laugh filled the air. Chills rippled over her skin as the door slammed shut and firelight flared around the edges of the hall. Celeste stalked toward them with a wicked glint in her eye and a vicious smile carving across her face.

"You really do make it too easy, Molinia."

Molly stepped beside Talie and lowered her voice as she raised her protection warding.

"You need to get out," she muttered. "Think of Sa- you know who. I'll distract her and you run for the window I showed you. The wards might let you out. If not, hide in the room you got me from."

"It's rude to whisper in corners," Celeste said.

Molly squared her shoulders and faced her. "I'm not in a corner."

"How witty. I had a feeling you would try to escape if given the chance, so I made sure to test that early on."

"Let her go and we can make some kind of deal then."

Celeste chuckled. "Her? What her? I don't see any her."

Molly turned her head to Talie and a gasp slipped out of her mouth. Ru grimaced back, his face pale and his eyes wide as he stood where Talie had been only moments ago.

"You- you didn't- we- oh orbs."

Molly pressed a hand to her mouth, mortification curdling in her stomach and bubbling up her throat. She swallowed hard as the shame burned across her skin.

He called me Molly, not Princess, I should have known. He didn't ask if I was okay either. Talie would have asked.

"As you can see, Molinia, I have complete dominion over what happens here."

Molly couldn't bring herself to even look Ru's way. He'd stolen her first proper kiss with Talie, or what she'd thought was her first. He'd joined in with Celeste's mind-trickery. A tiny part of her mind, the logical part, knew that even if he was doing it by choice, the alternative was refusing and that wasn't a safe option. She faced Celeste instead and tamped down on her sunlight gift with all her might as it fought to break free.

"Sure." She shrugged. "While you have the support of the nobles, it's probably not that hard to play cruel parlour tricks on me."

"You'll understand in time."

"Okay."

Celeste frowned. "You will. I couldn't risk you leaving and letting your friends hide you from me, not when we have so much to accomplish."

"Okay."

"That is not a full sentence."

"Okay, it's not. Are you done tormenting me?"

Celeste's nostrils flared, but she gave no other sign of irritation.

"For now."

Molly nodded and walked toward the stairs. As she started up, one hand braced on the banister to steady her limbs shaking from pure fury, she let her voice float back down.

"Okay."

She half expected Celeste to storm after her, but nobody stopped her as she climbed the stairs and walked back to her room. She shut the door behind her, the urge to cry burning her eyes.

Nobody saw. It's not even anything to be embarrassed about. I like Talie and I thought it was her.

It didn't lessen the discomfort inside any, but she would repeat it over and over until the horrible feeling passed.

She flinched as the door swung open.

"She made me do it, you have to believe me."

Ru stood in the doorway with his hands pressed to the frame and his eyes still wild.

"Did she compel you?" she asked. "Who did she threaten to kill if you didn't obey?"

She couldn't calm her bitter tone, the fury she couldn't unleash on Celeste lashing at him instead.

"No, but she's furious. She knows I'm on your side and I couldn't stand seeing her hurt you."

Molly scoffed and stormed toward him.

"She made you kiss me?"

He clenched his eyes shut for a moment, his face twisted in agony.

"No, but you've made it clear how you feel and I knew you'd never let me as me. Then you kissed me and I just… didn't stop you."

"That's not okay!" Her voice could have shattered glass. "You can't take advantage of me like that."

"I know, I just… I shouldn't have, but Molly you need to understand she's going to keep punishing you and using me to do it."

"Can you get outside?" she demanded.

"Of course not. You think she's going to let me walk out of here now? Only paid servants can come and go, and every way in or out is enchanted to do a glamour lift on everyone trying to leave."

She bit her lip. It would stop anyone she knew sneaking in under a glamour, assuming they did ever decide to come for her, and she couldn't imagine Beryl or any of the others posing as a servant just to get inside.

Talie would but I don't want her here. At least she and Sammy are safe.

"I can't forgive this," she said.

Ru pushed away from the door, both hands threading through his hair.

"I got carried away with the kiss, and I'm not sorry I did. I am sorry I have to be part of this though, part of her games. I'm doing everything I can to convince her to go easy on you but that's just made things worse."

"Clearly."

He sighed. "Can't you just try and see where she's coming from?"

Molly stared at him for several seconds, astonishment holding her captive. She had two choices, she realised. She could let her sunlight gift have free rein and potentially burn him and possibly the entire Menagerie to the ground, assuming it was that strong inside her, or she could take the moral high ground.

Fighting every desire roiling inside her, she took a deep breath and slammed the door in his face.

After a moment of silence, the key scratched sadly in the lock, leaving her with her embarrassment and the frightening realisation that she really was all alone.

CHAPTER TWENTY EIGHT

MOLLY

Molly watched daylight dawn from her hand hours after the altercation with Ru. She focused on practicing her sunshine gift to block out the sickening waves of fury and mortification that kept rising. Nobody had brought her breakfast, no doubt Celeste's attempt to further punish her, and she'd tried the door but it was still locked.

Kainen's words from when he'd taught her about controlling her compulsion gift were a gift all of their own, and she recognised what others might not, that both her sunshine and compulsion were controlled by the same process of keeping intentions specific. She could illuminate her body and manage to get the glow vaguely isolated to an arm or a leg if she really tried, but without risking using emotion to power it, she had to rely on mental control, which eventually gave her a needling headache behind the eyes.

The key sounded at the door and Molly breathed in deep, focusing on letting her glow dim back inside her skin until it was merely a gentle hum of warmth wrapping around her bones.

Sat on the bed with her wrists balanced on her knees, she left her hands palm up for all to see, the reddened skin still smarting from Celeste's icy torture. She had no way of showing the mental torture Celeste had given her the night before, but she wouldn't let them see they got to her.

The door swung open a second later to reveal a ridiculous amount of fabric in various colours, the pile teetering with the hint of booted feet peeking out from underneath.

Knowing Celeste wouldn't be seen dead in grubby boots, Molly swung herself off the bed and hurried forward.

"Should I take some of those?" she asked.

A muffled grunt echoed from the pile as it wobbled into the room.

"No need, Princess, although I may have accidentally eaten part of one of your sleeves."

Molly blinked, realisation settling. "Oh orbs, those are all outfits for me?"

The pile flopped unceremoniously onto the bed, revealing Lia behind them. A vague moment of embarrassment filled Molly's head as she remembered Lia having to help her up to bed after the nobles dinner, but the whole thing was a blur and she couldn't remember much, other than a lot of water.

"Yes, the finest gowns from the finest seamstresses in all the citadel."

"I don't suppose I can get you to take them back?" Molly groaned.

"No, that would not end well. I'll just hang them up in the closet for you, and you can pick your favourite. You also have a visitor."

Lia's smile faded as she nodded to the door. Ru stood leaning against the frame, arms folded across his chest and a painfully familiar smile on his face, as if his treachery in the early hours hadn't happened.

"You will have to concede to dressing like a noble now," he said. "You're royalty, Molly, whether you like it or not. The sooner you accept this and try to understand, the sooner Celeste will relax into giving you more freedom."

He was her enemy as Celeste was her enemy now and she plastered a fake smile on her face, letting the irritation fill her with venom.

"There is no freedom from her. You of all people should recognise that. Slaving after her like a puppy to a master, except you're doing it willingly. Or was the emotional manipulation and sexual assault last night by choice after all?"

Ru flinched. "It was just a kiss, Molly. I didn't have a choice, you know that."

"I don't though, do I? I'll never trust you again, ever."

"At least try one of the dresses on. I managed to convince her not to have Fae here at dawn doing your hair, so at least give way on this one tiny thing."

Molly bit down on her retort. The dress was important to him, which meant it was a specific demand from Celeste. He was being used to mould her into suitable fashion so that Celeste didn't have to waste time punishing her again.

She didn't want to admit defeat so early, but angering Celeste outright clearly wasn't working for her.

She glanced at Lia, who was busy sorting dresses into piles on the bed with a frown on her face.

"Any dresses in there with pockets?" she asked.

Lia paused to assess the chaos. "You know, I think there might be. Hang on."

"Bonus points if you can find one that looks like battle armour, or fighting leathers."

Ru groaned. "I'm warning you because I care about you, Molly, even if you don't believe it. Don't assume you can beat her. She's stronger than anyone can guess."

Because she's been siphoning from the well of power the artificers mentioned? Molly bit her lip. *If I play along, get free reign of the Menagerie, I can find out more by stealth than I can by interrogating nobles to piss Celeste off.*

Lia resurfaced from the pile with a triumphant grin.

"So dark the purple looks black, staggered skirts for ease of movement, pockets for daggers, and a bit of golden sparkle to dazzle."

Molly smiled. The dress Lia held up was exactly what she needed. Dressy enough to pass for nobility but with just enough sharp edges and darkness to give wicked queen vibes from the ancient human tales.

"It's perfect."

She flicked a dismissive glance at Ru. If he wanted her to play princess, she would give him the full experience.

"You can go then. I doubt anyone wants you hanging

around while I change, least of all your mistress. Doubt whatever noble she plans on eventually selling me off in marriage to wants others looking at their future pet."

Ru's face contorted, with pain or rage she couldn't tell as her door slammed behind him.

Refusing to feel any sliver of pity for him, Molly eyed Lia next.

"I can dress myself," she said. "I don't know if this whole royal thing requires me to have a maid or if you've just pulled the short straw, but it's fine."

Lia grinned. "As you say, Princess. I'll get the rest of these hung away."

She gathered up the rest of the dresses with no care whatsoever, and Molly smiled. If Celeste insisted on her having a maid at some point, choosing would be easy.

As Lia disappeared with the huge pile into the closet, Molly hurried out of her jeans and sweatshirt, dropping them on the floor and stepping into the dress. She pulled the front up and hugged it to her chest, baffled.

"It's got strings and stuff," she called out.

Lia reappeared. "Right, and?"

"What am I supposed to do with them? They're at the back. It's like a corset thing."

"Oh. Um… right, hang on."

Molly bit her lip as Lia walked behind her and started tugging at the strings with brisk hands.

"Lace it up, not unlacing it!" Molly squeaked.

"Right, right, got it. So this thingy goes through this bit, then that goes over there," Lia muttered. "Breathe out."

Molly breathed in then out, squeaking a strangled noise

as Lia cinched the strings tight.

"Thanks, now I can't breathe at all," she muttered.

Lia chuckled. "I think that's supposed to mean it's working. Let's get a look at you."

Molly lowered her arms and twisted to face her. She couldn't remember the last time she bared her shoulders, probably the last time she had to wear a dress.

"Is it okay?" she asked.

"Looks good," Lia grunted. "I'd give you a dagger if I had one to hide in those many pockets, but I don't have one on me. No metal allowed past the boundary since you arrived. Everyone's checked."

"I can protect myself if I need to."

She wasn't entirely sure about that, not against Celeste, and Lia didn't look too convinced either. But the dress was beautiful, so she gave the skirts a little swish with her hips and eyed the door.

"Any idea when they're coming to get me?" she asked. "Or is this some other punishment to make me sit in a dress all day for nothing?"

Lia shrugged. "Not a clue, Princess. Your young man there is the one issuing orders."

"He's not my anything, not anymore." She shoved her feet into matching slipper-shoes complete with sequins. "Might as well be dead to me."

"As you say. It might be a while though. There was a huge commotion going on downstairs earlier, something about an escape from the big doors, or one of them was left open, something like that."

Molly froze. "Big doors?"

"Yes, you know, the ones that sit at the far end of the main entrance hall, the ones nobody's allowed to go down. Got all sorts of guards on it and they say it's like a labyrinth on the other side."

Lia started fussing with Molly's bed, fluffing pillows and straightening her sheets, unaware that she'd set Molly's mind thundering.

That's where Talie went when the resistance stormed the Menagerie. I never even asked her what she saw down there, too busy storming off, then I wanted to protect her. But it must be where the fairies are being kept, or where that well of power is, or both.

She smoothed her hands down the dress, eying her normal clothes still on the floor.

"I don't suppose there's anything useful in that closet, like not dresses? Even a pant suit might do," she asked.

Lia frowned. "Didn't see any. Perhaps if you play nice with your mother awhile, she'll let you have some."

"Yeah, great. Eternal capitulation with added side of servitude in exchange for some proper pants."

"I'll have those washed either way." Lia bent down to pick up Molly's clothes. "The laundry might agree not to shred them."

"No! Leave them. They're fine."

Lia arched her brow. "If you like, Princess. At least fold them and put them somewhere out of sight then. The entire place is warded against people going in and out, other than through the main doors where servants have to announce themselves, so if you're planning on escaping you might not want to try doing it in a dress. Then again, what do I know?"

Molly smiled. Whether Lia was another of Celeste's minions sent in to gain her confidence and eventually get her onside, or simply someone trying to get through her day without problems, she made the depressing situation that little bit sunnier.

Lia took a step toward the door but her gaze flicked down to Molly's hands.

"I'm trying to get you that *liquin* like I said," she murmured. "It's taking a bit of trading for though."

"Don't get into trouble for me. I'll manage."

Lia glanced back as she pulled the door open.

"As you say, Princess. I have no doubt."

That simple statement warmed Molly's chest. As the door closed, her glow broke free, filtering over her skin and illuminating the golden strands on the dress until prisms of light glinted across the room.

Dress or no dress, it was an ideal time to use her stealth gift, mainly because Lia hadn't locked the door behind her.

She filled the dress's pockets with her paperclip pick and her privy pouch and checked the room for anything else that might be of use. Celeste had given her stationery but no sign of a letter opener that might double as a dagger. Short of strolling through the corridors with a lamp to batter people with, she was down to charm and sneakiness alone.

She pulled her stealth gift to the fore and checked the mirror to make sure she was little more than a faint outline. With a deep breath, she strode toward the door, determined to get downstairs and hopefully through the internal doors to the fairies before her gift tired.

She swept along the corridor and down the stairs. Several people in uniforms were moving about but none of them glanced her way as she crossed the entrance hall toward the towering black doors, both closed and flanked by guards.

Without any way of opening the door unnoticed, she debated whether to use charm to get herself in, or compulsion. As she drew closer, both guards bowed their heads. She whirled around, expecting to see Celeste, but the hall was still empty behind her.

"Anything we can help you with, Princess?" one guard asked, her tone wary.

Molly grimaced. "You can see me?"

"Er… yes?"

She's made the guards immune to my stealth gift as well. I bet she put conditions on it that she never told me about.

"Okay, just testing something." She sighed. "Thanks."

Both guards bowed their heads to her again as she walked away, her heart in her ridiculously slippered feet. She could compel them perhaps to let her inside, but then they would probably tell Celeste, or be immune to her compulsions by now. If what Lia said about the halls beyond the door being labyrinthine was true, then she couldn't risk getting lost either.

She walked back up to her room in time to see Lia going in.

Orbs, she's going to realise she didn't lock the door.

Molly hurried along the corridor and swept into the

room. Lia whirled around, a hand raised in front of her as if to defend from an attack.

"It's only me," Molly said. She closed the door behind her. "I won't tell if you don't."

Lia's lips twitched. "The mistress won't like you sneaking out, but as you say, I won't tell if you don't."

Molly tensed as Lia came closer.

"I have the *liquin* for your burns," she whispered. "I'll leave it with all the clothes where you'll find it."

"What's the trade?"

Lia frowned. "No trade. Just take a quick sip of the stuff and the pain will fade."

"A sip?" Molly took a step back. "No offense, but I'm not going to be drinking some unknown liquid. I take it Celeste put you up to this? Befriend me and get me to do something dim, like she did with the wine at dinner, and with Ru this morning?"

"I don't know about that, but the last thing I want to do is harm you."

She's Fae so she can't lie.

Molly folded her arms across her chest.

"Why? Why would you risk helping me?"

Lia started toward the walk-in clothes room.

"The Menagerie targeted my family and hurt people I love," she said. "I can't do much, but I'll help you however I can."

Molly bit her lip. She had one option and she really didn't want to resort to it, but she needed to know if she could trust Lia or not. She let her compulsion gift ebb forward.

"Do you-"

The door swung open before she could finish and bashed against the wall. Molly flinched but Lia jumped too, a small vial dropping from her hand onto the wooden floorboards of the clothes room.

Molly grimaced at the sound of breaking glass and turned her fury toward the door. Her pulse pounded as she glowered at Ru, not least because he'd stopped her before she could compel Lia to tell her whether the *liquin* was legitimate and if she could trust her word.

Ru saw the mess as Lia whipped off her apron to clean it.

"Don't be so careless," he snapped. "Clean up and go, and make sure there's no leftover glass for the princess to cut herself on. What was it?"

Lia's expression shuttered, the fleeting flash of hatred barely noticeable. Molly saw it though, felt it even, and turned on him.

"Leave her alone. Is this your new ego-trip? Got bored of tormenting me so now you're barking at people just trying to do their job?"

Ru scowled. "Your mother is coming to see you soon. It'll put her in a good mood to see you in suitable clothes, but please try to be considerate to her, if only for your sake."

"I don't recognise myself as having any mother," she retorted. "I don't need your tinpot advice either, considering where it's got me so far."

She breathed a tiny sigh of relief as Ru pulled the door shut and left without a word, his sour mood disappearing with him. Molly wiped a hand over her face and seethed through her teeth at the sting still in her hands.

"Thank you, Princess." Lia approached with her apron bundled up in her arms. "I can't let you out, but I would if there was a way." She veered close so fast Molly didn't even have time to flinch. "All I can do is promise you there will be something that will help you under the plant pot outside your mother's office."

Molly froze. "What is it?"

"Something that will help. I should go."

Molly chased Lia to the door, almost tripping over in her slippers.

"Are you part of the resistance?" she whispered.

Lia laughed sadly with her hand already on the door handle.

"I'm on the side of people I love."

Molly went to ask again but Lia opened the door and they both stumbled back as Celeste swept in. Without another look, Lia rushed out and shut the door.

"Ru has convinced me that I may have started our relationship the wrong way," Celeste announced.

Molly stayed by the door, conscious that it was still open as Celeste moved toward the fireplace and started fussing with things on the mantel.

"Didn't realise you were in a relationship with him. Congratulations."

Celeste sighed. "That humour may work on some of the nobles but I find it tiresome. I understand this isn't what you want, but perhaps we can reach a compromise. Ru tells me you like working with your hands, so how about we set you up a workshop of sorts here in the Menagerie?"

Molly stared. "What?"

"A workshop. Perhaps some people to work alongside you. We could have some artificers from the guild collaborate on your projects even."

Don't ask how many are still alive. Don't ask. Don't do it.

"You can't bribe me with a new workshop. I like my old one fine."

"Well I'd offer to bring your friends to you, but I imagine you'd see that as an attack," Celeste said. "There must be something you want. I'm not pleased at having to punish you."

Molly dropped her hand to the door handle.

"Oh, please. You already did and you'd do it again easily. You'd hurt me purely to get me to heel. Fae aren't dogs. What happened to the stolen fairies? The artificers that went missing? You think they don't matter, but they're people just like we are. You're so drenched in arrogant entitlement you use people. Phoenix was right, and he's just as dodgy as you are."

Celeste whirled around, her face shadowed with pure wrath. Molly saw her hand twitch and reinforced her own warding but something shoved against her and sent her staggering forward. She pressed a hand to the wall as Marcus strode in.

"It's time," he announced.

"Don't bother knocking then," she snapped, her gaze still fixed on Celeste. "Don't tell me I'm supposed to start calling him 'daddy' now in this sick little ode to yourself you've got going on."

Celeste took a deep breath, her fury reverting to a genteel smile as Marcus raised an eyebrow at Molly's tone.

"Perfect timing." Celeste lifted a hand toward the open door. "There are more nobles massing who've come to meet the new heir apparent. Let's go down."

"You're not going to threaten me so I don't play up this time?" Molly asked.

"Oh, I'm very much hoping you will now. These nobles need to see how I have no problem keeping anyone in line, even my own daughter."

Molly bit her lip as Celeste indicated to the door again.

She wins either way. I behave to annoy her and she gets the united front. I misbehave, she uses me to make an example.

Unable to do anything else, Molly swept out of the room.

First, I test which gifts she's immune to. Compulsion I know, and stealth I'm guessing, but charm she might not be, and she doesn't know about the sunlight.

With Marcus and Celeste flanking either side of her, and Ru waiting at the top of the stairs to the entrance hall, Molly lifted her head high and marched herself toward the next battle.

CHAPTER TWENTY NINE

MOLLY

Molly descended the stairs to the entrance hall under the gazes of countless nobles. She surveyed the crowd, her insides chilling at the sheer numbers. Several guards were dotted throughout the mix as well, and she fought to keep her hand steady on the banister.

"Welcome everyone." Celeste's voice filled the air.

Molly stopped most of the way down and turned back to find Ru inches away from her and Celeste holding court at the top of the stairs.

"For those who have not yet had the *experience* of meeting my daughter," she paused as the crowd laughed on cue. "Allow me to introduce Molinia Elverhill, heir apparent to the citadel and one day to the oak crown also."

Molly gulped as all eyes turned to her and her gut churned at the thought. She spied Lady Featherdown in the crowd but after what had happened at the dinner, she doubted she'd get any support there.

"There have been murmurings recently," Celeste continued. "We are getting reports that some errant factions plan to target Molinia and groom her to rule in my place. Now, I would hope none of those are gathered here today, but there are some loyalties that have been called into question."

Molly clung to her warding as Celeste prowled down toward her, eyes glinting with determination. She didn't struggle as Celeste placed a firm hand on her shoulder and guided her down to where the nobles formed a wide circle in the centre of the hall.

"It's time for a demonstration to ensure that nobody is under the wrong impression," Celeste announced. "Ru, would you like to do the honours? A chance for you to prove where you truly stand."

Molly bit her lip as Ru stepped beside her. He couldn't reach through her warding and his eyes widened when he tried.

"You won't be able to hold it for long," he muttered. "Let her have her fun and she'll go easy on you."

Molly straightened her shoulders and stared past him.

Celeste chuckled. "Of course, I don't expect Molinia to give in. She has our family's stubborn spirit after all."

She lifted a hand in Molly's direction and a puff of blue powder plumed from her outstretched palm. Molly held firm as it domed around her, the chill of the attack scratching at her warding and clamouring to be let through.

"Trust me, you need to let her do this," Ru insisted, his voice a mere whisper. "Orbs, Molly, I don't want to have to do this."

She didn't care what he wanted. She focused on Celeste, ready for the next attack.

A sharp scratch flickered at the periphery of her warding, a stab that had her whirling around.

Ru's hand closed around her wrist. She stared in horror as he held up a small length of metal.

"Metirin iron. It pierces wardings." He shook his head. "It'll be easier this way, honestly."

She arced her fist toward him without warning, but he'd taught her and had an arm out to block. As he twisted her around and stepped up behind her with one arm anchored around her shoulders to pin her, she glowered at the crowd of nobles, frustration and fury flowing through her limbs.

Celeste lifted her hand again and this time Molly had no chance to ward herself before the water swirled around her head.

She closed her eyes tight and held her breath, the icy water biting at her skin. The moment it sloshed away, she gasped a spluttering breath.

"It won't last if that's what you're worried about," Celeste announced. "Her face will remain as pretty as a picture, but believe me when I say the water will burn anyone else who tries me. I will not be as lenient as I have been with her."

The moment Celeste swept a warning look over the silent crowd, Molly dropped to her knees. Ru doubled over to keep his hold on her but she kicked out, a move Talie would have been proud of, or at least not mocked her for. He stumbled and his grip slid away. She rolled free and resecured her warding before clambering to her feet. Her compulsion gift leapt forward as she met Ru's gaze, hatred and hurt driving the words from her lips.

"You will never to touch me again without my consent." Her voice rang out through the hall.

Ru reached forward but his hand met her warding. Even with his stupid iron pin, the compulsion meant he wouldn't be able to grab hold of her anymore, warding or no warding.

She flinched as Celeste tutted loudly.

"Well that was silly. What difference does it make to me whether you're held or moving?"

Molly tensed as the water attacked again, a crashing wave battering her warding. She gritted her teeth and held firm against the power, each effort cutting wounds into her waning strength.

"I can do this all evening, dearest," Celeste sang.

Molly raced through her pitiful options. She could let her sunlight free, but it would show them a gift none of them knew about and Celeste would likely find a way to use it to toy with her.

The water crested away again and Molly sagged, exhausted. She couldn't use her compulsion on Celeste either and she couldn't compel a whole crowd of nobles collectively. It didn't stop her biting back.

"Well this is a delight," she announced. "I gain a mother I never knew existed and torturing me is her initiation of choice. Well, they do say we can't choose our parents."

One or two notes of awkward laughter trickled around.

Celeste smiled. "I did warn you not to test me. I even offered you anything you wanted, but you refused."

"You offered me trinkets and frivolities, nothing that matters."

"And what do you think matters?"

"Respect. Kindness. Honesty. Communication. None of which you've given me. Torturing fairies might be one thing for high-born Fae, but torturing your own daughter? Grim. I suppose that's the high-born way." She cast a glance across the crowd. "Do you all torture your children? Is this normal?"

Nobody answered but she didn't expect them to. She could see which faces were staring in anticipation and those that looked uncomfortable.

"I have splashed your face a little, let's not be dramatic."

"Oh Faerie forbid *I'm* the dramatic one. Dramatic is kidnapping Fae from other realms and bringing them into the citadel. Dramatic is torturing people for their gifts. Dramatic is being arrogant enough to assume you can steal gifts that aren't yours to take. How long before you start stealing gifts from the nobility? One wrong word, nobles, and the evil wannabe queen is going to get you."

She was ready when the water hit, stinging worse than ever before. It raged against her, infused with Celeste's fury and malice.

"Loyalty is for family, Molinia. You'll learn that before long."

Molly choked through the sting as the water receded and she faced Celeste with her eyes burning.

"Loyalty is earned. At least I found that out before I gave everything to the wrong side."

I should not have said that.

She doubled over and clutched her arms around her

middle, hoping with everything she had that Celeste hadn't understood the meaning of what she'd said.

"Tell me about this everything." Celeste's tone turned silky.

Crud.

"My loyalty lies with those who give me freedom to choose," she tried.

Celeste laughed. "Try again. There's something missing from the information we have on gift extraction, and that information came from you. It's almost like *someone* missed a vital step of the process."

"Sucks to be you then doesn't it."

Molly angled her head to scope out the stairs. She wasn't far from them. If she could get herself away with a warding, she might be able to find somewhere to hide.

It was an awful plan but the only one she had. That or fighting to the death.

"Lady Featherdown," Celeste called out. "If you'd be so kind as to assist me in getting the truth?"

Molly winced as a sour tang washed over her tongue, and she braced herself for another splash of torture.

"There was a step I left out." The words were pulled unbidden from her mouth. "The infusion is to be brewed twelve parts yew and three parts nightshade. Then swill it with oia residue, distil once and steep for three days. Then brew it one last time with two parts infusion to one part coalbane."

She slapped a hand to her mouth, but too late.

So that's what a compulsion feels like.

She searched the gathered crowd, her vision jumbling

until she found Lady Featherdown without a single ounce of regret on her face. No emotion at all.

"Coalbane, of course." Celeste chuckled. "Not easily obtained, but I know the person to get it for me. How wonderful. But what an indiscretion on your part, Molinia."

This time when the pain came, it rolled on and on in endless waves. Molly clung to the last edges of her sanity, her body splintering against the icy burn of the savage water Celeste encased her in.

She sought inside for something, anything, and found a tiny flicker of warmth.

Please, dry the water, the pain.

Her skin heated, the sunlight a softness against the savage attack of Celeste's power. She wouldn't be able to hold it for long, and she would let Celeste win because there was no hope of besting her through gifts, but she needed to make enough of a stand to make it believable.

The water fell away and Molly shuddered as heat cocooned her right to the bone. She lifted her head, revelling spitefully at the wariness in Celeste's eyes.

"What is that?" Celeste demanded.

Molly smiled. "Gifts from friends of the family. My family that is. You torture, they gift. Says everything I need to know about what side I will always be on."

She didn't see the whip of fire coming. It lashed from Celeste's hand into the side of her warding and she staggered back, her sunlight leaning toward the neighbouring heat. She fought to calm her gift, her mind spinning with the effort. As Celeste brought her arm back, ready to attack again, Molly dropped all pretence and ran.

She dodged Ru as he reached out for her, but the compulsion had him spinning away again before he could make contact.

"Catch her!" Celeste yelled.

Molly slowed as a couple of nobles moved to block her path to the stairs. Sheer panic drove her to inspiration and she slipped into stealth mode.

"What, she was just there! I saw her!"

Molly picked up speed again and shot between them. As she took the turning on the stairs, she looked back at the gaggle of guards and nobles all fighting each other to get ahead. A whip of fire slashed right through the banister as she fled up the stairs, the stench of burning wood filling the air.

Lia. Molly dashed along the landing as the crowd exploded into chatter. *She said she'd left something that would help.*

She skidded into the hallway that led to Celeste's office and stumbled to a halt beside the enormous potted plant. She ducked down, ready to heave the plant to the side, but nestled between the pot and the loose earth was what she needed.

I have to assume this is it.

She curled the small item tight in her fist and eyed the window leading out onto the beams. She couldn't get out, the wards wouldn't allow it, but she couldn't see anywhere else to hide where Celeste wouldn't find her.

"Molinia, enough." Celeste blocked her in the hallway. "You're only making the punishment worse by testing me.

I won't have you undermine my rule."

Molly let the hint of coolness in her fist anchor her.

"What now then? Keep toying and tormenting until you kill me?"

Celeste shook her head. "No, I can see what the best path through this obstinance of yours is now. You aren't swayed by treasures, but there is something you value."

Molly's insides froze. She didn't dare ask, even though she knew what was coming.

"I simply need to target what you love most." Celeste smiled. "Talie is very easy to find after all, and her sister."

A shadow appeared behind Celeste and Molly folded her arms across her chest, forcing an unconvincing scoff from her lips.

"What, and your precious Ru too?"

"If that's what's needed to make you see sense. You're angry with him, but you won't want him harmed because of you. I once said you had a stout heart, soft. How useful a thing it is now."

Molly glanced past Celeste to Ru, who stood rigid with an ashen expression.

He never truly expected Celeste to see him as expendable. She couldn't bring herself to pity him. *If I give in now though, she'll keep threatening them, or worse.*

A loud bang made her jump, and Celeste's fury turned to the now open doorway halfway along the hall. Molly clenched her fists as Lia paused in the doorway, her eyes wide.

"What are you doing here?" Celeste snapped. "Get out, before I make you regret it."

Molly caught Lia's eye.

"*Help, please,*" she mouthed.

Lia hesitated, one corner of her mouth pressed thin. Then she took a step back and closed the door again behind her.

Molly's brief flicker of hope died.

I can't expect her to do anything dangerous for me. We don't even know each other.

She faced Celeste and went for her last chance of salvaging some safety for Talie and the others.

"What about a trade then?" she asked. "You promise not to harm my friends, ever, and we can discuss the specifics of what you expect from me."

Celeste chuckled. "Now why would I need to do that when tormenting your friends will get you to cave eventually? If I have to wait for you to crack before giving in, so be it. Are you going to come willingly and accept the remainder of your punishment? Or do I need to have someone drag and chain you?"

Molly dropped her shaking hands to her sides. The punishment was inevitable and delaying it would only tire her out more.

There's no hope of escaping now. If they were coming for me, they would have done it already.

"There's no point sullying our dignity either of us," she said.

Celeste stepped aside as Molly walked past her. She wanted to stride with her head high but it didn't matter what show she put on, not really. She was about to suffer regardless.

The nobles were silent as she walked down the stairs, conscious of Celeste right beside her. She couldn't bring herself to look at Ru.

She let her gifts settle inside her, willing them to calm. If she was lucky, whatever pain came her way would be enough to render her unconscious until Celeste was done toying with her.

"Do you want me standing, sitting or slumped on the floor?" she asked.

"However you wish, dearest. I think I'm going to give you a taste of the pain your friends will feel."

Molly remained standing and closed her eyes, arms braced ready to catch herself when she inevitably fell. Kneeling would have been more sensible, but she would die before kneeling for her mother.

There was no warning. Her head split first, a buzzing pressure that became a fireball of agony. It spread down her neck, her back and through her limbs. She barely felt the thud of the hard floor against her knees and hands a second later. Through the haze, she had the faintest sense that Celeste had stopped but the pain remained, a simmering echo ready to be ignited again. She kept her eyes closed.

Talie. The others will keep her safe.

"She's hurting too much."

Ru's voice crashed through her ears and she lifted her head with great effort, her lips pinned tight to keep the wave of nausea from flowing out.

"She's had enough!"

She opened her eyes as Ru shouted again, in time to see

Celeste's furious face. With an irritated flick of her hand, Celeste sent him flying across the room. Nobles stumbled out of the way as he sailed past them and thudded against the wall.

Molly's heart lurched and sickness bubbled up her throat as Ru tried to get up but fell back down again. She blinked several times to clear her vision, just enough to see his chest heaving.

"Let that be a lesson," Celeste announced. "Molinia belongs to me. I will punish and reward as I see fit, and you'd all do well to remember it."

As Celeste turned toward the crowd, Molly lifted her fist to her lips and swiped her thumb over the orb hidden there.

"Molly?" The voice that answered was familiar, painfully so. "What's going on?"

CHAPTER THIRTY

TALIE

Talie raced through the lanes, ignoring all the people staring at her dash past. She hadn't thought to drop her glamour either, so it hardly matter, but her mind was in chaos as she staggered down Molly's alleyway and burst into Beryl and Harvey's home without knocking.

Everyone stared, Beryl, Harvey and also Kainen. He stood with a blonde woman Talie didn't recognise, all of them frowning at her.

"This is Reyan, my fiancé," he announced. "Talie is a friend of Molly's. I almost forgot what you looked like."

Talie glanced down at her Lia glamour and waved a hand down her front to vanish the maid uniform and the rest of the glamour with it. She couldn't get the image of Molly's terrified face out of her head, begging her to get help.

"Molly's in trouble, serious trouble," she panted. "Out of her hands kind of trouble."

"That's why we sent you in," Beryl said bluntly.

Kainen flicked a glare at her before softening his

expression in Talie's direction.

"We've already said we can't interfere. Is it life or death?" he asked.

Talie nodded. "Celeste has shut the entire citadel down, they were saying it in the kitchens. Nobody goes in now, not even servants, and apparently only a member of Celeste's blood family can get through the wards now."

"That complicates things," Kainen said. "Her blood can't get into the citadel without invitation, otherwise they break the covenant."

Reyan shook her head. "That's not exactly it. The covenant says royalty can't come in without invitation, nothing about bloodlines."

"Okay but even if someone invited royalty here, only her blood family can get into the Menagerie now, so even if we had enough help to go in with, we can't."

Talie slammed a hand against the doorframe, ignoring Aurora's resounding squawk. She bit her lip as Sammy came out with baby Aurora, but she couldn't wait around for pleasantries.

"It's now or never," she insisted. "Celeste is torturing her, mind and body. I'll go to Phoenix if I have to, I'll beg him, I'll trade, I don't know what but I will."

"Talie, Molly is strong," Kainen insisted gently.

"Yeah, stronger now you've given her the ability to potentially roast the entire realm," Beryl muttered.

Reyan twisted to face him. "What did you do."

It wasn't a question, but a demand, one that sent a look of sheepish amusement across Kainen's face.

"I might have given her a less-advised gift, but it was

on Demi's say so. Sort of. I took liberal interpretation of a few bits."

"What gift?"

"He gifted her sunlight," Beryl jumped in more than willingly.

Talie stared in horror as Reyan whacked Kainen with what looked like a rolled up piece of paper. Sammy only rolled her eyes and gave Talie a sympathetic look as she retreated back into the tiny bedroom.

"You. Gifted. Her. Sunshine?!" The words were punctuated by hits to his shoulder with the paper she was holding. "*What did we talk about!* Do you know how dangerous that is!"

Much like Kainen, Talie was wise enough to recognise those weren't actual questions needing answering.

"Screw it, I'm finding a way in," Harvey said.

"No you are not," Beryl insisted. "We've been told to stay put."

"Since when did you start following orders?"

Beryl might have snapped back, but two men materialised in the corner of the room before she could and almost knocked over half the kitchen. Talie didn't recognise the man that vanished again immediately, but the one that remained needed no introduction. Even Fae in the citadel would have recognised the king consort of Faerie, his presence no less imposing for the hoodie and jeans he was wearing.

Flaming wings framed his body and Talie could see the hint of resemblance to Molly now. Something about the set of the turquoise eyes or the determined jaw. While Molly's hair was a darker blonde, almost brown out of the light, they had similar messy waves.

"This is rash," Beryl told him, no hint of propriety in her voice whatsoever. "Does Demi know you're here, Taz?"

"I am not at liberty to divulge such information," the king consort retorted.

"So no."

"Technically, I do have my own authority," he grumbled. "What's going on?"

"Talie?" Kainen prompted.

The king consort's gaze flicked her way, as if he knew exactly who she was. Talie gulped, not sure if she was more concerned about his status as a royal or his existence as Molly's actual family.

"Molly's stuck in the Menagerie and Celeste is torturing her, physically and mentally," she explained, then realising what she was dealing with, "um, your majesty."

"Call me Taz, everyone else does. When you say torturing…"

"She burned her hands with ice, and she's got some kind of mind twisting going on. She's been trying to drown her, and she threatened me and others to get Molly to do what she wants. She's going to torture her now in front of the nobles to make a point."

Talie wiped a hand over her face, her insides tearing raw.

"Please, I'll do anything," she begged. "Pledge to some court or give eternal servitude, whatever you want. Just save her!"

Taz exchanged a knowing look with Kainen.

"That's it, I'm going in." He unzipped his hoodie.

Kainen was already halfway to the door.

"Don't be dim," Reyan snapped. "Demi would kill you. Then us."

Taz rolled his eyes. "I'm already dead when she hears what I've done."

"Oh orbs alive. What have you done?"

"I made the deal." He shrugged. "Everyone else was faffing around and this is a family matter. Might as well throw my own punch in."

Reyan folded her arms, eyes flashing with fury.

"You shouldn't even be here as it is! As for the deal, did you even figure out all the loopholes?"

Talie had no clue what deal they were talking about but she watched them squabble, high-brow lords and royals arguing like...

Like a family. No hierarchy, no titles, just bickering.

The king consort's wings splayed wide as Kainen gathered shadows around himself.

"Never mind the loopholes," Taz insisted.

Kainen nodded. "Yeah, Taz is Celeste's blood, no offense, so he can go through the wards and get Molly."

"Don't even think about it either of you," Reyan growled. "How are you even here anyway, Taz? You're breaking the covenant."

Talie opened her mouth to say something that would hurry them along, what she had no idea, but a flare of heat against her leg sent her hand flying to her pocket.

Only one person would be calling her orb because

Sammy was already with them.

She held it up, her insides icy as a garbled image flared into monochrome life and grabbed everyone's attention.

"Molly, what's going on?" she demanded.

A shuddering breath and what sounded like rushing air, or water, but no words followed.

"Molly, for orbs sake, talk to me."

"Talie? You... Lia said... she's almost destroyed me. I've held on as long as I can but my warding's shot. I might have said, some stuff. Made her really mad." Molly choked for several seconds. "You need to get everyone out. Please, you and Sammy, go to the house, Beryl's house, by the workshop. Hide there. Someone will come eventually, they'll get you out. Tell them I told you to."

"Okay, just hold your warding for me." Talie looked around the room for something, anything.

She had no hope of beating Celeste herself, but desperation gnawed at her insides as the king consort strode out of the room and off down the lane.

"Sorry," Molly whispered, the sound obscenely loud in the roaring silence. "Get you and Sammy out, promise me."

"Just hold on! Keep your warding up and play for time."

Before she could scream anything else or get her legs to start running, the orb-cast went dead.

CHAPTER THIRTY ONE

MOLLY

Molly stayed crouched over with her knees tucked into her chest. As Celeste hit her with another horrific onslaught of agony, she kept the cool surface of the orb welded to her ear.

"Just hold on." Talie's voice sounded distant, like a dream. "Keep your warding up and play for time."

Nobody's coming. Nobody can get inside.

A scream wrenched itself from her mouth. Her gifts spasmed inside her, roiling against the attack, but she couldn't ward, couldn't do anything other than feel and suffer.

"Nobody can get in, Molinia," Celeste crowed, her voice a focal point in the darkness. "Nobody's coming to save you. Yield, and I will stop. Vow to serve me, and I will reward you."

Never. I'll die first.

It was inevitable, she realised. Even if she tricked Celeste into eventually believing they were on the same side, she wouldn't ever be able to leave. Celeste would never trust her, and Talie was always going to be a target. But the nobles, they would talk long after today was over. Nobility flocked to the strongest leader, and while Celeste had power, she had lost control in front of them.

As the waves of pain subsided, she clung to the orb. Talie's voice was gone and she couldn't even be sure she hadn't imagined it, but it gave her courage all the same.

If I'm going down, I'll make her proud doing it.

Her mind swayed and clanged, sense warring with disorientation. She wanted to sleep. No pain in sleep. She opened her eyes with great effort, the light dazzling enough to hurt. She struggled to her feet, lurching about like a newborn animal.

Another wave of pain sent her to her knees again, the impact nothing compared to the agony Celeste drowned her in. It dissipated quicker than she expected, short enough that she could lift her head at the sound of yelling.

Her gaze wavered then focused on Celeste, and a flash of white and green haloing her head.

Not haloing. Attacking.

As Aurora took flight and swerved back round for another shot, her talons ready and feral cawing flying from her beak, Molly sought for her warding and pieced it around her limb by limb. It wouldn't hold for more than a second now against Celeste, but she would go out fighting like Talie taught her.

With her warding as secure as she could manage, she whistled a single note. Aurora heard it and backed off, her wings catching the light as she soared upward.

Molly inched toward Celeste, who had the gall to laugh

despite now bearing deep scratches and lines of blood all over her face.

"You're strong, I'll give you that, but foolish. What do you possibly think you can do to me in that state? Unless you have an entire army of birds like that one, you have nothing you can best me with."

Molly kept going, step after agonising step. A few feet away, she realised Celeste wasn't warding herself. She would only get one shot.

Celeste sighed. "Perhaps we should conclude our little performance." Molly swung her leg back. "I think your humiliation has been punishment enough, and I don't want to permanently damage you."

Her eyes widened as Molly's heel connected with her kneecap. As Celeste hunched forward with a huff of surprise, Molly staggered back. Nowhere to run, but the nobles were murmuring between themselves now, several concerned faces in the mix, including Ru's as he struggled through them to reach her.

Celeste reared up, her cheeks pink and her eyes flashing stormy.

With a savage shove, she sent Molly flying to the floor. Molly winced as her shoulders hit first, her head jolting. Pain radiated down her neck but it was a fleeting thing, nothing like Celeste's vindictive punishment.

"I'm disappointed," Celeste snapped. "Perhaps I have been too lenient. Some time in one of the cells will get you to heel."

Celeste loomed over her and Molly tensed inside her warding, fear freezing her down to the bone as a huge bang shattered her ears. Celeste veered out of sight and Molly lifted her head, the aches like shards of ice that stabbed through her neck and shoulders. She blinked through the haze of pain as a wave of icy blue light pulsated through the room, crackling with untameable energy to all except the one wielding it.

Celeste gasped and took a step back.

"How can you be in here?" she seethed. "It's impossible for you to get in without breaking the covenant, and I sure as hell didn't invite you."

The man framed in the doorway caught Molly's eye and winked at her, then grinned at Celeste.

"Royalty can't get in without invitation, that's true."

"So how?" she snarled.

"I abdicated."

Then the previously king consort of Faerie released a blast of fire from his flared wings that set the room ablaze.

CHAPTER THIRTY TWO

TALIE

"I still don't think this is a good idea," Talie muttered.

She glanced sideways at Kainen, who grimaced back as they crept along the beam that led to Molly's window entrance to the Menagerie.

They'd caught up with the king consort halfway along the main lane, and Talie didn't bother questioning how he knew where to go. All she knew was that he could get past Celeste's wards, and that was all that mattered.

"I know, but Taz said that Phoenix said that you were the best fit for this," Kainen replied. "That's the plan. He gets Molly, we get as much information and save as many fairies as we can."

Talie pressed one hand to the wall as she shuffled toward the window.

"Once we're in, what's the plan though?" she asked. "How is he planning to get Molly away from her?"

She didn't dare say Celeste's name so close to the Menagerie, just in case. The window loomed in front of them as Kainen sighed loudly.

"Taz is king consort of Faerie. Do you really think he's not one of the most powerful Fae there is by now? Let him worry about Molly. Our job is to go down to the core and free as many fairies as we can, and anyone else down there."

Talie's heart chilled as the memory of the tortured people stuck behind the black doors filled her head. She dodged to the other side of the window and pressed her back to the wall. The wards would still keep them out, but apparently his mighty highness was going to fix that for them as well.

"As long as he definitely is going in for her and not for some family feud or some kind of glory," she muttered.

Kainen's brown eyes darkened, a hint of shadow coiling in the depths.

"You don't know him at all then. Molly's family to all of us, even if it's not technically by blood for some. I'm not leaving here without her and Taz won't either, but we have to give the fairies a fair shot at escaping."

Talie gave him a grudging nod.

"Fair. How do we do this then? It's like a labyrinth and we don't have a map, or enough people, or a safe route out."

"Let me worry about that. I promise I'll do everything I can to keep you safe."

She snorted. "I can keep myself safe. If you've got something fancy up your sleeve then fine, but if I see Molly and nobody's helping her, I'm going for it."

"Fair," Kainen echoed with a smile. "I'd do the same for people I love."

Love. Talie shuddered.

Love was complicated. Serious. Molly likely saw her as a friend, or perhaps not even that anymore, but love?

The air shivered beside Kainen and she drew her protection warding tighter around her. Then her jaw dropped as the previously empty space beside Kainen was filled by a burly man with messy sandy hair, the same one who'd arrived briefly with the king consort before.

"Good to go?" Kainen asked.

The man nodded. "Do we know how to get through to the fairies?"

"That's Talie's area." He waved a hand in her direction. "Talie, Milo, Milo, Talie."

Milo nodded to her. "Hello. The wards should be broken now, but no telling how long for."

That was all Talie needed. She swung her foot slowly toward the open window to test the wards. When her foot sailed straight through with no resistance or rebound, her heart lifted. She pushed inside and dropped onto the carpet.

The corridor was empty but loud crashes echoed from the stairs. Talie led them through a side door instead, even as her heart tore at her to go the other way, to follow the noise and find Molly. Celeste would likely be somewhere near the source of the noise, or causing it, which meant Molly would be too.

Assuming she's still alive.

She broke into a jog along the servant's corridor and down the narrow flight of stairs that led to the laundry and the kitchens.

"How do we get past any guards?" she asked. "I can

fight, but not sure if lords generally know how to."

Kainen huffed. "Oh please. I have been learning combat since I was able to hold a sword. I could likely best anyone here in a fight."

"Your ego definitely could," Milo muttered.

He sounded out of breath and Talie shoved aside the adrenalin-fuelled urge to laugh as she stopped by the service corridor.

"There'll be servants on the other side," she said.

Kainen shrugged. "I'll compel those I need to and shadow us from the rest."

"And the metirin iron?" She couldn't remember if she'd told them that bit yet. "The cell locks are made of it."

"Ah yes, the Fae failsafe." Kainen rolled his eyes. "Will you please believe me when I say we have it covered?"

Talie didn't believe him, not entirely, but he couldn't lie. She had to hope he was talking from experience rather than lordly arrogance.

As she pushed open the door, a spark of inspiration hit. She waved a hand down her front and strode into the service corridor as Lia. Several Fae looked up as she walked past with the cacophonous banging shaking the walls from the entrance hall on the other side.

"It's this way," she announced, glancing over her shoulder at Kainen. "I'm sure the mistress has her reasons."

She kept the word-tangling vague, because of course Celeste would have her reasons but she never stated what for. Several servants scurried past but nobody stopped them.

"The guards on the doors will be a different matter," she murmured.

As they reached the end of the serving corridor, and the door which would lead them to the far end of the entrance hall, she almost didn't want to go further.

"No need to worry." Milo clamped a hand on Kainen's shoulder. "I can sense where we need to go."

Kainen grinned. "Wait here Talie, and when Milo comes back, trust him."

"What?"

Before she could step forward and demand he explain, the air wavered around them and in a flash of purple-grey, they vanished.

They can realm-skip. Without a skip-way.

She hadn't even considered that was how the king consort had ended up inside the citadel in the first place, but now it was the obvious answer. She bit her lip as Milo reappeared beside her.

"Hand or arm?" he asked, his tone turning shy.

"Huh?"

"I need to hold onto you to take you through the nether."

"Oh." Talie grimaced. "Arm then, I guess."

She tensed as Milo wrapped a sturdy hand around her upper arm and the corridor blurred. She waited for some kind of jolt or a sensation of 'things' unravelling, but even before she could wrap her head around the fact she was being realm-skipped, the swirl of nether dissipated and she recognised the firelit hall settling around them.

"Wow." She stared at the two guards unconscious and slumped against the wall as Kainen flexed his knuckles and seethed through his teeth. "Double wow."

He grinned and preened a hand over his hair.

"I do try."

"I'm sure she meant the realm-skipping," Milo snapped back. "Where to now?"

Talie ignored them both. They would follow her, and the doors back to the entrance hall deadened most of the sounds on the other side. Until she got the job done, she had no idea if Molly was okay or not.

"This way."

She dropped her glamour to conserve her strength and hurried toward the nearest cell, the one the woman had been in before. With her heart pounding, she peered through the bars.

The cell lay empty.

"Oh." She moved to the man's next. Also empty.

"There were two here, but they're gone." She pressed a hand to her throat, the urge to scream rising.

"Okay. You said you can fight?" Kainen asked. She nodded. "Then you're defence while I get these doors open. We won't be able to do all of them, but we take as many as we can before they come for us."

"Take them where?" She had to ask.

"Arcanium," Milo said. "Our healers will do what they can, ask a few questions, and send them home."

Assuming they're in any fit state to go home again.

Talie followed as Kainen moved to another door and looked inside.

"Hello," he said, his tone turning soft with charm. "We're going to get you out, okay? Don't attack or we'll have to subdue you."

He walked inside and Talie turned her back to the wall beside the door to keep watch. Kainen reappeared with a young man, barely any older than Talie if she had to guess. His eyes were wide and wild with untold horrors lurking in the depths, his lips moving over silent words.

Milo settled a hand on the man's shoulder and vanished with him.

"They will be safe now, won't they?" she asked.

Kainen was already off toward the next door.

"If you're asking are we going to torment them to get information, no, we're not." His tone turned fierce.

She shrugged. "I don't know you, so I have to check."

He pressed a hand to the next door.

"Hello. We're going to get you out, okay? Don't attack or we'll have to subdue you."

A subtle whimper answered him as he inserted something into the lock and wiggled it about. Milo reappeared alone, just in time for the cell door to swing open. Both men entered the cell and this time Kainen reappeared alone.

"He's going to realm-skip all these people out of the citadel?" she asked.

Kainen nodded. "I forgot to tell you not to tell anyone about him, but yeah, don't tell anyone about him."

"I won't." She tensed as voices echoed from the hall. "I'll handle this, get around the bend out of sight and keep going."

She expected some gallant insistence that he couldn't possibly leave her unprotected, or perhaps some scoffing remark that he was the one in charge and he would decide what to do.

"Okay. Holler if you need help."

He hurried around the bend that led them deeper as a guard came into view from the other end.

"Hey!" The guard strode toward her. "What are you doing down here? Who are you?"

Talie's insides sank but she pulled her mind-wipe gift forward and faced him.

"There were all these noises. I came in here." She put a touch of fear into her voice, feeling like an absolute idiot. "What are you doing here?"

She wished she had compulsion or charm like Molly did, or even stealth would have done.

"That's not your concern," the guard barked.

She frowned. "What's not?"

"Huh?" He shook his head, confused. "I… what are you doing down here?"

"Are you supposed to be down here?" she countered. "There's a fight going on outside and won't the mistress want all hands ready behind her?"

She had to phrase it as a question but the guard lifted a hand to scratch his head.

"I was sent here to check everything was clear."

"There's a fight in the entrance hall," Talie repeated. "Won't the mistress want all the support she can get from her guards?"

He nodded slowly. "A fight?"

"Yes, you'd better get up there quick! I'll make sure everything is as it should be here." She waved her hand at him when he hesitated. "Go, quickly! Before you get in trouble."

He turned on his heel and hurried away. He would forget the whole thing in a minute or few. As the door to the entrance hall opened and loud sounds of combat echoed through, she wiped her arm over her clammy forehead. She was supposed to go back to Kainen and Milo, but her heart twisted at the thought of Molly so close by.

Milo can get Kainen out anyway by the look of it if things go wrong, and Kainen's an actual lord with Faerie knows how much power behind him.

She froze as someone bulldozed through the door from the entrance hall, the face and set of the shoulders infuriatingly familiar. Her blood roared and she clenched fists at her sides.

Molly had mentioned sexual assault to her when she was pretending to be Lia. She'd said all sorts of awful things that Ru had done. Now as he came to a halt a wary distance in front of her, it took all her resolve not to launch herself forward and claw at his face.

"I should have guessed you'd be lurking around," he said, his tone bitter. "Celeste made me immune to your gift as well, so don't bother trying to wipe my mind."

Talie held in the curse brewing. It made life more difficult, but if she had to fight him to get past she would, and willingly.

"I won't." She hesitated. "Is she okay? Or are you so entrenched with her mother that you don't even care about her?"

Ru grimaced. "Everything I've done is for her."

"You consorted with her mother, lied to her, grabbed her off the street, tormented her, helped her mother keep her locked up here-"

"I thought it was for her own good at the time. Everything has been for her. She's always been my main priority. She's mine. She just doesn't realise it yet."

Talie stormed toward him and her warding clashed against his with such force it almost drove her back again.

"Molly is her own person." Going up onto her tiptoes with her nose an inch from his, she glared at him. "She chooses what she wants, and how, where and when. Beyond that, she's *mine*. I'll protect her from you, Phoenix, her mother, all of you, and I'd be willing to die if it meant keeping her safe."

Ru cocked his head as something undecipherable flitted across his face.

"Would you?"

CHAPTER THIRTY THREE

MOLLY

Molly could only stare as Taz sized up Celeste. She stood amid swathes of burning drapery as Fae poured into the Menagerie while the nobles vanished like magic and guard surged forward.

"How?!" Celeste demanded.

"How did I abdicate?" Taz drew a sword and swooped it in fancy loops, only slightly less fancy than the delighted grin on his face. "You should know, you did it yourself. Or did you? Who knows what the truth is. The oak queen certainly isn't forthcoming on anything."

"Oh, call her mother, you idiot"

"Why? She doesn't see us as her children. We're pawns. Then again, you sound like you're running the monopoly on using kids as pawns. No offense, Molly."

Molly grimaced. "None taken, I think."

"Good. I'm on your side," he promised. "I've already had Phoenix promise that you're off-limits, don't worry. No taking you as a hostage or their noses will drop off. Well, something will drop off, I wasn't entirely specific."

Molly clambered to her feet with heat and chills rolling across her skin, her head throbbing as she scanned the crowd for Talie.

Her heart froze and breath choked from her lips as Sammy raced through the doors right behind Harvey.

Celeste sent a wave of power radiating across the room but Taz swiped a hand to knock it aside. The fighting echoed with the shouting and stamping of chaos that bounced off the walls and shattered bits of wall.

Then Sammy saw her and changed course. Molly could barely take a step as Sammy dropped to her knees and slid across the floor, then shot right past her and slammed into an overturned table.

"That was risky!" Molly yelled.

She shoved her warding against someone rushing to attack them, but the effort sent her flying backwards until Sammy's arm came out to steady her.

"I couldn't let anything happen to you!" Sammy shouted. "Talie would kill me. She's been frantic."

Molly grabbed her hand and hauled her behind the nearest bookcase.

"I was going to say the same to you, she's going to kill me if I don't get you out of here," Molly muttered.

"Screw that for a pouch of percats!" Phoenix jogged past with a cloud of dust whirling from his palm. "She's got the king consort fighting her battles now apparently, so she's going to slaughter the lot of us for both of you being here at this rate!"

Molly choked over a laugh, even though she knew she'd never be able to trust him. As if tied by an invisible bond, she lifted her head above the edge of the table in time to see Talie running in.

Talie scanned the hall and found them. Weaving a hand out, Talie shoved someone running toward her, ducking so her shoulder shunted against their chest and sent them flying off balance. With a face full of fury, she weaved through the chaos the resistance were now causing, but Molly noted as Talie reached them that many of the nobles had fled already.

"Go home, now!" Talie yelled.

Sammy scowled. "No! I've as much right to fight as you do. So does Molly."

"You can't fight!" she shouted, even though her gaze was fixed on Molly instead.

"Rude." Sammy lifted a finger above the table while hiding behind it. "Molly would let me stay."

Molly grimaced. "No offense, but you should go home, it's not safe."

"Bugger that!"

Instead of arguing, or pulling them both out by force, Talie changed direction and launched back into the fight, her movements solid as she reached up and laid a savage punch to someone's shoulder to send them careening away.

Molly glanced at Sammy's grinning face.

"I did not expect that," Sammy said. "Maybe she's finally decided to stop treating me like a kid."

"Um... maybe stay here though, just you know, to keep watch."

Sammy eyed the carnage and her smile dipped.

"Yeah, okay."

Molly firmed her warding around her as she stood and found Celeste at the far end of the hall with her water whirling around two separate Fae. Molly tensed as her sunlight gift bubbled to the surface of her skin, but she couldn't trust herself to use it, not with so little training.

What use is a gift if I have no time to train it?

Celeste noticed her and dropped the people she was drowning as though they were nothing more than fleeting fancies for her to toy with.

Molly put all her power into her warding. Her limbs ached, her head was still swimming and her gifts roiled in her bones, desperate to set free, but either way she probably wouldn't survive another round of Celeste.

Before she could take more than a couple of steps, a wave of purple flashed in front of her.

"Molly, come with me." Harvey held up his arm so she could see the rainbow bracelet on his arm. "Sides are evenly matched but we need to get you to safet-"

The words sputtered on his tongue, his eyes going as wide open as his mouth. His body jerked toward her and she reached out for his rigid shoulders as he slithered to the floor. Even as she hoped he'd been stunned somehow, she read the truth in his vacant eyes. She fumbled to get his body steady and find a pulse, but she knew without a doubt that he was already dead.

She looked up to see Celeste withdrawing an outstretched hand, her attention solely on them. Thoughts of Beryl and baby Aurora thundered through her head, and every single muscle and droplet of energy she had went into dragging him behind the overturned table to Sammy.

A feral roar filled the air as Taz caught sight of them. A whip of fire lashed out, sparking against wardings as Taz blasted them all back. Only Celeste and Phoenix at the other far end of the hall managed to withstand the blast.

Molly couldn't contain the rush of breath raging in and out, her throat burning as another wave of fire sent Celeste staggering. With Harvey's body out of reach, Molly steadied her feet and stumbled forward. Anger coiled tight around her limbs, urging her through the crush, and she dodged everyone else with her eyes fixed on Celeste, who had the depraved indecency to laugh.

Molly staggered as she hit the edge of Celeste's warding, domed around her like a fortress. The burn hit her chest before she could grab control of it, the glow growing across her skin. Celeste caught Molly's eye and looked to the left, a pointed enough gesture to draw Molly's attention as Talie charged toward them.

Molly's heart lifted and she changed course, even as Celeste lifted a hand with a vicious smile.

"Get away!" Molly screamed.

Talie opened her mouth to argue, to tell her the same, Molly couldn't be sure, but she saw it happen before it did.

Talie didn't go rigid like Harvey had. She grimaced instead, frozen for one timeless moment before doubling over and crashing to the floor. Molly staggered the short distance between them and dropped to her knees with a pained whimper. Talie's body trembled as onslaughts of whatever pain Celeste was inflicting continued to wave against her.

"Let this be a lesson, Molinia," Celeste thundered, her voice filling the entire cavernous hall. "Everyone is breakable."

"Talie, get up!" Sammy screamed. "Get up!"

Molly reached through the blistered patches of Talie's fragile warding, her face contorted in pain as the unrelenting waves of Celeste's power clouded down around them.

"Talie, stay with me, just fight it until I can get you warded," she begged.

Even as Celeste whirled what looked like blue splinters of agony into Talie's side, she kept those roiling sharp edges away from Molly, piercing only skin that was not of her own blood. Molly sensed the raw pain but couldn't feel it, couldn't use herself as a shield against it, so determined was Celeste's intent to harm only one of them.

Talie's eyes flickered open, the hazel depths dimming fast.

"It was an honour, to be your friend," she choked out.

Molly tried to shove herself into the cloud but it held firm against her, resisting her. She rounded on it again. Again. And again, failing to even make a dent as it siphoned away the last dregs of life.

Talie's eyes blazed and caught hers, her lips lifting in a pained smile.

"In another lifetime maybe. For you, I'll make this an end worth dying for."

Molly remembered what Talie had told her in the letter she'd left for her after the last battle. Frantic, she clawed at the parts of Talie she could reach around the now dissipating cloud, her hand, her knee. As Talie's head lolled, Molly whispered those same promises back to her.

Then the quiet roaring in her ears grew.

She forced herself to stand on shaking legs, fixing her gaze on her mother's face.

"Anyone who values their life should leave," she shouted. "Right now."

It wasn't her words that stilled the crowd, but Celeste's laughter, the dismissive cruelty echoing enough to draw worried glances their way, to halt fights mid-battle.

"Anyone who wants to life leaves now." Molly screamed it into the sudden silence, loud enough to burn her throat.

Celeste raised one eyebrow, her face still bearing blood from Aurora's attack.

"What more can you do, child?"

Molly lifted her arms out wide, removing every doubt and boundary she'd ever placed on herself. Beryl had once told her sunlight could burn. She really hoped so.

Fae scattered as she began to glow, and she thought she heard the faint sound of Taz muttering "oh orbs" somewhere behind her. He would get Sammy out, or Kainen would. Although she didn't know either of them well, they at least would understand.

"Well?" Celeste snapped. "What harm can you do on your own?"

Molly eyed her mother and smiled, wicked and soulless in her grief.

"Burn."

CHAPTER THIRTY FOUR

MOLLY

Her sunshine gift burst, rays of pure power radiating across the entrance hall of the Menagerie.

Nobles and guards scattered the moment they felt the heat, but Molly squinted at Celeste through the glare.

A tide of blue powder whirled into water at the edge of her glow, but she wove the heat into her warding to burn the water dry. The sheer effort of it had her staggering back as Celeste advanced, more used to wielding her gift with skill than Molly was with pure grief.

"Molly, stop." Kainen's voice pierced the utter agony. "Let your shine dim slowly."

She wanted to say no, to fight and burn until everything was nothing but ash and embers, but the word tasted sour on her tongue.

Celeste's power forced her through the doors and into the lane but Molly fought against the chill of the water. She needed to get Talie, to force Celeste to back down, to apologise, to do something, anything to make it right.

"Molly, sunshine off, now."

Something in Kainen's tone allowed sense to trickle in. Her gift resisted her attempt to dim it and she dragged a pained breath in, the rattling gasp anchoring her mind.

"That's it, let it settle," he urged.

Her body chilled, darkness fringing the edges of her vision. The air was insufferably cold and something seemed to be easing her gift back down, calming it where she couldn't until her light dimmed back into her body and left her quaking.

"This isn't over," Celeste spat.

Molly flinched as the Menagerie doors slammed in her face, and she didn't need to test the boundary to know Celeste would have sealed herself inside.

Without the nobles to support her and guards to fear her, she's weak.

Shadows roiled around her as she crashed to her knees and stared at the doors. A hand landed on her shoulder and she barely had the strength to wriggle away.

"Easy, I'm going to help you stand."

She let Kainen shove his hands under her arms and haul her up, tears burning her chilled cheeks.

"We need to get her out," she sobbed.

He wrapped his arms around her shoulders, holding her tight.

"We can't, you know we can't. We need to get you out of here."

"But Talie, and Harvey," she choked. "Oh orbs, Sammy, and Lia, she's still in there, she tried to help me."

Kainen clung on as she wriggled to get away, her faded strength laughable compared to his.

"Talie wouldn't have had a chance to tell you. She was glamouring as Lia. We sent her in to find you a way out originally, but when Celeste started attacking you she broke cover."

Molly whimpered, realisation like a knife to her gut.

"We took her in to help us free the fairies," he added. "But we had to fall back and when we did, she was already out in the hall with you."

"Did you?" She couldn't settle her thoughts, a chaotic jumble of noises and memories. "The fairies?"

It mattered. Talie had done what they both intended to, what Molly hadn't managed.

"We saved most of the ones we found."

She shuddered. Most wasn't all, but it was better than none.

"Come on. Let's get you back. We can't stay out here. Close your eyes if you need to. I've got you."

She obeyed without intervention from her mind, shutting her eyes and letting Kainen lead her away from the doors. She didn't even open her eyes, not caring who saw her.

"Is she okay?"

She heard a male voice but couldn't place it, her eyes shut tight against the tears still flowing.

"Molly!"

She lifted her head and opened her eyes as Sammy dashed toward her.

"I'm so sorry, she- I-"

She couldn't get the words out as Sammy threw tight arms around her middle and clung on.

"It wasn't you," Sammy insisted, her shoulders shaking with sobs.

A lumpy sheet lay on the sofa, and Molly's insides caved at the sight of Beryl kneeling beside it, utterly silent with her face twisted in anguish. Beside her, Taz had an orb in hand with Queen Demerara's face illuminated out of it.

"The wards are down on the citadel," she said. "Nobles are already fleeing to other courts."

Molly held onto Sammy and drew in a breath. The ache inside didn't seem to stop growing, but Talie would want her to be strong now, to make sure Sammy survived this.

As soon Sammy's asleep and I know someone is looking after her then I'll go. Once it's quiet, I'll call Celeste out and finish this.

"More news is coming in," Demi added. "Phoenix has publicly declared the resistance are now in control of the upper levels."

"Yeah, that was the deal," Taz admitted. "I had to strike it to get them to come and help storm the Menagerie."

"What were the terms exactly?" Kainen asked.

"Continuation of freedom of control from royal rule for every level above the Menagerie."

"We'll be with you in a minute," Demi said.

Even through her grief, Molly could hear a familiar note of pain in Demi's. The air shivered as Demi appeared with two women in tow. Their wild hair colours were similar to Beryl's, as were their tearful expressions. Molly shuffled Sammy back against the wall as two men appeared next, one of which could only be Harvey's twin.

She inched Sammy toward the door, suffocating in the sudden cries and waves of grief filling the room.

"Molly, in here."

Demi walked toward the box room and indicated with a hand that she should follow.

Molly took a step back but Sammy clung on, so she guided her into the box room and leaned against the wall.

"Their family will take them home to grieve there," Demi said, her tone utterly broken.

She sagged, face utterly weary and in that moment Molly saw a young woman with the weight of Faerie on her shoulders.

"Both Phoenix and Celeste will be fighting to resume control of the citadel," Demi continued. "That means they may well meet and strike a deal to work together to get the citadel locked down again. I imagine I'll become their new enemy now, despite Phoenix's deal with Taz."

Molly lifted a shaking hand to wipe her eyes.

"Celeste is in league with the oak queen. Someone she trusted told me that." She couldn't bear to think of Ru.

Demi nodded. "I've feared as much. Once Beryl's been sorted, we'll get you out as well. Kainen offered you sanctuary at his court, right?"

"Yeah." Molly glanced at Sammy, now silent and still from shock. "We've only got each other now."

Demi frowned and dropped to sit on the edge of the bed.

"Well none of us can stay now."

"I did sixteen years without anyone, I can continue on doing it."

Demi grimaced. "I thought you might refuse to leave,

but it's open-ended. If you want to come with us, Sammy, we'll look after you. I'm sure Reyan has stuff you can help with at her court, or you can come to Arcanium."

Sammy lifted her head. "I'm not leaving Molly. I'm not leaving until that orb-muncher is rotting so far in the earth even the nether can't find her."

Molly folded her hand around Sammy's, squeezing tight.

"It's going to be dangerous," she said.

"Life's always dangerous," Sammy murmured. "I don't have to be any bother. I can move into the workshop if it's easier. We need each other now."

Demi sighed. "Take this place. We need to know you're both safe, and I can ward it well enough before I leave. We can't return either and I don't know how often Kainen will be able to check in with you."

"What about the rest of the citadel then?" Molly asked. "Don't they deserve to be safe? Or is this just because of who my mother is?"

Demi wiped both hands over her face and rubbed her temples.

"Those are the worries that keep me up at night. Phoenix has taken the upper levels as per his agreement with Taz, which I had no idea about. The lower levels will likely end up as a squabbling of nobles. Celeste will do her best to claw back as much power as she can, but that will start from the bottom. You have a small amount of time, but whatever you plan to do, Taz's abdication is now officially rescinded and we can't interfere again. I want to, orbs alive, trust me I want to, not for me but for the people."

One look and Molly believed her without a single shred of doubt.

"It's almost better if the whole rotten social structure of the citadel is brought crashing down and rebuilt from the debris," she muttered.

Demi reached into her pocket and held out two silver bracelets, rainbow beads woven on wire.

"There are still a few of my people dotted about here, hidden in the system. Take these and look out for others wearing them to know who to trust."

Molly took the bracelet. She slid one onto Sammy's wrist first, then her own.

"I need to go out."

Demi frowned. "I guess I can't stop you. Is that wise though? How do we know it'll be safe?"

"Nothing's safe anymore, but I have to do this. Taz said he made a deal with Phoenix, that he can't target me anymore. That's one enemy that I can handle now. As for Celeste, her time will come."

Sammy wiped her face. "Bring some food back with you. I don't feel like eating but we need to look after each other now. You take the main room, I'll take this one."

"Okay."

Demi stood and opened the door. Molly wasn't surprised to find Beryl and the others gone. The only person left was Taz, and he gave her a sad smile.

"You said Phoenix can't target me?" she asked.

He nodded. "He can't, and he can't use the resistance to do it either. If you offer willingly, that'll be different, but I don't get a very trustworthy vibe from him."

"Neither do I, don't worry."

"I will worry, but Kainen or Reyan will be checking in when they can. I'm thinking Celeste will probably lick her wounds for a while then make an attempt to catch you, so if you are going to go strolling about, pick a glamour and a story."

He took Demi's hand, both of them standing together as they said goodbye and vanished.

"No tears." Sammy sounded like she was close to breaking her own rule. "Go get food. We can have time to mourn, but we need to start thinking of a plan."

Molly nodded. "I know. I'll be back in a bit."

She couldn't hold a glamour for long without help but Celeste wouldn't attack immediately. She would be too busy clawing back her control of the nobles and likely the guilds too once the news spread.

In the alley, Molly made sure the door was firmly locked and strode toward the lane. She couldn't tell if people were looking at her or not, but the news would spread all the same. Some would fear her, some would try to ingratiate themselves because of who she was, but all would be whispering in corners about it.

She found Phoenix in the gym. The sign on the door said it was closed, but it opened when she pushed. He sat on the edge of the nearest training ring and said nothing as she approached.

"I have no intention of ruling anything," she announced. "The king consort's deal with you stops you from using me, but if you're going to try somehow, you'll be on my hit-list alongside Celeste."

Phoenix shrugged. "I have no intention of getting you involved. His deal has obliterated any chance of that, but if you want to fight Celeste, you'd do well to consider being our poster girl."

"No. Do you even care? She…" The words wouldn't come.

"I have to be practical. Soft hearts don't build dynasties, but I will miss her."

Because she was useful. Molly resisted the urge to burn him alive. How easy it would be, or to compel him to throw himself into a wall.

"You focus on playing lord of the citadel then," she spat. "I'm not done kicking the ashes of the old one. Consider this a warning. Leave me alone."

She strode out before he could dredge up an answer. He would try to find a way, she had no doubt, but that could come another day. Her feet took her down to the park and she traced her steps to the bench where it all started, where Seymour the artificer had died.

"Molly!" Mary hurried over from the kiosk. "I don't know what's true and what's not, each tale is more ridiculous than the one before, but are you okay?"

Molly bit her lip, hard. She couldn't bring herself to speak so she shrugged. Mary patted her arm.

"Come on, I owe you some fare for past work done. You've more than earned it."

Molly didn't have the energy to argue. Sammy had told her to get food and Mary was offering it. She wasn't even sure how they'd feed themselves now. Opening the workshop again would be rash with Celeste lurking, but she only had a small amount stashed away for emergencies.

She stood at the kiosk counter as Mary ferried far too much food into bags.

"One meat pocket without the meat, please." Someone stepped up beside her.

Molly gave him a brief glance and tensed to find him smiling at her. As he extended his hand to put money on the counter top, the light caught a sparkle on his wrist.

A silver wire bracelet with rainbow beads.

She took a closer look and couldn't be sure, but he looked suspiciously similar to the man who had appeared with Harvey's twin earlier and disappeared again like magic.

"Not much time to cook when I'm working all hours at the library," he announced.

Molly hesitated. Demi had told her to look out for the bracelet and here it was. As she stared at him, his expression softened.

"Bad business all this what's happened recently," he added. "But there are some interesting books on the history of the citadel in the library, although my boyfriend isn't so keen on dusty old books."

Molly lifted her hand to tuck her hair back and shook her sleeve down enough to show her identical bracelet.

As Mary bent over to ferret around in one of the fridges, the man leaned closer.

"I know who you are," he murmured. "I'm on the front desk at the library most mornings now, sorting out the absolute travesty that is the previous custodian's filing system. Come by tomorrow at nine and get your new library card."

"Oh, I don't- I mean, thanks, I will."

He turned to walk away with his food, but a thought flickered amid the haze in her head. The library was a cavern of sorts, a sanctuary where someone could likely work and hide in relative safety without anyone noticing they were there.

"Can I also get a library card for my… my sister?" she called after him. "Her name is Sammy."

"Consider it done. Tomorrow. 9am, ask for Milo. Oh, and don't be late please!"

Molly took the horde of bags Mary pressed on her and promised she would be careful. As she started the walk back to Sammy, she let the future spool out in her mind.

Celeste would be hunting her in the coming days. Phoenix would be looking for ways to turn her to his advantage. Demi and Taz couldn't interfere, but they had left her some man called Milo and access to the library.

The core of power. Sneaking into the guild seemed like a lifetime ago. *That's what Celeste is protecting. I bet she's using it as the conduit or something to extract gifts.*

To storm the Menagerie a third time, she would need nothing short of an army. She would consider siding with Phoenix if it brought Celeste down, but first she needed to grieve, eat and rest.

She pulled her privy pouch out of her pocket and found her necklace. Beryl and Harvey's home shared a wall with her workshop, so she could knock through easy enough.

Perhaps if she had some friends left, like Mary, she could do commissions secretly by word of mouth. She would need all the goodwill she could get before taking on Celeste, but she would do it.

As she approached the front door to what was now to be her home, she stopped to put on the necklace.

Talie's gifts settled against her chest, a reminder.

I won't let Celeste get away with this. I'll take her down or die trying.

She pushed the door open and forced herself to be strong, for Sammy's sake if nothing else.

Celeste's time would come, and soon.

ACKNOWLEDGEMENTS

A huge thank you to every reader who has walked with me through Faerie and is still coming back for another visit! To those who've shared on social media, done ARC reads or just given me compliments about the book to keep me going, thank you!

To my family and also my writing family as always, your support means everything to me – Aerin Apeltun, Katina Wright, Estelle Tudor, Anna Britton, Sally Doherty, Marisa Noelle, Emma Finlayson-Palmer, writing Twitter, the amazing ARC readers (who have caught so many printing blips it's not even funny…), the wider writing community and everyone who joins #ukteenchat, WriteMentor, SCBWI, and especially libraries and schools who've taken a chance on the previous books, shops that are still stocking them and giving this indie author a chance to reach more readers *deep breath* and most importantly to the readers who will find these books in the future:

THANK YOU!

ABOUT THE AUTHOR

While always convinced that there has to be something out there beyond the everyday, Emma focuses on weaving magic realms with words (the real world can wait a while). The idea of other worlds fascinates her and she's determined to find her own entrance to an alternate realm one day.

Raised in London, she now lives on the UK south coast with her husband and a very lazy black Labrador who occasionally condescends to take her out for a walk.

Aside from creative writing studies, an addiction to cake and spending far too much time procrastinating on social media, Emma is still waiting for the arrival of her unicorn. Or a tank, she's not fussy.

For the latest news and updates, check the website or come say hi on social media:

www.emmaebradley.com
@EmmaEBradley